About the Author

Isabel Moet was born in England in 1965 and has lived in London for most of her life. She studied Graphic Design at Kingston University and worked in advertising and design, also assisting with the production of pop promos and commercials before discovering her love of writing. She won the Richmond Poetry Prize in 1980. This is her first novel and she has written several other short stories.

The Lute and the Lyre
& Other Stories

Isabel Moet

Published 2010 by arima publishing

www.arimapublishing.com

ISBN 978 1 84549 448 3

© Isabel Moet 2010

Printed and bound in the United Kingdom

Typeset in Garamond 11/14

Swirl is an imprint of arima publishing.

arima publishing
ASK House, Northgate Avenue
Bury St Edmunds, Suffolk IP32 6BB
t: (+44) 01284 700321
www.arimapublishing.com

To my Godmother Isa who was an English Teacher

We are both only fair to middlin"
I can't use my knees + Staffy has legs
that wont work. Consequently we don't
go very far. except go shopping at
The nearest Asda. every Friday. We go
from door to door by taxi. I cannot do
my gardening any more. + I really loved
it all of my life. We have a gardener
but I try to keep tubs of flowers on
the patio — + That's bad enough.

I don't expect you to write back soon
because, like me, you've gone off writing
altogether but do send a card when
any Thing thrilling happens to you.
                    Love
                    Aunty Isa

Contents

The Lute and the Lyre

A different point of view

As the lift passed the numbered floors you could watch the horizontal concrete and carpet go by through the sliding expansion lift doors. It stopped at the right illuminated number and she got out, sliding the metal catch closed after her. Hotel atriums and old buildings are a good source of interesting lift reference. The Dallas Hyatt has an amazing glass car and there is a hotel in Barcelona, which springs to mind with an open caged shaft surrounded by a grand staircase.

Riddle:

Q. Why did the passenger get out at the seventh floor and walk to the Penthouse?

A. Because he's a dwarf.

Dubois looked at the Venice Beach web cam before writing her letters – a couple of cars and a skater passed in the freeze frame then disappeared. The palm trees jumped in the wind and a wave broke catching the sun. TV shopping channels, Marlboro green, delis and diners, all day coffee, hash browns, jazz at Shutters, breakfast in Santa Monica, downtown comic book heroes and muffins in Manhattan Beach. A director friend had taken a photo of them with Dubois' camera at a forty five degree angle through the restaurant window. [The action looked good].

They walked along the Hollywood Boulevard walk of fame and ate by Mann's Chinese Theatre, then drove up the Hollywood Hills, the sign diminished by the distance.

They had driven two hours to the desert to Palm Springs, freeways and routes, and then came to a crossroads with a silver mailbox. Palm Springs appears very small at first on the horizon, just a few lights and then out of the big space the city swallows the road up.

Windmills stand between the cactus on the desert rock hills on the way back to the Joshua Tree. About fifty to one hundred metres tall they tower above you against the dramatic solarised Ford Coppola clouds. Up close they make a hypnotic rush of air as the blades turn.

Dubois had to write to a business in Notting Hill to cancel a delivery as it clashed with the carnival. Salt fish and beer, lots of people, heavy reggae bass and steel drums, costumes feathers and flowers, Dubois was going away for the weekend. She made some rose tea. The kitchen still had Macdo bags from people's lunch. She had poured her wine into the end of her soup and drank the 'chabrot' from the bowl. A kitty syndicate of twelve names pinned to the wall was the usual visible reading matter as she waited for the kettle to boil. She walked back to her desk. An idiomatic last supper, she thought as she wrapped the pretty little floral tag around her finger like a cigar brand anilla.

Riddle.

Q. Why wasn't the surgeon allowed to operate on the boy in the car accident brought in by his father?

A. Because the surgeon was the boy's mother.

What do you call a female chef?

The DRTV advertising duty free had quality products, beautiful people and shopping musak. Dubois admired her new matching hand luggage, checked her tickets and the departure times on the screens in the lounge, flight TZ6721 was leaving from gate twelve. She had been to a Hayden recital the night before and had packed in a non-conservatoire frame of mind. The flight was on time and virtually empty. Only twenty passengers and crew sat in the 737's seats.

'Good morning and welcome aboard. This is your captain', said the announcement, giving altitude conditions and speed. He advised it would be possible to spread out and sit in first class and that the stewardesses would be serving champagne. The cello and piano played in waves as the plane took off, the bow moved across the strings producing an unusual sharp phrase of notes and the violin played Allegro and Valse Russe. About half and hour into the plane party everybody was enjoying their champagne, the 'extinguish all cigarettes' light was switched off and the cabin lights turned on. The passengers thrown together by their minority in a usually packed environment where the normal behaviour is to pretend other people are not there, became very sociable. Three Robbie Williams fans who had tickets to a concert were talking to a pepper and salt checked businessman and enjoying the in flight movie. The two DJ's booked for a gig that night were talking to a young woman in a hydrangea print dress and her husband – newly weds going to Rome for their honeymoon.

'Do you know anything about Veronese?' Dubois looked up. One of the nuns from across the aisle touched her arm. 'Veronese? The artist Veronese? We are going to see the Allegories of Love.'

Dubois smiled and stopped reading about the origins of Stones Ginger Wine and the Liberty and Burdett Riots, freedom of speech and nineteenth century Parliamentary Reform in the 'in flight' magazine.

'No, do please tell me more.'

'The silks are the most beautiful colours draped and blown by the breathe of Zeus the goddesses have soft virginal flesh and little cupid holds his bow in one hand and arrow in the other floating above the characters. This is a picture'. She handed it to Dubois enthusiastically enlightening her on the symbolism of scorn, respect and the conjugal couple.

'Beautiful skin, jewels, gold chains and these marble statues'.

They commented on the male figures large muscular stomach described by the yellow silk covering it and the tummy button emphasised by it's clinging nature like yellow rubber armour.' When were they painted?' asked Dubois.

'Quadraphonic pictures telling a story on four great walls. I do like champagne'.

'This is sister Marjorie, she's from South Africa.'

By the end of the flight sister Marjorie had inspired Dubois with the Limpopo, blood and orange rivers, giraffe, zebra, wildebeast, elephant, lion and buffalo. The baobab, milkwood and acacia trees, the flowers and blossom in the garden state where hippos graze on the lawns in the sugar cane and banana plantations.

'Kalahari actually means desert' she said before describing the diamond mines, bushmen and casinos in the busy townships.

'I mustn't forget to mention the Namaqualand quiver trees –'aloe dichtoma' – 7.30 matins'.

Dubois enjoyed the Purcell legroom and shared her recipe for black forest gateaux as the bronzed savannah stewardess handed her another glass of champagne.

Tube philosophy.

Poetry on the tube, health insurance ads and film posters, four sheets, eight sheets and twelve sheets. What lies beneath? Three blind mice. Book reviews, new titles and seasoned experts at reading newspapers in confined spaces. Leave behind and compacts. Sharing people's lunch, their bags of shopping and flowers. Dinner, wedding rings and red berets. Ghost trains, rush hour, luggage and travel in transit. Mail and make up bags, late for work, routine or one off, the portable survival kit of make up and mirror. Dubois tried to apply mascara on the tube once and found it too difficult. Had she washed her ears? Moscow chandeliers, shoes and exits in the overcrowded space. Primula processed cheese spread or toothpaste moving through the apertures, Norman Parkinson's hat and moustache, the concertina windows of the adjoining carriages move along the rolling tracks turning corners as the electric cables pass by. A Pakistani in a white hat and beard stands in the frame of the golly gosh carriage, a Japanese tea ceremony – one minute to Hainault and sliding doors.

The Aviary is Obverse

The prediction for Sunday was twenty eight degrees, Saturday was twenty three, Dubois decided to visit Seaford after sourcing some information on the internet from the English National Tourist Board. Coastal Paths were a topical theme discussed in her group last week and she had felt cravings to feel the sand between her toes and salt breeze on her face.

Sunday morning was going to be easy. Heating the brioche under the grill and making some tea, she heard a noise from the next room. A pigeon had come through the door and landed on her tambourine, it hopped around it's shiney silver edge like a parrot on a unicycle hitting the little discs. Slightly worried the pigeon would crap on the stack of CD's next to it Dubois offered it some brioche as it gave her a Hitchcock crow impression. She packed the Saturday paper, a book, some oil and a sarong in her bag and caught the two minutes past ten train from Victoria to Seaford changing at Lewes.

Small cream, yellow and green spiders with jewellery legs, caterpillars and bugs decorated the yellow daisies, elderflowers and thistles. A fine example of Balthasar accompanied by invisible grasshoppers. Red and black, black, white and orange butterflies flew around knee height in the Beachy Head grass growing either side of the paths following the 'roller coaster' chalk cliffs.

Dubois walked up the path to the first stage where the white cliffs had carved names. A group of RSPB twitcher's with high tech telescopes lined up along the seawall watching kittihawks, gulls and puffins swooping and diving in a circling vortex over the blue and green water. She had never seen a puffin, there were none at Bristol or Regents Park zoos. The Maine Adopt a Puffin paperwork, which had arrived from New York nearly matched the price of a business class season ticket when annually renewed. Dubois tried to identify a puffin it would have been nice souvenir for the day, she loved their cute cheeks and scallop bills.

About twenty minutes further at Seaford Head a plaque read 'This bench is dedicated to Archie Hughes for you to enjoy the views'. Although it was better worded than that. Small Karakuri sailboats on the horizon fulfilled its message.

Square
12.15am

At one end of the garden square soft leafy patterns danced on the paving where the dedicated benches were re located in the shade to the south. A water pump and trough probably for watering horses stands in the middle in front of a bicycle park. Early lunchers can select the best seats and relax in the afternoon sun. After five minutes there are two women in discussion and a girl sitting in a cross legged lotus style, exercising her ease at yoga and reading, undisturbed by someone joining her, next to her a big soft, camel leather bag. A fat old man with a cane sitting opposite watches people arriving half expecting a game of boules. You could hear the Mediterranean politics being argued under the trees, the distant murmur only broken by a passing car.

By 12.45am the square would be full of baguettes and sandwiches, nurses' picnics, name badges, briefcases and the buzz of earphones and mobile telephones. Three halved yellow/green galia melons looked very tempting. Three large flower beds full of white, pink lilac full blown roses at each end are divided by a path. Hollyhocks and blue stocks stand taller than the textural grasses and bigger leaves of tropical varieties among the denser trees at the northern side.

Enough semiotic daisies for a very long chain and some dandelions gave away the need for the lawn to be cut, along with a piece of broken glass where a four year old girl in a pink dress with a blue ribbon in her hair was playing. The glass was found in time to avoid spoiling her day.

The buildings surrounding the square are a mix of red brick and white marble fronted Georgian town houses with elevated entrances, pink marble buttress balconies, columns, chequered tiles and Paladian structures divided by coaching stable courtyards.

'Can I join you?' a girl in a big shell necklace asked the group on the grass as another woman, a nurse in uniform, commented ' I didn't wear tights today it's so much cooler'. Somebody else was 'having a mid life crisis.' The dislocated comments were lunchtime small talk after a mornings work en route to somewhere out of context.

1.15pm

The park was full. Hermione could hear a piano playing New Orleans style jazz from a first floor window. Leaving the square with her dandelions, a rapid Spanish football commentary covered a piece of action enthusiastically from a balcony window, continuing the soundtrack in one long joined up phrase to an unfamiliar ear.

Dandelion tea:
25 dandelions, 1 litre of water, 1 tablespoon of sugar and lemon juice.

Last supper, can you remember what you had for breakfast?

The local Tobago fishermen bring the painted boats up the sloping beach and dry their nets pulling them in, a line of men about one metre apart, laying them on the sand in the sun. This has to avoid the three metre wide turtle nests identified by disturbed areas of sand, the nests are dug at by the night by the large turtles awkward and slow flippers throwing the sand everywhere before laying their eggs. In the morning the equatorial clouds sit on the horizon of the massive sky, their perspective distorted by the position of the sun.

Frobisher was on the telephone ordering some new laying breeds. The plan was to corner the market by introducing ring neck pheasant and turkey eggs, Rhode Island Reds, Plymouth Rocks and New Hampshires. It was going to be Dubois' new business venture when Frobisher was away. She was busy watching a goose trying to pick up an apple, rolling it along with its orange beak.

'They have red feathers and lay brown eggs, 'read the catalogue text'. It had taken three days to notate the research of the dozen chosen varieties at boiled egg dinner parties with Hermione. Burford Browns, Aracuna, Marans, Duck, Goose, Quail, Frizzle, Turkey, Ostrich, Emu and Leghorns. The blue green Aracunas and alabaster duck won. The goose had the advantage of being twice the size of the others, but the duck's transparent, finer white and creamier yolk was desired more.

11.15am on Thursday the new coops arrived. Dubois had busied herself with the house to forget her bird-brained pipe dreams, behaving like a bodyless head of figures running round coping with national supply. Her enthusiasm returned with the profitable realism and the three-month trial contract with Selfridges and Fortnum and Masons.

The French buy five and a half million pairs of tennis shoes every year. Dubois shelved her other business plan for highly trained mobile shiatsu teams in the city delivering efficient Japanese workforce ethics and morale to the hands, necks and feet of desk bound employees. £15 for ten minutes. Each team would visit a company for about one hour. They would probably manage three times ten minutes, giving a total of £45 an hour times five people totalling £225. Which at eight hours is equal to £1800.

Allowing for scooter transport and investment and no overheads, employees could start at £150 - £200 per day giving a £800 profit per day.

The translation of shiatsu is 'Shi 'finger' atsu- pressure.

Tai Chi before work in big Japanese companies also appealed to Dubois, she wanted to participate in the free flow of chi and blood to improve her immune system. The introduction of air conditioning to buildings can raise the absenteeism by sixty percent.

She looked up at the file and then at the bookends, heavy objects with a value and aesthetic but static purpose. Paperweight and doorstop.

Dubois wandered where to buy them. She was in a people and profit mind frame.

'Bull moose 'Theodore Roosevelt said:

'Kermit had kept about a dozen trophies for ourselves, otherwise we shot nothing that was not used either as a museum specimen or for meat – usually for both purposes. The mere size of the bag indicates little of his achievements.

There was no river of doubt today. Dubois started her Citroen. It's unique handling took about a mile to hydraulically adjust. They were the first European cars to be mass-produced. It was definitely singular and its battery was possibly older. She drove to the library to return some books. One was overdue.

As the lights changed the passenger in the car next to her looked at her strangely. Was the exhaust smoking? Remembering being reliably informed about the twelve eyes in a rastapharian back bone she hit her horn at the next car she pulled up next to and waved at its back wheel, making the driver get out to check his tyres, then she drove on feeling much better. The overdue book looked like a rejected time lapse hamburger, solarised after a damp spell.

She parked outside the library and returned the books. The librarian stamped them with the rotating inked stamp and she paid the fifty pence fine. Dubois needed a book on chicken breeds. She was in the Michelin guide section, walked further through the j, k and l's scanning their spines. Biographies reference and guides. The layout was confusing, Roosevelt had his own pig skin covered library sent to him during his African Safari in 1909. Dubois ordered a book from microfiche and was told to come back in two days.

Typhoon Season.

'There's a place called Silent Pool near there,' said Hermione, 'somebody took me once, it's difficult to find. The rock face side is quite tall and the spring is surrounded by woodland with grasses and wild flowers. A lady of Shallot or Ophelia location, I'm not sure of it's exact geographic and artesian formation.'

Dubois could hear the familiar sounds of pans, plates and cutlery coming from the kitchen through the French doors. A Mediterranean mistral carried the smell of fresh herbs and food out to her as she sipped her Bordeaux. Prevailing church bells were peeling over the sound of someone's jazz, a Charles Trenet song and a piece of conversation. The smoke from her cigar blew across her view and the breeze carried dandelion clocks in the sunlight. The mistral is said to last for an odd number of days, lasting up to three months. It is known as 'le vent de fada' the idiot wind or master' as a literal translation which is caused by a cloud vortex resulting in cyclonic circulation from Sicily to the Gulf of Lions at Marseilles.

Tarquin had enlightened us on the seventy types of wind at the egg survey last week, Diablo, Maskan Matanuska, South African Cape Doctor, Greek Eros and the South Mexican Tehuantepecar which squall one hundred metres out to sea.

Lunch was going to be a cucumber sandwich, lentil and Roquefort soup with large homemade croutons. Lyonnaise and aiglot potatoes with fine and broad beans in mustard. Dubois poured some more wine.

They were going to a Schubert recital of Die Schöne Müllerin at 7.30pm. Dubois did not have to do anything all afternoon. The week had been unusually busy and she was in 'le septieme ciel', they had spent the morning in the Japanese gardens, where small black rabbits and peacocks walked and hopped on the surrounding lawns and around the plants whose leaf size and proportion are considered and planned, balancing with the low bridges and waterfall whose moving water flows into the still water lake with fish and shallow edges. Dubois had followed a peacock out to the tall Italian mazes trying to take in the blues and greens, the different feathers and plumes with eyes and its crown. She liked the hidden statues and Capability Browned an empty pot by training ivy around a wire frame to make a topiary heart.

They ate the food and drank more wine; Dubois hoped that the Indian summer would last another two weeks for the nature reserve meadow seeding and haymaking. It sounded like hard work.

She had lied about the cat when she took the warm body to the vet and promised the children an ice cream. In Reykjavik they drown women for perjury, adultery and infanticide. It's nine lives were up – no 'Angel of mons.'

Maron Glace.

Dubois spent the following morning in her office checking paperwork and filing. Her tickets had arrived for the flight next month. She pinned them to the board next to her laptop between the picture of Tarquin on his bicycle and the phone bill, knocking a postcard from Turkey off in the process. Another flood was on the news; there was a feature about looting in New Orleans and the local basketball team shooting at fish in a barrel. She added a burgundy to her cork collection. It had bold certified initials on it and an iconic crest. Some of them had script and numerals or pictures with unknown names. They had a certain interest, which amused Dubois like the scratched words in vinyl on the inside grooves of records and finding an additional track at the end of it. She would stick it with the others later when she could be bothered to look for the glue. A plate needed fixing and she had kept the chip somewhere.

She never kept the champagne corks just watched the size and rate of the little bubbles, some rising from the middle of the glass and some from around the edges and wandered where they came from.

She needed to get some food essentials and went via the park finding herself at the Lubetkin Penguin pool in London Zoo again watching the penguins walking up the shallow steps and slope paths around the eye shaped building, then sliding down and eating fish being fed by their keeper from a bucket. Little groups on one side diving in and swimming. Black and white trembling bottles toppling off the shelves, shaken in a little Greek earthquake. Tectonic bodies at an airport waiting for flight.

Important little decisions, time and motion directions and motivations, tracking their short fat bodies. There was no apparent danger as the glasses jumped across the table, the first floor balcony did not feel safe, and there was the possibility the building may collapse.

On the way back Dubois parked and went to buy the food. Surrounded by produce propensities – apple, cherry and mandarin glace fruit, glass counter gateaux windows, marbled cake icing and ice creams with desirable names, tutti frutti and maranello, sliced sushi, spices and coconut ghee – Bhutan buddhas, Bertolucci buddhas and last emperors.

Dubois returned home to the clotheshorse, with the laundry hung on its simple clever design, which folded flat and disappeared when she did not want it.

Moguls.

The nature reserve haymaking started at 11am. Three times a year the large meadow full of wild flowers, butterflies, insects and bumblebees needed the long grass cutting to make hay before the blackberries and brambles take over. At least a dozen volunteers are needed to clear the grasses and help build a safe permanent pathway with wooden steps around the sloping land and natural spring. The small pool with bullrushes and lush green weed made an afternoon of raking and dredging, to remove the large lily rhizoid, like giant articulated spider crab claws crawling out of the water as it became visible the surface was noticeably disturbed by flies not breaking it but lightly causing a lateral displacement.

Through the rosehips Tarquin could see the other volunteers cutting the waist high grass making sweeping movements with their tools. It was nearly done by lunch at 1pm, work stopped for crisps, salad, chicken, tomato flan, chocolate biscuits and sharp apples from the heavily laden tree in the corner of the meadow, its branches pulled by the weight of the fruit. After lunch the children helped to collect the cut grasses and pile it up. Then amused themselves by rolling down the slope. In the car on the way back they played snap with their smarties. New hexagonal packaging replaced the round plastic tubes and lids with clever integral, perforated and engineered ends. Hermione liked the little plastic pyramid packs but could not work out how they existed without any joins. They stopped at the stables on the way home. Nobody was visible in the cobbled muse, most of the horses would be out on a ride. They looked in the back room, which smelt of straw and leather saddles. Rows of hats and boots sat on the shelves and quilted jackets hung on the hooks. Hermione called out and a girl appeared in muddy jodhpurs.

'Apples for the horses.'

'Thanks'

Hermione sliced a large pumpkin and put some of it in the oven with onion and sliced apples, made some soup and curried the rest. Tarquin had carved one for Halloween; the children loved it's little glowing face illuminated by tea lights. They had made some chutney and bread and had java apples to try. Subtle fragrant, white fleshed with pink waxed skin, their pear shaped sliced outline made a William Morris Sanderson wallpaper or frieze in a MoDa collection.

Dubois, Hermione and Tarquin had very large glasses of wine, listened to the Beach Boys and talked about space tourism and Bhutan rockets.

'We'll have elimination astronaut training game shows this time next year' said Hermione.

'What's today's rouble exchange rate, the flights are £100,000 – which is slightly more appealing than queuing for a potato if you don't mind a fifteen thousand waiting list.'

Dubois hesitated on air, changed the CD to Fluke and admired a book on Oscar Deutsch Odeon Style on the credenza. Tarquin looked up from the paper he was reading,

'What about investing in a frankfurter factory? America's hot dog consumption will rise dramatically after the 2008 cricket world cup, the US is gaining notable and increased success although it's a niche sport there – in a three day test the average spectator could eat up to three or four times as many hot dogs compared to a three hour baseball game.'

Tarquin's eyes returned to the paper. Noticing Hannibal was scheduled for Sunday afternoon he carried on,

'Alternatively Dubois needs a backer for the Dial a Drink delivery service. Most people would be in a better frame of mind after 11pm to part with twenty quid than finding room in a full trolley at the supermarket'.

Last week Hermione had thrown a large fillet steak into somebody else's trolley when he was not looking. She got another bottle from the kitchen, feeling like a field of mustard in her yellow dress. She had often wandered what it was like to walk through the tall plants with little yellow flowers, having only seen them from a distance. Hippocrates had first discovered their curative properties in 460 BC and the Keen and Dix families brought them to Norwich in the late nineteenth century making them a Coleman packet.

Two days later she swam twenty lengths at the gym, inhaling the heat in the steam room and alternating between a telescopic Tignes balcony hot tub surrounded by snow and a roof top Delft Jacuzzi in Dallas.

Belle Epoque.

The willow pattern lovers locked themselves in their little blue house. There was lichen on the hazel coppice woven fences edging the gardens. A sign that the air was good. Hermione had new lemon trees, she had never had lemon trees before. They finished the wine, planning the next Belle Epoque. Dubois sent a text to the designer to say that they were pursuing the political tide and that she would see him on Thursday. Tarquin planned to occupy himself with carp fishing. He had not been since his visit to the French lakes when Hermione Fawcett had exercised her rights to threaten divorce if he did not go. Tarquin praised the Suffragette Society and her priority of economy.

From the air the River Argens and its tributaries [it might have been the Rhone] reflected silver in the sun against the fields and forested hills. A flat layer of cloud covered the sea and formed a tall physical skyscape through which they navigated to the tiny white villas and blue square pools that cover the rock.

Seventeen degrees is warm for October. A heat mirage affected the view over the wing of the plane as it refuelled, you could just see the ground crew loading the baggage onto a small truck through the leaking fumes.

Mercredi matin - a few rollerbladers joined the groups of fishermen along the pebbled Baie de Anges. Rows of palm trees and white railings, blue chairs and white gulls, blue shutters and white balconies, blue sea and chic white awnings lined the promenade where the bars and elegant hotels with gold names regarded the paradise de plage.

None of the ticket machines were working. There was a long line of people and only one counter to buy tickets . The train announcement said the train was already at Nice. The queue would have to speed up .

'Je m'excuse.' said Tarquin to a woman and explained they were late for a meeting and could they go first. The little Blue Train arrived on time. The small stations along the route line had pretty flowers and plants. The cypress trees in the villa gardens, inspiration to Van Gogh and Cézanne, did not move in the still windless air.

As the train travelled along the Côte D'Azur it went through little tunnels each time appearing in a different bay, Villefranche Sur Mer, Eze Sur Mer, Cap D'Ail. The sunset turned the sky rose and the small boats sat very still on the tranquil sea. The train rocked slowly on to Monaco.

At Monaco the lights from the hotels and apartments gradually came on as the sky became dark and covered three sides of the harbour. They walked through the smart squares, passed the casinos and white boats. There was a slight smell of diesel and seaweed, Tarquin didn't find it unpleasant as trod the Grand Prix circuit. Everything seemed to be paying attention to itself.

Tarquin, Hermione and Dubois ate scallops with Celliers de Dauphin, toasted Devota with champagne and enjoyed a jazz quartet which was playing a new arrangement of a Hungarian folk song. The waves of double bass played over the drum rhythm and when the melody became freer Dubois concentrated on the quality of the grand piano. Sometimes it got as confusing as her 97/98 Irish Tax Guide.

She turned her attention to the shimmering view of strategically placed yachts suspended in the moment of the beautiful evening. She had hated her music teacher at school and lessons at school but enjoyed the success of the musically inclined girls. Her spanish guitar lessons were invaluable, she could play a minuet, andantino exercises and Love Me Tender. Her friend could play The Streets of Loredo and Lord of The Dance. She also had a tamborine she played badly when no one else was around.

Dubois had owned about a dozen Elvis singles bought from someone's Roddy Doyled collection , but they became dislocated along with Bill Hayley's The Twist that cost 1p from a jumble sale aged five and a Theatre of Hate LP that got stuck behind a cupboard in Ladbroke Grove. She was horrified because it belonged to somebody else and she couldn't unscrew the fixtures to retrieve it, the only solution would be to knock the wall down. And so it stayed there like a Fred West victim.

Snares

The breeze from the windows between the tube train carriages made Hermione look up. The elderly Pakastani gentleman wearing a traditional brimless hat with a white beard and a grey suit stood perfectly framed again as the train wobbled and shook behind his head turning at a bend on the line. It continued noisily through the tunnel until they pulled into the platform at the Angel. They walked down the hill to Sadler's Well's.

Hermione had seen some great photographs of the Peschawar Hat Market where the bazaar storytellers recount far-fetched myths and allegories. She wanted to know the name of the brimless hat worn with the starched white neru style cotton collar but knew no Pushtoo or Urdo to ask. They had been arguing about the name of and origins of a chef's toque, their black and white chequered trousers and white twill herringbone cotton neck scarves and how the little toque high hats ended up as presentation on racks of lamb. And why shepherds waited until the evening to wash their socks, which would not be dry by the morning necessitating a second pair.

The Lyon's Ballet started at 7.30pm. The first piece was called 100% Polyester 'un objet dansant a definer no 36'. Adventurous, inspirational and expressive, two choreographed white dresses are suspended on hangers and joined at the sleeves to make one piece. A row of fans blow the fabric making it dance to an electronic mix by DJ Food. Allusive Apollo phrases move the minimalist hypnotic performance into another dimension.

During the interval Tarquin got the pre-ordered sandwiches. He had not known how many rounds they would need for four people. He took the advice of the person serving. Existentialist rounds of sandwiches and paper rounds and the increased circulation of the Guardian from 5,000 to 180,000, x 30,000 since the 1911. Manchester corn law wars occupied Tarquin as he made his way back to the balcony table. He had lunched in the city and was struck by a piece he had read by a retired banker Mumtaz Iqbhal as he waited for the arrival of the people he was meeting.

'The revelations of peace can be as bewildering opaque as the fog of war.'

'Brass hats shouldn't make the mistake of thinking that the seat of intelligence is in the chin.'

They re-entered the auditorium, another voyage into the unknown. An eccentric Jules Verne voyage to shape their realities for his two hundredth anniversary. 'Jules Verne is the fourth most translated author,' interrupted Hermione, 'less known for his inventions like the Pan telegraph facsimile machine and Gas Cab. I defy you the distance to The Reform Club. Bring the wine.'

High Hat

Hindu for hat Hermione discovered is Tu Pi. The rose had transparent onion skin lucidity, un peu nacarat in the atmospheric lighting. Chelsea 3 – Madrid 0. It was 9.30pm. Hermione needed her notebook and racked her brains where she had left it.

A kissing couple stood next to them on the two hundred and fifty metre observation deck of the Eiffel Tower as the 2002 celebration lights were switched on writing out the numbers on the great icon structure. They had eaten lunch at the Jules Verne Restaurant earlier when Monmartre and The Sacre Coeur was hit by a rainbow. Hermione took a photograph and texted Dubois. She remembered criticising the amount of packaging used for some topical product or souvenirs in one of her recycling phases as she stuffed her bags onto a spare seat. Vacuum packed and vacuum moulded items with excessively engineered boxed outers.

She refilled her glass and bosonova'd from the table to the kitchen to the brushes on a steel drum kit. Her long hall had a runner, which thankfully had a slip proof under mat perfect for her mambo moments.

Barry the Crab

'The fishmonger caught a crab in my jambalaya,' said Hermione. 'His body was honey brown and about 1.5cm across, 5cm including his legs. It was only a small pot of shrimp. I've seen better-looking plaice. You should have seen the one that got away.'

The crab was perfect with a little serrated exoskeleton like a circular saw with a jagged edge. Its surface was slightly tortoise shell. According to her source the males have an inverted Y shape to their abdomen likened to the Washington Monument and the females are more pyramid shape. The information source also mentioned the Capital building. Each set of four legs has a flat fan end. The others are articulated with four joints plus a front claw. The front separated pincer is either red [male] or blue [female], neatly wrap around, hug and protect its little vertical aperture mouth. When looking underneath a contrasting V shaped six packs blew some little bubbles. They are capable of walking forwards and diagonally but they usually walk sideways. No real explanation was given for this.

If the tides are right you can find them washed up on the Thames beaches [notably SW8]. She recognised her skill requirement for a £40,000 a year job counting them for their migration studies in the Caribbean and made a note to add it to her CV.

Crab Nebula 1054 AD supernova is four times brighter than Venus [mag-6] and was discovered by John Bevis 1731 and Charles Messier 1758 and added to the sky atlas.

Turpentine trees and turtle soup.

Tarquin spent the afternoon carving two massive orange pumpkins and filling them and all the available vases and glasses with small tea lights until the house resembled a temple. The trail of flickering flames reminded him of the scene from the English Patient as the pumpkins sat and glowed with spooky faces. Hermione's kitchen was full of everything seasonal. Chestnut, goats cheese and spinach salad, Teriyake with eryngii Japanese mushrooms and roasting pumpkins. She stopped cooking and made a paper hat out of newspaper, found some French brandy and toasted Nelson. It was the two hundredth anniversary of Trafalgar. Retreating to her laptop she reread the response to her weeks activities. The mobile brand had been tested for new marketing possibilities. PR exploitation of the advertising campaign utilising the latest cabtv, phone technology screens and electricity free cardboard film sequences, advanced lenticular footage. They drove around W1 testing their cab as a target audience and passed the breaking news 'future wireless' locational technologies – below the Coca-Cola sign at Piccadilly which gives the time date, temperature and cryptic text messages. 'Info chic clique loquacity. Love Babel …….side by side, unbeatable happy birthday … fashion victim …..' New roles for future audiences' psycho geographical games, mobile technology to construct knowledge 'buzz buzz.

Boardroom back biting and budgeting. One late night, two missed lunches. Hermione was glad it was in production.

Chestnut soup and chestnut ice cream.

They had celebrated with Dim Sum. Steaming Har Kau pink and white prawn paper wrapped parcels, chiew chow glutinous rice dumplings with pork and very finely sliced bright green vegetables, chillie chickens feet and sizzling ducks tongues, scallops, cheung fun and Chinese tea.

Halloween firecrackers, ghosts, ghouls and spiders. The food smelt of cinnamon and oil. Cherry and cranberry blood red cocktails with rose petals were waiting to be prepared.

'Are the kids ready? Let's go trick or treat. I'm taking them next door for a couple of hours have you got the tricks?'

'How are they? India's got them ...'

'Great.'

Epiphany threw some firecrackers and rang the bell.

'Trick or treat!'

'Hi, what do you plan to do if I have no treats?'

'I have a spell book. There's a red ribbon and a green candle with a $1 note to influence daddy's investment. I've got a coin in my shoe and India has a ear of corn.'

'You'd better come in and have some chocolate eyeballs and skeletons then. We've got apples on strings for some reason and some in a bowl for apple bobbing.'

The children played, made spells and watched some cartoons.

There was plenty of pumpkin at dinner and enough for soup.

'We can have Tiffin tomorrow with muffins, toasted tea cakes and crumpets.' said Hermione as she served another bowl of chestnut ice cream.

' I have to renew my V & A library membership in the morning. I'll put some Louis Jordan on. Basement trumpet. Ground floor for chivalry, stationary and leather ware. As smooth as a piece of galaxy with the wrapper still on it. There are fourteen tunnels and seventeen viaducts on the seventy two mile Settle to Carlisle railway. Ribble Valley viaduct pullman. Do you think you've enough head of steam to last until Guy Fawkes and bonfire night? I might be drunk.'

Perforated photocopier paper

Hermione gave Dubois three wishes. She replied:
1. To visit the places I have not been to yet.
2. Then to visit the ones I had not been to before and
3. To wear chinoise.
What are yours?
    1.   More apartment blocks with swimming pools.
    2.   Eating Russian caviar everyday.
    3.   Hearing no complaints.

Dubois bought some poppies and they walked past the Christmas windows stopping to look at the knitted toys in one armoire lifestyle display. It was Remembrance Sunday, they had observed the minutes silence at 11am, shopped then stopped for tea and parkin. Hermione took a letter out of her handbag with her evening class graduation details on,

' I have a date for the Diploma graduation ceremony. It says there's a reception.'

'Hermione you're nearly as old as the perforated paper these pins are stuck in, is there a need to change its presentation to a contemporary design or has the original a more respectful message?'

'Good question Dubois. Maybe Monsieur Sabor could design a poppy carpet for the knitted thing. Je t'aime mon petit.' Hermione took the toy to the till pour l'acheter et Dubois fait le bruit des baisses.'

'Tarquin the cuckold,' said Dubois, 'this is not soft toy monogamy then Hermione. He will grow Monsieur Molieres horns.'

Hermione smiled and paid then added the little bag to the others.

'On y va! Il y a autres tapis de voir.'

R'n B

Tarquin sat at the keyboard and played a few bars of honky tonk jazz to the Blue Note CD that was playing adopting the Cinque Port privileges and liberties in his own upright jurisdiction, importing, exporting and trading notes. The journey back from Carlisle was snow all the way. A brief encounter with steam and Wensleydale cheese.

'There's an early train from Portsmouth to Liverpool Street station which brings a container of fresh salt water to the Hotel Spa there,' said the ticket collector as he showed them to the dining car. 'Here is your table, by the window sir.'

Tarquin checked his mobile before turning it off. Someone had left a message on his answer phone. A long message which he listened to twice and then passed to Henry for an Agatha Christie option.

How urgent was the Indian ladies request for someone to call her back, it sounded like she knew them very well. They forwarded the message to the department for their reaction.

They changed at Leeds and left their Orient Express without any BR sandwich clichés. Tarquin had been a hero once, stopping someone walking off with a friend's luggage on a nine hour journey in Spain, but it hardly met the detection or literary intrigue of the classic crime writers.

Captain James Cook had named Hawaii 'The Sandwich Islands' after the 4th Earl of Sandwich when he discovered them. He gave the settle valleys an 'Aloha' as he ate his escargot and chateaubriand lunch and then rang himself at home to leave a message to remember go out and buy some milk.

Vermeer

Hermione walked slowly around the exhibition lingering at the Dégas Jockeys at the start of the race, studying the composition, cut off at one side and vertically divided by a post.

'Only three horses. What are the odds? Which one is the favourite? Where are the other horses?'

'Hello India. That's another picture dear. They probably only had a frame that size. Have you seen the ballerina's rehearsal rooms?'

'Yes the prettiest colours.'

'Luminous.'

India rented Hermione's flat where she had lived before she met Tarquin. The flat was her grand plan, a property investment for her financial independence as a modern woman. She would keep it as a business to maintain her independence when she married. Or sometimes depending on her partner situation she had a baby from a passionate affair, which she took to briefings – working from home. The rent from her friend who lived with her covered the mortgage payments and she only had to work two days a week to live a very nice lifestyle. Then she met Tarquin and dropped plan B like putting down a good book on rabies and picked up a healthy income. Hermione and India ordered coffee and Absinthe and discussed Ascot, peeling quails eggs, hats and watching front fence as the hooves charged by on the touted turf.

India had recently visited the Cardamom Mountains in Cambodia and the million elephants of Laos. She told Hermione about the paddy fields, flowers, plums, rivers and bridges, bicycles, rain and fish with chillies and coconut.

'L'amour l'après midi' is on at the ICA,' said Hermione.

'Good film I would like to have seen it when it came out.'

'1972. Every opinion at it's start is a minority of one – Thomas Carlyle – a British politician, I've just been reading about today. Look …….' The Everlasting no 'refusal comes to the centre of indifference' and eventually embraces the everlasting yea – a voyage of denial to disengagement to volition, an existentialist awakening –Calvinism.'

'Your usual irritating self Hermione, I'm glad to hear.'

They finished their Absinthe and put a bet on the Cheltenham Cup winning £5 each. Hermione pulled some Christmas cards out of her bag.

'Yours is in there or you pay me for the stamp.'

She posted them before India had a chance to answer.

Tarquin was 'at home', his feet on the upholstery.

'Stool pigeons and decoy ducks,' said Hermione as she put her coat on a hanger.

'Have you eaten? I could eat clays. India has made me hungry. What have you been doing?'

'Trying to play the notes made by the birds in this picture on the electricity pylon wires. I found my guitar. I'll play it for you if you like?'

White Chocolate

Made with their premium espresso roast blend and soy silk milk it is a high return personal investment in caffeine sex, at £2.75 the Grande is worth the little extra.

Hermione's research stated the company contributed $1.8 million to education in Indochina, Ethiopia, Kenya and Guatemala, and $750,000 to conservation in Latin America and Africa, an investment they share with their customers. The product launch was two days away.

1.30pm meeting with the Olympic logo designer at The National Gallery Café, its new restaurant. The just opened vast space was very cool and white. The meeting was to discuss the inspiration for the meeting the following day. There was a Valentines theme for the week as they walked through the rooms enjoying the oxblood-buttoned chesterfields with low, firm, well-upholstered upright backs dividing the two sides and returning either end. They watched Japanese tourists with lay-by picnic chairs and sandwiches discussing cupid and clouds. Hermione and the designer stopped to listen to a talk given to a small attentive group. Gainsborough's Lovers Walk, post wedding breakfast stroll with loyal hound to symbolise their union, powdered wigs and idyllic scenery, Pintaricchio's Penelope and her suitors. They left the blushing art historian with Psyche being adorned with gifts by cupid flowers, ribbons, silks and scents under the glass ceilinged room with bold colour and glorious gilt. The designer was accurate and edited his muses and fiery mimesis to supplicate his Olympic flame with didactic information.

Hermione returned to the office and checked her diary. Valentines Day – Baccarat, Bolanger, Banco and Banquet – this year was a Wednesday. She drank her white chocolate mocha, made some publication bookings and emails and confirmed her date for the evening. Message from India – dinner confirmed. Epiphany would get the New York vibe on the coffee, sugar and cocoa exchange prices. They had been to the Moda silver studio museo tessuto to see the Beaux Art textiles with some visiting guests last summer. She recalled their mostaccioli and rigatoni jackets.

The remainder of that afternoon was spent looking for other places to dunk your cookies.

The shirt worn by Hermione's date matched the surface texture of the bar's interior. She found it slightly distracting.

The following day the Olympic logo meeting was a successful presentation which continued over lunch in Charlotte Street where the chef keeps his fungi and mushrooms outside, displayed on a cloth in the February temperatures. Big, beautiful gills, soft folds in pale brown, pink and yellow. The gym was quiet in the afternoon; Epiphany did fifteen minutes running, fifteen minutes weights and fifteen minutes bicycle. Her yoga class had changed to Thursday. The office was buzzing with gossip and telephones when she got back. Chelsea had left a memo on her desk – Celebrity client needed press statement for alleged incident and break up.

Selecting an evening class with the Weatherman had been an amusing exercise, he brought a floodlight with him that day, and it was an amusing digression while waiting for lunch. That was three months ago. Now Hermione had to tailor her diary around it and found herself sounding slightly odd 'I can't make Tuesdays, I have French evening class.' The Weatherman was now an expert on philosophy and cinema.

Five degrees centigrade. The dawn crowing had woken her as usual, the chicken houses needed extra insulation for the winter ,the sudden drop would affect their laying. Dubois fed the ducks and geese with some corn, rice and the end of a bag of spaghetti. One of the legbar cocks was being a bully she would have to check it for red mites. Then she completed boxing the Rhode Island Red order, collecting the alabaster shells in her feathered apron, moon boots and Fendi hat.

She ate a goats cheese crepe with coconut and lime salad while her Christmas plum pudding soaked in ruby port. Icefish and coconut stew waited for dinner. When the delivery was taken she drove to drop some toys off for the children's Christmas appeal. She tutted at her split ends and rang to make a time to have them cut off. Her straighteners would disguise the overdue visit for tonight, instant sleek and shine. She took the tickets off the pinboard for the theatre later and put them in her purse.They were meeting at 6.45 pm. It was a small theatre with three tiers of balcony boxes, very tall for it's width. The play lasted two hours including the champagne interval. Two critics were discussing the set and making notes on the interior, its choreographic use of space in conjunction with the furniture, doors and windows, effective variety of lighting - English summer sunlight, evening and electric.

'A living Grierson documentary. Great selection of music. Did you get a list of credits ?'

'Yes I'll send it later. Sailor suits. Textiles. U.S. influences - been watching too many films !'

'18th century Napoleon and archeology in Egypt ..Yes....the scale of the pieces is incredible. Are you doing anything on Saturday ?' asked Dubois.

'We'll be in Scotland.' replied Hermione.

Tarquin and Hermione were visiting a castle for the weekend. The reindeer park at Aviemore was always a favourite with Epiphany .

Dubois smiled to herself. She was making a list of resolutions and wants and started to write them down on the programme as they waited for the safety curtain.

Dear Santa ,

How are the elves? Hermione and Tarquin have both been good children.

These are some of the things I want for Christmas [first draft.]

Trips to Kashmir, Vietnam, Egypt and Moscow.

A sleigh ride in the snow with sleigh bells and fur.

A train over the Ribble Valley Viaduct.

A city capsule living experience. Japanese hotel style micro flats featured in an article last week.

A new car she liked the Citroën's latest concept 'air' something.

Navy shoes and underwear.

A bigger house and the silver hob canopy repaired. [It only needed a new filter but she kept forgetting when she was in the store.]

A longer run for the chickens.

The kitsch yacht front minibar she looked at every week in the shop on the way to the tube. [Her own little port and starboard].

Turtle soup.

And macaroni.

Resolutions: To keep her diary tidy.

Eat jellied eels and stop noticing men's wedding rings on the tube.

Then Dubois read the back of the programme.

'By immersing himself in the personality of others he forgot his own is perhaps the only way not to suffer from it. 'Flaubert.

It was a full moon, brighter than usual; there was a reason she had read earlier.

A bowl of raspberries .

In the toy deparment the 00 train chuffed on it's tracks around the perfect scale signal box, trees and static model people in typical plastic poses. Outside the festive chandelier Christmas lights belied the start of the festive semiology which exists from November to January. Valentine's Day, Cadbury's Cream Eggs, holidays, heatwaves, Halloween, 5th of November and January sales. Cards and commercial calendars, guilt trips and excuses to celebrate. The ice skating rink was full of laughing people wearing hats, scarves and mittens dancing to music, drinking hot chocolate and watching the flames in the square.

Waiting for the white winter weather from Narnia as the season slowly neared, people were present buying, receiving party invitations and booking holidays. Hermione bought some skatewings from the ice mountain fish counter. Blue tag, beautiful white flesh angels wings. She added some bright silver sprats and little pink skate cheeks for a fish stew. Tarquin studied the penguin paradise.

'Boiling peppermints!'

'FAA - iheihe. Tahitian for making yourself beautiful,'said Hermione.

'Yellow dress again and navy shoes.'

The assistant serving held his apron lace at his stomach like a Beuckalaer fishmonger. Fire, air, earth and water .The prodigal son in the background leaning on a group of debauched women. Tarquin surveyed the surrounding signage of escalators and departments for a signpost to Chaucer's nunnery.

Hermione was finishing her coffee.

'How about this one for Henry. Downing Street doorman - £15,000 plus benefits and pension. 2 years experience, apply in writing or email including CV.

3 month trial contract .'

'Intrapreneur dreams of entrepreneurial expansion - Freudian trip.'

They passed the hanging game, wheat bundles and floured rustic loaves, hare terrine, ghee, sushi, caviar and canapes.

'Any goose or duck eggs?'asked Hermione .

'No .'

She turned back to Tarquin.

'They have no Rhode Island Reds either. Remind me to contact their buyer when we get home .'

Festive frontier

The following day getting to Scotland was a literal Hadrian's Wall of a hurdle. Hermione's wisdom and basic instinct told her to make some posset for their souvenir hangover. Minerva's wisdom had given the Athenians olive trees, the flute and the art of taming wild animals. Hermione lent her roman 'CODONUS' cure to avoid sounding like the talking grave at Lambeth castle cemetery. She could not reach her Delftware which was made in Lambeth at the nearby factory, without climbing on a chair and decided to avoid further damage so early and used some glasses instead. She gave some posset to Tarquin. Conquering the circus maximus journey would be more like his usual Solomon island canoeist who navigates by underwater lighting.

Dubois had a lunch meeting at the Eel Pie and Mash Shop. She parked in Boss Street near the Design Museum and took her paperwork to see her jobbing accountant Amen.

Amen otherwise known as the Egyptian God of the unknown and unseen, as reliable as the rising and setting sun.

'Hi I'll be brief, the dog and bone needs a charge, I'm just parking and I'll be there in five minutes..'

She checked her boat race in the window, and walked up a short flight of apples and pears, tucked her Hogan plates under the table unbuttoning her whistle as she did.

From Tower Bridge you can see all the bridges to Charing Cross revealed through their arches. She knew the vast pumping rooms and walkways. People were walking along the embankment enjoying the riverboats and flags in the sunshine. The yellow and cream Wellington stood out. Dubois fancied an office on the elegant funnelled boat along from the Latin bar decks and conference dining. She made a note to visit the Tea and Coffee Museum samovars to buy some Russian Caravan.

Amen arrived.

'Hello Amen, I've brought you two dozen duck and geese eggs, try not to break them and the 2007 hard copy.'

'Dubois hi. Thanks. Forms. All you have to do is sign here and here .... Good that was easy now food. This is much better idea than the office.' He looked around. ' I have some Slivowitz in my bag to make it Kosher. What do you want, a mug of tea?'

'Tea, jellied eels with mash and liquor.'

'Make that two with one pie as well.'

Amen scanned the net and gross.

'Where are your totals?' then he mumbled something about percentage forecast and clauses and said, 'Content or not Content?'

The food arrived.

'Content' replied Dubois.

He put the paperwork in his bag and his bag next to him on the wooden and iron bench and they ate then drank their tea.

Clean green and white tiles covered the walls. A photograph of the original owner hung with an 1880 date. Around the dumb waiter there were three dimensional relief tiles with pink flowers and the staff wore smart green and white overalls. Behind the counter they had pictures of celebrities who had dined there, Victoria Beckham and Roy Orbison.

'You must come to our Christmas party Dubois.'

He wrote the time and date on his newspaper next to a humorous article she read later which gave Pijin Polynesian translation 'Mi kam to meresin long klimik iq, mi no kam to faki, I came to this clinic for medicine not sex. Duim hambag – to have sex.'

'Thanks!' said Dubois, 'I'll make some Advokaat.'

Tambourine

Dubois went for her usual thirty minute run; she ran three or four times a week or swam. Listening to dance music on her discman disciplined her pace and pushed her faster. When she got back she checked and fed the chickens then ate her porridge with a shot of malt whiskey.

Amen's party was that evening. She made some advokaat and started the armoire archaeology of black dresses. Paul Costello, plain wool with long sleeves, Egyptian sandblasted glass necklace, gold eye shadow and camel coat. Amen's motorbike was outside the restaurant. Inside the Christmas tree was covered in gold and white lights. You could hear carol singers and French horns coming from a few doors away over the music and talk.

'Hi Amen, how's tricks?'

'Fine, hi. The party's arrived. Dubois come and get a drink. If I had a pound for every toilet roll wrapper basket I've shot I would be a very rich man. I could have played for the Harlem Globetrotters. I have nothing else to throw. Wembley Stadium is packed tonight as you can see'.

'You're in a good mood Amen.'

'Writer's block, another clichéd stereotype in the way, most of them are trying to get published.'

They left the glowing icicle Christmas tree and walked through the groups of cocktail dresses and conversations talking about stadium budgets and schedules, 2012, the Christmas number one and the latest film release.

'Canapes, fishcakes, Russian eggs, cantuccini and cheeses.'

'Hermione and Tarquin said to say hello and Happy Christmas they arrived in Scotland about an hour ago and Epiphany has already made a snowman. Cheese looks interesting.'

'It taste rancid.'

'Poets have been mysteriously silent on the subject of cheese' – political comment by a politician, I can't remember which one, Chesterton or somebody like that, about cheese or the government. The French have two hundred and seventy two different types of cheese and did you know that Marlon Brando was particularly partial to brie. You need a particularly large vat to make a decent amount, rennet and enzymes and a good thermometer. I was given a tour of a fromagerie in Tignes last year, they have massive cowbells, and I was surprised at the process handling the curds to put them in moulds. Great cheese. The dairy is very helpful for contacts and supply. They gave me some sample rennets to produce my own cheddar. It takes a while, about a month for a ripe one. I have my own baby thermometer now. Did you ski this year Amen?'

'Yes Slovenia and Austria, snowboarding, jet skis and husky's, I bought a new white and silver jacket with built in goggles, LCD altitude read out and compass for cross country. It's great you can vanish into the snow like a magician's dove, skiing to music. We skied floodlit at night and took part in a torch lit parade. Here's your drink.'

The party discussion continued around Henry and Hattie's tattoos, Bambi and Thumper, a heraldic horse and a rattlesnake. There was a great deal of dancing and singing around the piano –let it snow, I'm dreaming of a white Christmas and Etienne sang silent night in French..

Left or Right of the Dealer.

At 2am they called a taxi and Dubois left with Henry and Hattie passing Amen's motorcycle parked outside. She got home and mixed a drink, found a sweatshirt and scrubbed her little Egyptian face then emailed Hermione.

Hi Hermione,

Excellent party. Wembley's budget was popular with the profit and lossers. Thought for the evening about the £757 million – the umpire will have to write a cheque for injury time before the match and toss a coin at the end to see who will foot the bill. Another channel tunnel story to distract from the trains being on time in the newspapers. Maybe they should strike on cup days or when everyone's in front of the telly. Daisy did some snake charming and belly dancing, which she'd learnt on her recent trip to Marrakesh. Everyone got presents; I played the tambourine and ate belinis and angels on horseback. I didn't spill anything and Amen has promised to take me out on his motorbike in the New Year and to see Goal 2 when it's out.

Dubois xxxxx

Amen has asked Dubois if she understood why anyone would tie a ribbon around his bike mirror. It would not have bothered him but it made him remember someone had tied one around his office phone about five years ago and it gave him the spookiest feeling that he was being watched. Dubois told him to stop behaving like an obsessive paranoid from a bad movie.

Tarquin kissed the snowflakes, which had landed on Hermione's eyelashes as she leant her head back looking up at the sky. They walked in the snow through the Narnia landscape with frozen lakes and ice cream dripping from the fir trees for about half an hour and returned to the castle for coffee and mince pies. Mistletoe hung in the hallway.

Hi Dubios,

The offside rule does not apply to ballpark budgets. When the only team player over the line in the penalty area third shoots at goal, it is not allowed. They could threaten to pay them in penalty kicks. We had the cutest asparagus forests filled with cranberries and goose. Epiphany liked her presents. We spent last night with Alexandra and Monty.

Love Hermione xxxx

Dubois got some last minute shopping and watched the organic turkey web cam in Harrods.

Christmas eve. Midnight mass the church was packed. Red and gold robes, choirboys and candles gathered around the stained glass, stone sculptures, nativity and Christmas tree, the congregation wrapped up in fur coats and woolly hats. O come all ye faithful, O little town of Bethlehem.

Hermione, Tarquin, Dubois, Henry, Hattie and Hermione's sister Sydney spent New Year's eve playing cards after a dinner of stuffed squid and risotto with fish and vegetables. They sang Auld Lang Syne, drank champagne and made cocktails. Henry shuffled. The atmosphere around the butter mountain table was intense and buzzing – everyone had a butter knife up their sleeve, Tarquin looked across the attitude, concentration and cigar smoke at Henry attempting to judge his play and memorise the cards with an expectant charge.

Sydney was distracted from her cards by the green emerald pieces of glass in a small window. The jewel like facets caught the candlelight and danced on the wall. Hermione had put coloured glass in all of the interior windows, rose, blue and a rare yellow – she often caught herself staring at them, day dreaming absent mindedly as they shone in the morning sun. She had found the small panel with emerald jewels in a shop for £40.00, it fitted the larder cupboard perfectly, 25 x 35cm.

'Sydney it's your go,' said Hermione.

'Tarquin has just laid the King of hearts.'

'Oh right. King of diamonds.'

Sydney was useless at cards and Hattie told her.

'Sydney you're useless at cards.'

Sydney gave Hattie one of her Michelin Hotel Inspector business cards. She had a purse full of a selection of publisher, journalist and health and safety inspector for party people.

Hermione's latest remodelling project was working on a laminate vibe. She had wanted a wooden wall in her office to go with some sixties furniture she had seen and a glass bead curtain she had which made reassuring music when you walked through it. Tarquin was used to her sticking pictures and samples of colour on the walls. An intercom with a light, which buzzed for telephone calls, proved amusing starting point to her theme. Hermione found herself with a playful inclination to push the loudspeaker button in Sainsbury's as they left the checkouts. Some of her other projects involved a rich crimson room with glowing floors, and painting a wall in the kitchen black – it sucked you in like a magnet when you stood next to it and she loved the sunlight on the marble walls through her muslin curtains hanging from their silver finials.

'Any scurvy?' asked Hermione, talking to Tarquin as he walked up and down impersonating an electric toothbrush, brushing his teeth and gums. He could never stand in front of the mirror in the bathroom like some people. He usually forgot to brush them when he had been drinking.

'No scurvy.'

He had toothpaste economy. Why did people automatically use the amount shown in the ads?

He spent about an hour once explaining how if the aperture's diameter were changed by 1mm we would use 250,000 extra tubes of toothpaste a year if we persisted in using the regulation toothbrush length of toothpaste. This would make the manufacturers an additional £750,000 in increased sales; alternatively they could reduce the aperture and not charge the price and still sell more toothpaste. Hermione fell asleep.

Lemon Grass

Dubois inspected the cornflowers and little fir trees in her window box as there had been a frost, the temperature had got quite severe. She was reading My Family and Other Animals by Gerald Durrell and wishing the days were long and hot. The book was sitting on a plain wooden chair with an embroidered cushion, small cross stitches in pale blue, red and yellow , hearts and lovers tokens around a green circle that looked like a crown of parsley. Outside the branches and twigs moved in front of the window with ghosted shadows, purple judas trees giving away the time of day as the sun went down and came up. At this time it was as bright as the Galatas Limomodasos lemon tree forest on Poros, birth place of Theseus and home to the Temple of Poseidon, carnations, springs and watermills. She hid under a patchwork blanket with a cup of hot chocolate and left the shallow anchorage and Russian dockyard behind. She thought about making some eggs for Chinese New Year. One Thousand Year Eggs, first boil, crack shells then soak in soya sauce, remove shell to leave a Ming vase laquer surface of age lines. The alternative was to dye some red which the Greeks do for lent for their supposed protective powers. The first dyed one always belongs to the Virgin.

Dubois finished her drink, it was still early. She listened to The Archers then crawled out, found her Toast socks and put Underworld on. Skyscraper I Love You .

Before the New Year countdown Dubois had watched a documentary about the Big Ben clock. A presenter was talking about the clockfaces with clips of Buster Keaton hanging from the clock hands in Wall Street. The Big Ben tower is reached by climbing up a narrow spiral stairway which involves a medical questionnaire and disclaimer for heart conditions, claustrophobia and epilepsy. Dubois' experiences of Mexican pyramids and Gaudi churches was enough to put the idea aside although she wanted to stand inside the analogue window, awed by it's scale and deafened by it's timekeeping. She had been introduced to Buster Keaton's

[BK's] editor at a breakfast meeting in Santa Monica on a trip to Hollywood ten years earlier. Maybe Hermione's sister Sydney could get a press pass to get around the 'no members of the public' rule for visitors.

She opened a bottle of Limoncella and put the ten eggs in water to boil. She selected them from a large bowl next to an article on lemon varieties and Henry's design for Dubois' Dozen two storey egg box scribbled on a serviette .

Thick skinned or wedges.
Bergamot
Verbana
Harvey
Eureka [fewer thorns]
Meyer [introduced from china in 1908 thin skinned and less acid]
Lisbons
Prior
Old line
Ponderosa
True
Dorshapo [bumpy rough peel]
Armstrong [skin used for oil]
Berna [elliptical]
Bearss [flavouring and candles]

Technically the lemon is a berry prized for its medical properties, relieving colic, originally grown in 1193 by the Sultan of Egypt and introduced to the Mediterranean from India. It was then taken to America by Christopher Columbus in the nineteenth century. Lemons were rationed to the British Navy to combat scurvy giving them their 'limey' name – lemony would be more accurate confusing them with an over ripe lime.

The Limoncello was made from the oval type of Sorrento.

Dubois contemplated bitter anathemas: whether floundering lemon sole ever felt the people looking at them looked intelligent or stupid, lemon squeezer faces, Phillip Stark kitchen items, mechanism-less individuals form and function. At one time she had about three classic glass lemon squeezers but could not find one.

As the eggs boiled she drank the sour, syrupy chilled liquor. She drained the eggs and put half of them in cochineal, the other half she cooled and rolled with her hand cracking the shells and then put them to soak in a Soya sauce to make Thousand Year Eggs. [Nine hundred and eighty six years, give or take a few – the soya beans are only kept buried for fourteen years – who's counting?]

The oyster shells she had kept from a dinner two days before were still sitting to one side, she melted some tea lights and made some little candles with them replacing the wicks.

Winter sunshine turned into early evening. Hermione rang Dubois on her way back from a swim in Fulham and arranged to go for a drink.

Tarquin's hangover was making the room rollercoaster with scenes from seventy's horror films with padded cells and spiked shrinking walls. She left him to his Universal Studios reconstruction and rollercoaster until he recovered. Sometimes it was rounds with Mike Tyson or birdcage floors. They sat and toasted little pink and white marshmallows. The sugar burnt like a spacerocket on re-entry. Hermione had cut her leg shaving, only half paying attention, as the water hit the shower curtain she watched the blood go down the plug hole Psycho style. They ate the marshmallows and brainstormed the feasibility for a fun Fashion Cafe/Restaurant for the eighteen to twenty five youth market. An interesting identity venue for people who wanted to be seen and pose. It had been topical at dinner, would it be a realistic business venture or a floundering flatfish?

'Orange and goats cheese salad, chestnut and spinach salad ......'

'Parsley and beetroot vodka sorbets, food with flowers and belinis,'interrupted Hermione .

'Catwalk vibe and ambient music.'

India had been somewhere similar abroad which she raved about. Models and wannabes, fashion student fever. She had also eaten in a typical American rail carriage diner somewhere in Covent Garden when she was drunk and couldn't for the life of her find it again.

They had nearly finished the bottle of Limoncella .

'Any baseballl pitchers in the budget?' asked Hermione. 'Baseball pitchers should be aware of 'Lemon List activities '- the dollar men who did not keep up with the indexes in the 2000 crash were on Henry's 'Lemon List '.'

Dubois impersonated Henry, 'Belief based' not 'evidence based 'pitching improvement was required by trading to boost velocity, longer hardballs or weighted balls. Weight training was advised for pitchers.'

The scent of the sugary citrus hit her as she poured another glass.

Punjab

When Hermione returned she discovered Tarquin had made Tandori chicken. He had found the red food colour and mixed it with yoghurt, spices and chillie and taken great care and pleasure in slashing and covering the meat screaming 'Beetle juice! Beetle juice! Beetle juice! As he did it. His hands and fingers the colour of blood.

'Do you want some? I've found an evening course in Indian Cuisine and reserved a place online. What do you think?'

He showed Hermione the page. She read the write up and tried some of the vivid red chicken.

'It's amazing. I'm impressed.'

He had been going through a gold Medici phase, first floor Tuscany living, truffle hunting, Italy's rice bowl, risotto's, pork and bean stew, and wines from Elba and Napoleonic battles. Charged by the Palio horse races, the gold painted hooves which race over a ninety second course and the Lucca coastal locations of the 1930'a golden era of movie stars. They visited the National Gallery with Hermione's sister and picnicked with strawberries in balsamic vinegar by the Spanish Fountains in Hyde

Park last summer. Hermione was capable of finding herself disorientated in the many rooms of the gallery, but always managed to navigate her way out once she found the large seascape ports of Carthage before the Medicis, Bellinis and Botticellis, halos and shining armour, Bermejo's St Michael slaying the devil in a crimson silk cloak. As they lay on the picnic cloth in the sunshine, the strawberries all eaten, Sydney screamed as something landed and crawled on her. She suddenly confessed to murdering a massive spider when she was about four by boiling it and skewering it down a drain until she was sure it was dead. She said it was like The Incredible Shrinking Woman.

Tarquin lit her cigarette as she fumbled with her matches.

It was about 5.30pm when the sun started to go down. They packed up the picnic and walked back through the park, groups of people were playing football, frisbee, roller-blading and boating and a pony club dressage event was presenting rosettes.

Tarquin's checklist:
Spices and rack
Seeds
Chillies
Pastes
Yoghurts
Limes
Fresh herbs

They grow lots of coriander but Hermione's chilly plant wanted to remain ornamental.

Haggis

The first spring day in February with the recommended daily intake of 5000-lux light bathing hours. Amen took Dubois out to Cambridge on his Ducatti motorbike. He lent her a pair of gloves, a jacket and a helmet with walky talky intercom and she held onto the back of the racing panel and mirrored his moves staying warm behind him. They walked through the college squares, lawns and surrounding stone cloistered walkways with people reading in windows, college scarves and bicycles everywhere, books tied up with string in their baskets. Amen made a crown out of pussywillow and put it on Dubois' head. She looked like a Lady of Shallot as he punted her along the river Cam with swallows diving in the water and mermaids sitting on the riverbanks. They were too old to jump off the bridge in the après ball tradition but agreed to return in the summer. Feeling hungry they found an agreeable restaurant and had half a dozen oysters and half a pint of Guinness each. Amen suggested a Ukrainian wedding tradition of ducking the bride and groom's parents in the river instead. He took some of the bread and fed her then drank to their liaison by putting his arm through hers and trying to drink leaning forward over the table with their arms linked and getting Guinness on Dubois' nose.

The following day was Valentine's Day; she had three cards and a bunch of mixed white flowers with daisies and roses. Hermione sent her an email –

Hi Dubois

I've just written to The Times to praise the little cages which catch the post as it comes through the letterbox to stop it landing on the doormat because it makes you realise you've just wiped your feet when you butter your toast.

How many cards?

I'm still craving haggis, the whiskey and porridge is a good replacement until I have another one.

See you at 1.30pm

Hermione

Seeking culinary karma on his first Indian Cuisine evening class Tarquin was introduced to about ten other students mostly wearing suits after work [minus their ties]. An actor and a politician's wife. The chef talked for about twenty five minutes about two handled 'karahi' concave cooking pans, light chat snacks that translated as 'lick', paneer cheese made by curdled milk and lemon juice and the different regions, spices and trade. Trades like paper mache, silks, carving and pashmina shawls made from cashmere with embroidered paisley patterns representing cypress trees bending in the wind. Items and jewels, which were prestigiously presented at the 1851 Great Exhibition and kept in the 'nations attic'.

Tarquin laid out his curry leaves, saffron, ginger, cardamom, coconut, cashews and almonds. He had an egg timer, a wind up alarm and sourced a digital clock on the oven as well, he started to prepare the paste and fry the meat in flavoured oil.

When Tarquin arrived home Hermione had lit some incense and put on some silk sarong trousers. He explained everything to her across the candles.

'It's a bit like ringing up directory enquiries in Scotland to get the number for the take away in the next street.'

'What are we having next week?'

Dummy

Dubois was starring at the Polaroid's of clouds stuck on her board, each one unique, she always found herself wanting to catch them all.

She returned to reading the paper – 'enhanced awareness of personal predestination' and 'common bigotry' was the opinion of the new Russian nationalism.

Seasonal affective disorder SAD was a topical post Christmas article, winter negatives and treatments. She had not opted to go for a solarium that morning before her swim. The mother and baby 'water babies' class slows the changing area down with Maclaren buggies and luggage for a week. Little faces with glazed expressions in towel hoodies and blow-dried hair, swimwear with saggy gussets and my first pull up pants.

She flicked through the pages of the paper.

Weapons Inspector.
Pension available £14,500.
Class 1 armourer 5 years MOD.
Environment equipment.
Standards care being applied.

It sounded like the British kitemark small print on the toys in Hamleys.

Speech working solutions new technologies – speech and handwriting recognition for handsets [headline and two column text] – teething uses probable.

Art installation at a Cork Street Gallery – visitors book graphological analysis of comments.

Dubois checked her emails and replied to some customer enquiries and orders. The egg box packaging people were still developing the feasibility of the two storey egg box.

Chocolate Blanc

The Winter Olympics dominated the sports coverage on the TV, the Ski Sunday music and cowbells were familiar to Hermione, she knew the names of three British skiers. Epiphany was an expert. She enjoyed skiing but was lousey at iceskating. They had traversed the Alps the year before on a cross country epic through forests making clean tracks in the untouched snow. They were buccaneers, like pirates on the ski lifts following the signs and runs, taking cable cars to different levels and stopping for hot chocolate and schnapps, arriving in the next valley late afternoon to catch a bus back to their chalet. Tarquin was Captain Morgan freeing them from the morning's ski lesson. Slaves to the subtle latin rhythms of the samba and salsa slopes as unique as the different Caribbean islands themselves .

Tarquin booked his car in for a service. He had adjusted the Karma Sutra fan positions and directions for the change in weather. Something was obviously trapped in it that made an annoying rattling noise. There was also a loose runner under the passenger seat which moved very rapidly before locking unexpectedly. He pointed to an illuminated button on the dashboard.

'Turn the ejector seat off would you.' he said teasing Epiphany and opening the roof.

It reminded him of copying a scene from a James Bond film when he climbed through the apartment window on holiday. Hermione had locked the bathroom door from the wrong side because the window wouldn't shut. Then she had fallen asleep drunk. Tarquin fed several sheets of toilet paper under the door beneath the key, then pushed the key through the lock with a hairgrip he found in Hermione's makeup bag, so that the key fell onto the paper which he then pulled back under the door into the bathroom successfully getting the key and using it to open the door from the inside.

Dubois had mountains of paperwork to do. Her Easter orders were double the usual amount. Although she no longer had receipts and invoices savagely spiked in a Dickensian metropolis of carbon paper, a slave to the cash colomns .

She spent the evening melting chocolate and making eggs, rabbits and chickens in little plastic moulds, smoothing the joins with a spatula. She wrapped some up in foil for Amen. Mixing business and pleasure was always a good thing.

She emailed him with some questions about some equipment she had bought from Ikea. She had sworn to herself that she would never go back there because it took all day to get round. She had also read that women forget the pain of childbirth due to a hormone the body produces.

Without it half of them would never go through it again, with or without drugs .

'You give me fever.' Dubois tuned into the radio. Sixties female vocals and lounge jazz lifted her spirits. Hermione had played a similar CD at a dinner with Henry and one of Tarquin's colleagues. They had all drank too many Bacardi and Cokes, Cubra Libras and Mojitos after a play about Guantanamo Bay and Cuban detainees. Hermione was celebrating the publication of two pieces she had written on London theatre and hotel bars, their writers in residence and journalists, critics and actors who were part of the furniture. She had enjoyed researching the interiors. The glass Waldorf Dining Room, the small bar at The Savoy, The Adelphi, champagne at Claridges and tea at The Ritz. She used to go to a bar near The Strand after work where Richard Harris drank and had spent ten years collecting names and places from endless sources. Irrelevant facts were essential in the pursuit of an interesting piece. She had learnt this when somebody had asked her to contribute to the research of their book when she was fourteen. Her and a friend had had to see how many bites they could take out a small soft centre chocolate. They managed seventy two tiny nibbles from the tempting confectionary.

Aquatint

The accuracy of Big Ben is kept using old pennys. It has only ever been slow twice, once in 1949 due to snow on the hands and once in 1962 due to birds. Another notable occasion was in 1902 when Suffragette protestor Emmeline Pankhurst was held in a prison cell half way up the three hundred and ninety three steps, the incident write up did not say why .

On the news they announced the approval of twenty four hour drinking. Tarquin wandered whether Balfour would have approved as he put his 20p in the slot of the telescope on the opposite bank to the Houses of Parliament restaurant. He had decided to walk at early tide. One of his favourite things including the wide Festival Hall staircases and the decorative 1920's gold lift cage in the British Museum.

'The revolution starts at closing time.' Where did the generals go when they all left the game?

Fifteen years earlier when Hermione was still single a taxi dropped her home at 11.30pm, passed the curried goat shop on the corner, a front for selling cannabis, always suspiciously empty. She told the taxi driver to stop two hundred metres early to protect her destination. Exiting the outside, she took off her shoes and walked around the flat. She had spent forty days and forty nights in Thailand without talking to anybody or eating anything. She did not shave off her hair, neither call herself Jim Morrison. Instead she made sweet rice in banana leaves and knew where to find remote beaches and islands that had supply boats only once a week, mangrove swamps, tree houses, bamboo water gardens, temples with flowers floating in water and beautiful silks. She Gillrayed a cartoon caption bubble -'chemical karma,the single woman in paradise' as she entered the kitchen .

'Damn !'

Her tax return was due on the 31st and her aspic terrine was ready to turn out of the mousse ring mould. India was her little hermit crab now .

Mitigating circumstances.

8.45 am stables. Hermione took Epiphany for her ride. Tarquin and Epiphany had driven back through the city the night before, through the narrow deserted streets, the massive money making power base of skysrapers, illuminated jewels left for the night to shine and burn until the next day. The park was a Siberian wasteland, there was ice on the lake, it was like crossing the Moskva as she walked over the bridge. One snowman watched a snowball fight. The horses slid a little on the ice, their steaming breathe visible in the cold air as they fought the diluvian temperature, they were happy to run when they reached the sand. Hermione put the collar of her military style coat up. She was wearing a fur hat and big boots. She adjusted the camera aperture and photographed the gold and pastel baroque crocus and black caviar berries. A few solitary people walked passed wrapped in coats and scarves with briefcases giving away their journey and work destination . No park bench meetings or waiting Mercedes.

How not to take it the wrong way.

A light appeared on the dashboard indicating the petrol tank was on reserve.

Tarquin stopped at the first petrol station taking a slight detour from their journey. He put on the complimentary gloves to fill the tank, the mechanical figures ticked around slowly. LCD figures are a potential fire risk along with mobile phones and not allowed as he found out once. Hermione needed some milk and wanted a Vogue or Marie Claire. She went in to pay for the petrol and read the headlines waiting for the queue of two people to to be served.

'Pump number three please.'

She questioned herself if it was impolite for the Indian behind the counter to hold out his hand for the money before she had even touched her purse. Or was the gesture taken offensively. She decided that as the same thing happened at her local convenience store it was possibly curteous and convinced herself not to take it the wrong way, although it immitated pictures she had seen of beggars in Delhi. He gave her a receipt and served the next person in the queue. There is no CCTV in the Esso station on the Bayswater Road.

Dubois and India were discussing going to Marrakesh for Easter whilst looking at Vernet landscapes and African camels, with chechiahat, babouches, slippers, kaftans and fezs. There was lots of white and red against gold sand and palm trees. Hermione had found them in the Wallace Collection, sitting on a round buttoned and fringed red velvet settee, sectioned in triangles from the shared central backrest. On the other side of the room was The Laughing Cavalier. For five years his eyes had followed her along the corridor at school where she went to hang up her beret every morning. Twenty seven years later, there he was, Franz Hals, the real thing. Hermione was absolutely gobsmacked.

'It's 1.45pm shall we go and get some lunch ?'

They descended the staircase passed the tapestry, gilt chairs and turbanned busts of black slaves to the petit fours, gateaux and palmiers.

When Tarquin was eight his aunt died of a heart attack and he cried for a week. They used to make waffles, drink Stone's Ginger Wine, play with weegee boards, watch Psycho, smoke cigars and party together. He had not seen her for a couple of days because she had a cold. He discovered they had locked the house up and boarded the windows .Tarquin had made a get well soon card, but it was too late to deliver it. He might have felt slightly better if he had been able to say hello. And then he didn't know what to do with the card he had made. As result he made a point of staying in touch with people and became fanatical about Birthdays and dates. Hermione drank her coffee. Collodi eventually reached a happy ending for Pinocchio. Satre and existentialism seemed an appropriate subject discussed by the two red faced gentlemen on the next table to compliment the decorative surroundings.

'India looks beautiful in her dishdasha,'commented Hermione about a self depricatory remark made regarding her on a previous occasion.

'If you can cope with the souks, you can find some really nice ones.'

'Uniquely ubiquitous and very useful in a sandstorm.'

Before going to meet Tarquin and some friends to eat, Dubois and Hermione stopped at the Buddhist temple to light some insense for new year while the dragons chased the bad spirits away. Candles, chimes and chanting filled the temple. This was the year of the dog. They followed the example set and removed their footwear. Dubois was wearing an old pair of cowboy boots with cuban heels and steel bars in the souls, an old pair of Levis and a shirt. When she bought the boots the staff in the shop had showed her how to put them on by wrapping your feet in plastic bags and filling them with talcum powder and pulling the plastic bags out after. The heavy stitched leather was very stiff and made it difficult to get the right size to fit comfortably at first. They were twenty years old now. She took them off to kneel on the small prayer mat and bowed her head. The prayer mat reminded her of a rug at home that had a dollar bill under it. She knew it was there and thought of it everytime she walked on it .

They ordered sake, rice and fish ball dumplings, turtle soup and lemon fish.

Above the table the lamp flickered on and off. It looked like a fringed pool table light .

'Do you think the wiring's OK or are the spirits trying to make contact?' asked Dubois shuddering.

'Maybe there's an electric storm.'

'The body reaches thirty seven degrees centigrade during exercise and returns to twenty four at rest,' added Hermione, full of useless information as usual.

Tarquin poured some hot sake in the small blue porcelain cups.

'Don't worry I can recommend the food.'

Hermione's sister lit another Sobranie cocktail.

'The lighting was wrong at the opening yesterday. Some Rsoles had used the wrong fuse for the neon. Ambient is nice in the right place .'

'I rather like the seance.'

'Don't start dear!'

'Confucious says on your bike!'

At home the noise the fridge made was not the usual sound made by a cooling motor, which made it stand out. It made Tarquin jump and take notice. He had become used to its quiet hum and the new rhythm caused his feet to stop. Some silences can be deafening. Somebody had told him to praise the engine of your ten year old car when it was driving like new or you will only notice when it goes wrong. This was before he had read about the clouds in Blake's book of Urizen and felt thunder and turbulence on a plane.

Whilst touching on the subject, he wouldn't say boo to a goose. Their honk is worse than their bite. Inside their bright orange bills they have several rows of tiny teeth and their seasonal, migratory instincts bring them silently in V formations, thousands of miles to the same nesting wetlands; game fanned in the oven and on a plate.

Creole.

The Haemophilliac Society meeting was on the second floor as the Pre Election meeting came to order. Tea and coffee on the right, wine on the left. Candidates and photographers mixed with the manifesto and pamphlet holding public and balloons under the chandeliers and attractive pale blue and white ceiling. At 7.30pm the candidates took their places at the long table to address their constituancy audience who sat on gilt conference chairs. There were questions from the floor with roving microphones, lots of opinions, comments, facts, profiles, dictaphones, personalities, party policy and priorities. When the evening of general disatisfaction and complaints was over Hermione felt less inclined in any direction .

Tarquin had ordered cajun chicken in the Mexican restaurant. It made a change from the tortillas, guacamole and Caesar salads. The salads were always freshly prepared with egg and anchovy at the Yucatan tables. A Dixie band had played whilst they ate and the music carried over the trees and river. He was occasionally partial to Patum's Gentleman's relish. A ceramic jar of it had sat in the fridge for about a year. It became a complacent and integral part of it.

Tarquin always liked fish on Friday, whether it was small whole silver anchovies, as shiney as mirrors with their little heads on fried in lime, gumbo, cockles, lobster tails, sea bass, stupid pommefret, red snapper, sabre fish, octopus, squid, clams with china men's hats, jet lagged tuna steaks, cod or red herrings. Salt or fresh water tourists, filleted, gutted and grilled at customs, the Billingsgate arrivals and departure lounge was one of his favourite subjects.

Travel exercise number two.

The broadcast travel information service suggests adding half an hour to your journey. North and South Circular weather conditions become an electric blender, mortar and pestle of slowly grinding traffic in the rain. Today it is sixteen degrees centigrade/ sixty one degrees Fahrenheit and will brighten up by midday.

Throw a lot of salt over your shoulder before you leave and take regular rain checks. The commuter metropolis pipes people from the platforms to their offices and tourist destinations along the umbrella pavements with pretty colour canopies and crowds of black classic city Renoir's. They follow the financial pheromones and have Gilbert and Sullivan for lunch.

Lowest duck feed share prices. Wild duck dies of bird flu.

The french poultry enterprise went into red alert following the first case of asian flu. Dubois put eighteen months of preparation and investment for expansion on hold.

Hermione was at a book launch of Caribbean Cricket Heritage at the Jamaican Consulate aimed to coincide with the next World Cup planned to be held there. Women who qualify have been allowed entry into the MCC for the past ten years although the tradition has tried to maintain its impression of masculine domain and domination. She took a sip of her rum punch and smiled at herself, giving the buffet a suspicious look. No voodoo chicken's feet. Someone taking offense to 'whitey' had served her a dodgey burger with aloe relish instead of gherkin from a beach bar once. It kept her awake all night with tummy cramps. The food was better than OK. Salt fish, conch salads and tropical fruit. Not like the goat belly and cheap chicken from the market 'higglers' talking local slang and secret coromantee over goombay drums and reggae shouts of 'skyjuice','peanuts' and 'wrigleys'. Hermione ate plaintain, callaloo and deep orange pumpkin and was enlightened by the twenty eight different varieties of birds in Jamaica by the Ambassador's secretary.

'I still have some Jamaican dollars with a picture of a particular bird of paradise. The use of different design styles, national emblems and industries on bank notes are a bizarre interest of mine.'she replied .

'Does the Ambassador play cricket himself ?'

In addition to the best dressed goat and donkey being reserved for the yam festival, she discovered that, 'yes' the Abassador did play cricket and she would be happy to introduce her to him when he arrived.

Hermione adjusted her jacket and shut her bag, then looked around the room.

Where the elegant table had stood, a picture of perfection, stood a devastated landscape. Localised attacks on banana bread, pineapple, sugarcane and shellfish could be seen from the few diminished pieces of food left on the platters. This lead to 'shoot to kill' photographers taking pictures of fashion 'faux pas' and other victims making general assaults on the watermelon and attempts at humour. Hermione could count at least twelve casulties around the room starting to dance from side to side to the gentle reggae in self defense. The celebrity cricket players were pinned down by interviews. Hermione had put her dictaphone safely in her bag and noted the corrupt sweater and logo bag, worn by one interviewer, despite it being a good copy it was definitely not Chanel.

As Hermione returned Tarquin was mid target practise with a double barrel shot gun he had made from toilet roll tubes and a plastic milk carton using its handle for a trigger. Henry shouted 'pull' as he emptied the compressed coffee from the coffee maker. Henry's niece was asleep.

I live by the river.
Skyscraper.

Tarquin arrived at the office early. The person with the magenta pink décor in the Panoramic opposite does not know how striking their taste is, a North Star landmark when you get in and the light pollution prohibits the stella visibility. The river's luminary reflection makes a dematerialising transporter deck, awaiting enterprise, inspiration between the party boats and container tugs, the weather and surface conditions determining the depth of the beams. Unlimited hours of tidal traffic and astrology, watching Sleepless in Seattle and Powergen ads – office lighting jewellery settings.

Crossed by the harp suspension bridges from Battersea and Chelsea to the city, the figureheads at Vauxhall and pretty little bulbs strung along the embankment in between them. Seasonal rush hour of barges and Dunkirk migration, the roads tail light and transport like arteries in a Paul Simmeon painting and moving around the ant farm glass structure, Hitchcock heaven, roof gardens in the sky. Light photosynthesis seeing in or out, balcony breakfasts, ambient aura, penthouse party people, a pair of Pekinese, modern architecture lifestyle, marble entrance, fountain and best of breed underground parking, fish eyes, lifts and corridor cloisters, concierge cool.

Running the embankment , three to five kilometres daily, to Parliament past river boat cafes and the Hiedelburger fountain early enough to avoid commuters and tourists and back through the park gardens if they are open, twenty pence for the telescope opposite the Parliament restaurant, passing Russians in raincoats and front row benches for the Tate from Lambeth. A ten minute walk to Charing Cross there are canoeists and sailing boats on a Sunday, [business plan ideas for river taxi gondolas and docklands jet skis never put in motion, not knowing enough about traffic laws, speed restrictions and right of way post Marchioness. All very easily avoided by taking the tube.

Latitude 0

Week two, Madras, fish curry and spinach dhal. Tarquin laid his spices and ingredients out in regimental bowls ready for manoeuvres, with the ammunition and explosives for the oven and hob. Chef gave a display of frying oils using lime juice in an open flame to make sparks like a dragon breathing fire, and making flat breads rolling the dough with expert control employing the palm of his hand on the flat surface and cooking it on the hot plate. Tarquin found his confident slicing and handling of the equipment and food attractive, it expressed his personality and inspired him to master the techniques. It was world cup 'labboro piedi', giocco calcia, colour and chemistry. Lime and milk turning into yoghurt, he was back in the lab at school with a guru yogi open to new experiences. He drew the line though, at abdominal pools of blood made by knifeless Indian yogi operations and pulling strange humours out through someone's nose, which he had seen in a TV programme in 1975. Chef put on some Bangra music by the Asian Dub Foundation and some ambient music to accompany their cooking. The politician's wife had enlightened them on the sixteen decorative bindis she had learnt about on a visit to Jodhpur with her husband. She was wearing some very attractive ethnic jewellery and talked about the beautiful flowers and gardens. Chef promised to include some recipes and ice creams with flowers and delicate saffron and made everyone some jasmine tea. Tarquin was looking forward to the bottle of Château Neuf de Pape, which he had bought to go with the madras.

He was sharing a table island with Keith which developed an amusing coalition as they discussed the cricket, Indian interiors, four poster beds with white curtains blowing in the hot breeze in walled palaces on islands in lakes, Angpor, Taj Mahal.

General Field Marshall Bogdanovich Barclay de Bolly awarded himself the order of St George and a red paste mark between their eyebrows. Brigadier Kitchener Lloyd Khyber survived the stressful battle without a scratch. England were 256 for 6 in the second day of the Sri Lanka test match. World cup 2008 in the Caribbean and a Caran Dache demonstration of protest march banners for eternal tea at the MCC.

Apparently the man who sets his watch by the BBC World Service in Beijing is more accurate than the man on Westminster Bridge as the chimes of Big Ben are broadcast at the speed of light. It's four faces and copper hands [minute and hour only – the second hand is reserved for timing rather than telling the time] are lit by fifty five watt bulbs, only one changed in the last four years, allegedly, it's original opaque glass was damaged in WW11 replaced temporarily by white cardboard panels.

On the way back from the stables, driving past the church on conveyor belt wedding was leaving as another arrived, the campanologists were on double time ringing their bells announcing the joy of couples' unions. As Epiphany took off her boots, Tarquin asked her to ring directory enquiries and get the number for the fishmonger to see if they had any red herrings.

'If my socks smell it isn't intentional.'

She knew that Tarquin hated the improper use of the word sorry.

'Hai zi! confusious says learn Chinese.'

'I've written a book' added Epiphany. 'Sydney emailed me to say she would show her publisher. Here, do you want to have a look. I'll make some chocolate.'

Justin Case.

Justin Case tied his laces, just in case he tripped his paces and
Justin Chase had a hanky, just in case his nose got manky.

Justin Case had a case and in that case he had some string just in case his flies went ping.

Tarquin read on …….. Justin grew up to be a millionaire, so there!

Epiphany reappeared with two   hot chocolates and a plate of manchego cheese on toast. He had found reading Vanity Fair and the Herald Tribune interesting comparing the way the house styles differed from conversational film genres and the Americans he knew. Living with a Jewish New Yorker for two years when he was twenty five being the most notable.

'Has Sydney discussed any percentage yet? I can always check her maths.'

'Sydney …' said Hermione interrupting their toast. 'She is eating orange skin to combat her cellulite this month. Trying to prove one of her theories and avoid liposuction scars. Pith, paraffin, marmalade and vitamin C. Fuel for her fat pockets and botox buddies.'

'Epiphany wants to go into print.'

'Great.'

'Sydney said the proposals and dummies go to the book fair in May or they secure a publisher before. She has a couple of names in mind.'

Later they went to a Barbour PR event organised by Keith's girlfriend in the observation room of Wellington Arch, and drank champagne as models were photographed by the press cat walking under it. Keith had arranged for their names to be on the guest list. The arch and it's once famed live in feline, now available as a soft toy ginger tom, usually houses a museum and has great views down the mall from its balconies. Keith and Tarquin had both had trouble removing the red paste from their skin.

Fifteen minutes early. This week Tarquin was making chicken korma and coconut chicken with butter gourds and okra. He had finely sliced the fresh, soft, pink ginger and skinned and chopped the bitter sweet almonds. Keith arrived as he was reading how to make the paste. Keith's phone rang and the cicarda ring tone made Tarquin smile .

'Mi piacci ascoltare grillo,' said the politician's wife outloud to herself .

'It's such a wonderful sound. But you can never see them. Semiotic or onomatopiac. Sunshine, long grass, farfelli, api e vespi.'

Keith listened to his ansaphone messages.

'Chelsea won 2-0 v West Brom. I could kill my girlfriend, she's just confirmed that she's booked some tickets that coincide with the semifinals.'

'Despite a recent application in NW9, Saihti was abolished in 1891.'

Chef was not going to be an accessory.

'If I die,' he continued, 'my wife is unlikely to even notice, she could never give up George Clooney and follow me.'

'Light my fire!' said Keith .

'Jim Morrison would turn in his grave,' added Tarquin.' Between the Mercenary Moroccan Barbary pirates stealing US trade and with thanks to Dave Gilmour, the eldest daughters of Canada, New Zealand and

Australia rushing to the Mother of The Free in 1914, we are supposedly winning the battle against terrorism. Hermione will leave a legacy of speech marks. Mind you, there's a definate economy in a joint wake, but I don't see much future in it.'

Chef put on a CD.

'Try this, ' he said giving Tarquin some garlic .

'I grew it in my kitchen garden.'

'Is it easy to grow?'

'Yes, easier and quicker than the topiary and Capability Browned bedding design next to it. The stocks, canna lilies and ornamental cabbages are much taller and the rich colours make the little white flowers stand out.

'I might have a go, it's not something often found in a typical English country garden. But that's being grossly complacent. Historical compost and feasting rituals in Papua New Guinea under pressure from trade and progress. I'll be slaughtering pigs in the office next. Thanks.'

Tarquin downloaded Keith's cicada ring tone for his phone and fried the chicken with oil and onion. Keith was going to miss the last week of the course due to a week in Goa.

Two weeks later Hermione was in a restaurant with Dubois. She was still recovering from seeing her first Klimt. They had been looking at De Hooch's room with rear view of a woman wearing a bonnet and apron holding a glass up. A ghosted figure in the background had been painted over. Someone's phone rang in the restaurant, with a cicada ring tone the same as Tarquin's. It was strange, strange like the historical recognition she had felt noticing the plagiarised background signature line in Picasso's Colombe taken from Van Gogh's Sunflowers.

The cicada did not spend long chatting, he said he had a pig to slaughter in the office and switched it off returning to the attention of his pretty friend.

Someone handed Hermione an IFAW awareness leaflet for the campaign against seal culling. She had not renewed her WWF membership. Epiphany had sponsored a tiger named Malaka and had its picture and certificate. The organisation kept in contact with information on the reserve in Africa. Hermione usually ignored people with flyers but recognised the logo and felt responsibility to her blue tag credit. They had just got off the train at Victoria as the Orient Express pulled in. Low altitude clouds of steam chuffed from the huge engine on the next platform where a crowd of passengers waited. Hermione gave Epiphany a letter to hold as she looked for a stamp in her purse. She posted it in the box next to the ticket office. Epiphany waited by the new turf accountant's shop with television screens, posters and machines.

'It's Ascot, can we put on a bet?' asked Epiphany.

'Revolutionary.'

'Does that mean yes?'

'No that's the name of the horse Dubois mentioned. OK.'

They got a card and looked at the race times and put £1.25 each way on a horse each. The race was in five minutes.

The Department of Fisheries and Oceans can no longer be held responsible for the decline in cod stocks, read Hermione.

'I think about 5% of the seal pups are killed every year, they have few predators and the polar bears are suffering from melted ice flows, dying from exhaustion trying to swim to land. Yuk.'

She looked at the picture and looked away.

'It's 11.30.'

'Sinatra' was ridden by a jockey wearing red and blue stripes. Hermione kept her eyes on a horse called Roman Nose, with pink and white silks. Inflation was the favourite. As the horses thundered around the course the camera angle showed a close up of the hooves, too many to know which ones belonged to which horse. In the background you could just make out the hats in the stand. Two furlongs to go and Epiphany's horse went ahead to win. They stuck a rosette on his sheepskin noseband and Epiphany got £10.50 including her stake.

A private compartment in a cream and brown Pullman to Vladivostok on the Trans Siberian railway with studded leather chesterfield chairs and red velvet walls and white lace and linen was still waiting an embarquation from a platform in Hermione's head. It stayed on the buffers with the hatboxes, Louis Vuitton luggage everywhere.

Tarquin realised that he was hungry.

Epiphany arrived and handed him the betting slip.

'I won £10.50 on the 11.30 at Ascot.'

'Henry says Allied is looking good. The FTSE 100 index passed through the 6000 banner yesterday for the first time in five years at it's close. Allied WBFC's take over merger totalled £575m and 250 jobs were axed at QQ to save £1.5m.'

'What are they a share about £2.25?' asked Epiphany. 'I could manage about five then. Who wants tea? I made some Florentines, they're on me.'

As India handed Dubois a mug it fell to the floor and she was left holding the handle.

'April fool! I should have thrown it out. I don't mean that ...oh dear! I stuck the handle back on with glue, I forgot. I'll get another one.'

Dubois continued to whisk the crumpet batter until all the bicarbonate of soda frothed into little bubbles then poured the stringy dough into little round cutters and cooked them until the bases were black and the dough like rubber. They ate them with butter and tea.

After their late breakfast/brunch Dubois and India went for a drive in India's new navy and silver smart car. She was made up with the contrasting panels and city economy. She parked it with ease and they walked from the Hurlingham Club to Putney Bridge. The crowds were about three or four people deep. People were spilling out of the pubs onto the pavements holding plastic pint glasses, discussing when and where to meet on mobiles like a rave.

'Go left, go right, see you there.'

There was a good party atmosphere, people were buzzing with race vibe under the blue skies with thick white puffy clouds, the first decent spring day of the year. India had been to a Nunca party and was enjoying the progressive focus of the event.

They walked along the embankment past the stripy scarves, umbrellas and zoom lenses. Someone was chaining his bicycle to the railings, too much to cope with in the crowds.

'We should be on the other bank at one of the boathouse parties India,' said Dubois.

'If I'd known earlier I could have spoken to Sydney, she can usually do something. She's away this week.'

The gun went off and the coxes started screaming. The boats pulled away chased by team launches, journalists and photographers. A helicopter hovered overhead and the crowds cheered with every stroke. Cambridge won. Oxford, in dark blue were not punching the air.

'It's 4.30. Do you still feel like going to the photography before the book launch?'

'Loads of time. No need to rush we can cruise it.'

Dubois' hangover was better.

In the entrance a small boy about seven years old was playing a steel harmonica with the confidence and skill of a concert pianist. He was sitting at a table. Informally looking around, leaning on the table, his mother was about five metres away; she called to him in French. They were the only two people visible. India and Dubois walked through to the exhibition impressed by his playing. In the restaurant a jazz quartet plucked violins accompanied by a cello. They read the paper and ate scrambled eggs with sour cream and caviar in the acoustic marble hall.

'To Cheadle Defense Regiment manoeuvres at 21.00 hours love x' Dubois read the personal column out to India.

'The talk starts in forty five minutes. I'll get this and ring to say we're on our way. Hermione said she would reserve us seats.'

India rang her cat to tell it to make its own tea because she was out, that there were some biscuits in the bowl and she would bring home some milk. Dubois rang her ansaphone to remind herself to go out again and get some milk. They had drunk it all the night before with coffee. She remembered telling the floorboards to 'shh!' reminiscent of a Tom Waits song as they crept about laughing and dancing with the music low.

'Holding music, Gershwin not Greensleeves for a change.' said Dubois.

'I used to practise everyday,' Amen was in a good mood.

'My gran has a picture of me aged seven looking like concert pianist. I still haven't worked out how to get the harp out of the box. My piano teacher used to play symphonies to me and talk about his coloured layered sand pictures in glass jars but kept their trade secrets. She brought me a stick of rock with the seaside going through it. Solid sugar candy from Winchelsea. I think this one's Tchaikovsky or Rachmaninov. It's not Beethoven's 5th. What do you think?'

He put the telephone on conference speaker.

Dubois agreed, 'it's definitely not Beethoven's 5th. They're not answering. Must have gone for the day. I won't leave a message. I'll ring on Monday. Shall we go and meet Hermione? What's the time?'

'It's 5.30 what time are they going to be there?'

'6.30/7'

'Fine, let's go.'

St Katherine's Dock was heaven away from the traffic and noise. It was the first warm evening of the year and people were enjoying the European exterior seating without the aid of space heaters. British optimism towards pavement cafes with awnings and nice umbrellas, which make a bar, look inviting. Pubs in Soho were spilling into the roads in good spirits; it was crazy like a drive in pub.

'Wouldn't it be nice if it was all year,' said Dubois 'people are in much better moods, how can we destroy the ozone layer to increase the temperature permanently?'

Hermione and Sydney had been to a talk on Conflict and Cooperation in Israel. Sydney brought it up again while Hermione visited the powder room.

The river Jordan is bordered by Jordan, Syria, Lebanon, Israel and the OPT. There is an asymmetry between Palestein and Israel's share of the rivers aquifers. Israel has 86%; Palestein however has many existing wells.

Competition appears to be a preferable option to conflict, which has previously stood in the way of finding a solution to the political impasse existing since 1967. De Fabia Diabes from International Waterways said: 'International levels of advocacy were developing new motivations, stages of cooperation, pseudo reasons, ad hoc and long term vision and initiative in national liberation and identity.

A protracted mature transition agreement will be necessary for the essential waterways, which are too precious to fight over becoming the new oil source – conflict which is cheaper to cooperate over. Allowing the future of culture core and power.

Sydney liked its vibe. How to make statistics sound sexy. Getting around the stereotype prejudice of existing opinions of a warzone. Henry and Tarquin were walking around the harbour boardwalks past the moorings. The water was black and smelt of diesel, which pleased Henry. Lots of small lights illuminated the restaurant exterior and reflected in the water.

Conversation carried across the warm air from a party on board a large cruiser where beautiful people were drinking Crystal. Launchings and lunches, Hermione liked the flowers on the Perrier Jouet bottles and Tarquin's theory about the bubble size and speed ratio to central or random origin of source. Henry preferred Krug. He had tickets for Saturday semi-final at Wimbledon. Between them all they had to organise was where to meet and when. This took two minutes.

'India's got a friend who's working as an official linesperson this year,' said Dubois, 'apparently there are about fifty makes and types of tennis balls including high pressure balls for playing at high altitudes and they have a seventy five minutes on/off concentration time. If she qualifies as a chair umpire she might be at the 2015 finals. Service speed will probably increase by then and the climate change may effect the frequency covers are pulled over and the WWF might comment on the baseline grass erosion.'

Saturday was fine weather again. The grounds were immaculate. Corporate green ivy, neat white trellises, Odeon liner style stairs and railings with portholes doors and cool ash silver players' areas. Journalists and photographers with zoom lenses had taken their positions for the first matches. Hermione and Tarquin arrived at the water cascade after walking through a small crowd big enough to prompt a dress protocol and etiquette warning shot.

'Sydney. Is it still appropriate in South Africa to wear short sleeves for casual meetings after work? I thought visitors are advised to refrain from wearing national costume.' said Hermione.

'Yes Hermione. Welcome topics of conversation in Mexico dear – scenery, history and football. Avoid illegal aliens and religion and the US Mexican war and it's consequences. If you receive an 'abrazo' bear hug relax, participate, you have arrived.' answered Sydney.

'An Italian would never wear unfashionable or scuffed shoes. If in doubt always wear the best pair you possess [that go with your outfit]' added Hermione. Then she went on to say 'Do not grunt when the players serving do, restrict crowd noise to oooh and aaah and sharp inhalations and exhalations of air between the teeth to express shot reaction. The more experienced will appreciate this.'

Strawberries and cream,

'New shoes Dubois?' asked Sydney.

' I bought them yesterday. But not technically brand new. I had to practise standing up in them in the house for about an hour last night. I see Diamond Christian Diors are still popular this year. That's a nice green Fred Perry visor.'

The unavoidable uterus.

'15th of July is Bastille Day,' said Hermione, they were walking through a market in Brittany .

'Jules Verne had a globe artichoke for a head and as it's Bastille Day. I think we should all have one for dinner - freshly guillotined. Around the world in eighty days and on a plate in eighty minutes. With eggs and cider.'

They walked by the sea and watched the fishermen and rose coloured sky. Hermione gradually forgot the BAAF project she had been briefed on last week .The PR launch of the British Adoption Agency was a conversation piece. Epiphany has considered having a brother or sister and India started discussing her termination again. Dubois was more concerned with catching contagious fertility from the jersy fabric stretched over the bulging baby baring bodies smuggling foetus futures, doing ashtanga yoga in the sunshine and whether there was enough sunblock to go around. There was an archery competition in the park. The competitors were using hitech light weight bows with telescopic sights like the ones in the Olympics used by Britain's airian looking silver medalist. The slow deliberate way the bow is raised and aimed looked very professional.

Dubois had tried it on a management training day about five years before and she said that it wasn't easy. They stopped for tea and cake in the shade and sat in Lloyd Loom chairs commenting on aspiring businesses built from industries and souvenirs in Indonesia. The weaving techniques and designs that typify English summers, linen baskets and nurseries.

In Cap Sizon the men wore fishing sweaters, there were blue and white striped Bretagne tops and blinds, Sabot shoes and coiffure lace filled the shops. They booked a boat trip to go Atlantic seal watching the following day before going on to Guernsey and Sark.

Tarquin had looked like the Cheshire Cat when they saw seals rolling around on the rocks like stuffed squid in Cardigan Bay and wanted to get a closer look some time .

In the restaurant they ordered the artichokes and played back some photographs. Hermione had still not found any Bryndza Polish Cheese recommended to her by a photojournalist called Simon at the press launch.He had talked about contextural photography for about an hour while they ate and had their glasses politely refilled .

'There is no destinction or boundary in photography,' he said, 'either in a static hidden idea or as in photojournalism with the story in the subject. It's source is the mechanical eye, the photographer is involved, he is either expressive, connected or disconnected to the realism or mechanism.'

Hermione had to concentrate to keep up with his train of thought and long sentences and had written done the name of the cheese and slovakian Liptovska gnocchi recipe so she didn't forget. She couldn't find it anywhere and foresaw an inevitable trip to Eastern Europe until she consumed the said item and was sated by it's intrusion into her life. Hermione and Tarquin ate their artichokes and drank their cider and the sun went down on the harbour horizon .

Dubois spent the morning planting lettuce and tomato seeds. The bees on the lavendar made her want honey beer and reminded her she was seeing Henry later. Last time they went out he asked for the Ethiopian instead of the Sommalier after the second bottle of wine. Tonight they were going to a wine tasting at the French Institute. The chickens were laying OK, the accounts were completed to the end of the month and all the orders were ready. Dubois had tried some Rhode Island Blacks with ackee fruit, salt fish, banana bread and callaloo after watching the carnival on TV. The tins had been in the cupboard for nearly a year. Henry had picked her up at 2pm to go to the one day county match at Lords first.

'One of the batsmen had been arrested for drugs. The newspaper headlines have gone mad.I hope you like rosé.'

'LBW in the dock? - he wasn't caught then! What's that on your windscreen, something's crapped.' said Dubois. God knows what Hitchcock feeds his birds on but I wouldn't like to clean their cage out. By the way, could you stop at a Post Office I have a WWF tiger adoption certificate I'm sending to India with her tenancy statement.' She paused for a second then said ,' Yes I love rosé.'

The invitation stated that a concert followed the tasting.

Pays D'Oc, Shiraz, Grenache, Syrah and Rioja varieties of rosé of differing depth of colour with their labels covered up, stood lined up with elegant glasses on the table in the hall. Their crisp pallette and soft strawberry flavours were degusted with soft camembert cheeses, conversation and interesting facts. Namely the origin of the cheese, it was reputedly first made by Marie Harel in 1791 using a manufacture 'secret' that she had been given by a priest. Of the two hundred and seventy two types of French cheese, Marlon Brando preferred brie. The red skins were left in the barrels for only twenty four hours to achieve the rosé status instead of six months. The host spoke in English with a French accent which Dubois liked. Henry exercised his fluent rust, feeling like a Porsche that had just been waxed.

'C'est mon première degustation, 'explained Dubois to the woman on her right who having tried the wine stuck her hand out and requested 'le plein si vous plait.'Inferring her glass was a petrol tank and nous sommes were chêz garage .

'Have you been to the Isle of Wight ?' she asked.

'We were at Cowes last week for the regatta, absolutely wonderful, beautiful weather. A flotilla of starched white sails that disappear diminishing into the distant sunset like an army of ants moving a large leaf in sections. Everything depended on the wind, weather and instincts.' she checked herself then added,' Bad analogy, ants can't swim very well, maybe they evolved from pond skaters and can disperse their weight on the surface tension of the water.'

'And boats are pretty useless on land too, 'added Dubois .

'Have you ever noticed how ducks propel themselves ? It's quite different from other water fowl. They use a sort of bicycle pedalling motion with their webbed feet whereas pelicans glide forwards by propelling both feet together. Swans are like ducks without the diving action – no rear view micros for the D.A.'s. They must have adapted their long necks to avoid this, they are slightly bigger and a bit pigeon toed when they walk usually shaking their tail feathers at the same time.

Seagulls are very big too. The black ones, swans that is have beautiful red beaks.'

'Are you a member here?' asked the woman.

'No Henry and I were invited by one of his client's who's in imports.'

'You should come to the classic Burgundy's next month.'

Henry appeared and came over holding a plate of cheese.

'The concert is starting in five minutes,' he said 'shall we take our seats?'

'This is …. I didn't get your name.'

'Daisy.'

'Pleased to meet you, do have some camembert Daisy and come and sit down. Lady Curzon insists on relaxation as well as recreation and work.

Hermione looked around the room, the diners were demonstrating a variety of styles of eating. One man was lifting his bowl to his mouth eating with chopsticks. He did not appear to finish one mouthful before he put the next one in. His dinner partner was savouring each rice grain's texture slowly before it went passed the little epiglotis punch bag in his throat.

The dishes they had ordered arrived with varying punctuality reflecting the continued controversial trade route wars affecting the economies in Kashmir, Afghanistan and China. The restaurant filled up over the busy lunchtime period with customers who had a taste for travel, taking over tables like independant states, giving orders and making strikes on other parties. We have control of the TV station and will use it to broadcast our manifestos and demands, then help rebuild the damaged infrastructure. They got the bill and Tarquin asked the waiter to 'total it'.

They needed one hundred and fifty press packs. Each one was quite substantial. Enough pages to require additional recycling bins and reaforestation in North America. Hermione had visions of lumberjack shirts in the office, it only needed one person to start it off. Alternatively they could start making papier mâché dishes to sell to tourists. The Little Chainsaw That Cried would be published by the WWF.

Chelsea had saved some money to buy her VAT free size five tennis shoes from the children's department. This made her happy because they were half price. She was going to the Albert Hall later with her boyfriend who had a large Union Jack. They were going to see his brother who was playing cello. Then they returned to the office to continue orchestrating the press pack production. Handel playing in the background.

'Try one of these.' Epiphany handed Hermione some olives .

'I found them growing on a tree in the Edgeware Road.'

'Thanks. They're great. Get some more and we can press them and make oil.'

Hermione put the Proms on the TV. Epiphany was making muffins.

'Chelsea is in there somewhere waving a Union Jack .'

She looked at the audience as the camera panned across the swaying people .

Then she went to the refridgerator and pulled the ice cream out of the freezer compartment. It made sled tracks in the ice as the plastic scraped on it. She put it on the table shouting 'mush!mush!' as Epiphany's chocolate chip muffins cooled on the little rack. White wolf huskies with black wolverine rings around their pupils were watching from the dark side somewhere.

'Where's Little Red Riding Hood? Would you like some ice cream to go with them ?'

The next day was Thursday. Epiphany's O'level results were due. In future the results would be put online. But Epiphany had to look for them on the notice board. There was a big group of girls there, all asking and pointing and exchanging results. Most of them were smiling. Epiphany was elated. She thought she had messed up her Chaucer but she still got an A. Dubois had invited her to the Literary Society to a talk by Zadie Smith to celebrate. She had to choose which A levels to do although all she wanted to do was ride. English and languages probably then Oxbridge. Tarquin and Henry thought it was a good idea to do something practical and had taken her to the Stranger's Gallery in the House of Commons for the reading of a foxhunting bill. There were lots of protesters and the outside broadcasting camera crew with journalists. Epiphany liked the idea of working as a diplomat in an embassy in an equatorial French speaking paradise. She watched Sigourney Weaver in The Year of Living Dangerously twice one weekend. Hermione liked the idea too.

Stuck behind a tractor.

Hermione was sitting on the hay bale, which was being used for an urban PR event. She Jane Mansfielded herself with a piece of straw in her mouth and mentally changed into a white blouse with a fifties bra and serious cleavage. A saucy postcard from the High Chaperal. They had been working late on the market research for a press pack for a major soup brand. All new cans would have ring pulls taking the Coca-Cola and sardine initiative, making can openers redundant. Hermione imagined watching a call my bluff programme in the future with Epiphany's children looking at a strange mechanical object, which had no obvious function. She was glad to be at an event and sitting on her first hay bale in the fresh air.

It was Friday, tomorrow she would put on her authentic coolie hat from Mayan Mar, her Road to Mandalay and plant some garlic in the kitchen garden. They were trying to grow some rice plants in a water garden and were planning to try tea. The two chillies plants were turning red and the olive tree was bushing out. Tarquin and Henry were investing in a vineyard and a farm. This year's thing to do. Hermione's inner smile said ear-to-ear haricot beans. In addition to the gardening she had to post her entry to the National Poetry Competition, which had kept her preoccupied with hotels, one hotel in particular the Avalon they had stayed in on Miami Beach. Pink and blue art deco squares, big tiled sinks with taps from another century and shower roses under serious pressure. The likelihood of her winning was less than the chances of anything coming from Mars. She would post it anyway and ask the Irish Embassy if they wanted a cerebral cup of tea again.

The 'have a try at milking a cow' was very popular but chaos. There were hay bales everywhere and a couple of pantomime cows with the promotions team who were handing out flyers, alcoholic ice cream samples and slogan T-shirts. 'Don't drive the cattle they are over the limit.' The girls had milkmaid caps and aprons and the boys wore tweed smocks and wellies. Chelsea was on the company mobile to the office, 'is it possible to get any more hay bales at short notice? What do you mean No! Men jump over cows in Kenya to prove their manhood. It's called cattle jumping and they whip the women.'

A T-shirt walked past saying 'Country Road Cones', its wearer was eating an eggnog advocaat scoop. Epiphany's favourite was the 'Red Sky in the Afternoon Shepherd Spoke Too Soon.' with red wine. Hermione was happy she had a bottle of Frascati which Dubois had recommended from the wine tasting last week.

Still stuck behind a tractor.

Hermione had received the soup brand research. Fifty per cent of all tin can manufactured food was now being produced with the new 'ring pull' openings which was to be their launch benefit along with the new packaging design. She talked through the consumer selection psychology of widening customer choices with the new 'easy opening' versus other products and the importance of the design investment to get ahead of other brands in the same market. They wanted to include something about the endangered can opener and it's inevitable extinction when all tins became 'ring pull'. The first tin opener was designed by William L Lyman in 1870 following the 1810 introduction of the tin can for preserving food. Since then there have been several serrated, mounted and electric alternatives ranging between £1.99 and £32.75. Hermione read out a lot of statistics about x million households with at least 1 opener per household which meant alot of can openers. In addition to this she had found sales on ebay of 65,000 units in India, Taiwan and China which was just one of twenty notices selling more can openers.

Then there was the stock in shops and repeat orders to be considered. She gave up on the maths and emailed it to Henry along with a suggestion that maybe the African markets could do a deal to help lower third world debt. She had covered the Make Poverty History campaign with Chelsea and went to Nelson Mandela's speech in Trafalgar Square. Overpowered by his infamy as he got into a Lincoln Limosine in front of her and drove away.

The most popular can openers retail at £2.50, the metal type with a flat handle. He could have done with one of them in jail and might have got out sooner .

Hi Henry

Tarquin said you were going away again. Enjoy your trip. We're going to see the Canterbury Tales next week. I'll send you a review. Do you know anybody who can recommend a critic?

Regards

Hermione

Chelsea was discussing the new blue tennis courts with Karl. Which ones were better, the red clay, grass or blue ones.

'It's easier to see if the ball is in or out as the blue and white gives a stronger visual contrast on the optic nerve.'

'Is that right ? Where did you hear that ?'

'I didn't I made it up. It sounds logical though.' Chelsea paused, 'And why does Rembrandt's drawing of an elephant look like Rembrandt. It was a bit of an odd one out at the exhibition. He did a lot of self portraits, and fancied a change I suppose. Why don't elephants play tennis ?'

'I don't know. Why?'

'Because they can't hold the rackets!'

'Why aren't elephants allowed to drive in the USA?'

'Because they think the trunk is at the back !'

The soup brand press pack dummies were being presented next week and Hermione needed to go over the brief .

Contents

Soup can board game .

20 flavours : crab game, lobster, turtle, artichoke ....

Ready in five minutes heat and serve .

Four servings per can .

Five minutes to shoot the cans and win [with dice] .

'It says here that the earliest known board game is called the game of Ur 177BC and played in Iran 2500 years ago. It has round counters and a stick dice on a two halved board with square sections. Chelsea where are the samples of the magnetic timers and are the branded versions ready yet? These are the menu suggestions and recipe cards from the soup brands cordon bleu chef. And has Karl got the aprons and oven gloves?'

Chelsea finished typing the briefs for the game and sourcing the items by 1.25pm. Then they went to lunch at a new Japanese restaurant.

'Kon nichi wa.'

'Kon nichi wa.Yoyak o shite arimas.Terebu san chushok. I'ved reserved a table for three in the name of Darlington.'

They were shown to a table behind an occidental laquered and enamel screen with birds and blossom. The novel tables were very low, about fifty centimetres off the floor. Western customers with arthritis and stiff joints would not be able to cope being too used to couch potato lifestyles and soft furnishings to bother using their spines.

They sat down and ordered.There were beautiful pictures of Beijing bicycles on the walls and lots of little rosette wantons .

The compact rice and rolled bean curd started Chelsea talking about the straw grass rolled up in Hyde Park which ressembled a Dorset wheat field and smelt like a stable. Owing to the current drought the dry grass posed a serious fire risk and had to be cut and bundled.

Overtaking the tractor.

Bank holiday Monday Tarquin and Epiphany went for a bike ride to Notting Hill Carnival and to visit some friends. It was early, about 11am, before it got too busy. They locked the bikes up and went into the flat just as some paper streamer bombs went off. On the walls was a picture of a lobster, a Campbell's Soup can print and some geometric Islamic art with emeralds and sapphires.

They sat down with banana leaf plates of fish and mango cooked in rum. Epiphany had a banana daiquiri and some mint tea and tried the shisha pipes. She liked the ceramic lights, which made patterns on the walls and the little suspended coloured glass oil lamps. You could hear the calypso music; a lot of drum bass, football whistles, cowbells and horns. It was just possible to see the dancers, costumes and the roof top camera crews from the window. Tarquin was reading out the personal column from a newspaper – 'To Mr and Mrs Hammerhead from Leighton Buzzard love red stockings from Aylesbury.'

The hostess interrupted 'I looked everywhere for an album once,' she said shutting the window a little. I had to try and sing calypso 'Wine Miss Tiny to two teenage boys wearing band T- shirts serving in a small vinyl shop in Kingston Apple Market. My cheeks were bright pink. They managed to find it in a catalogue though and ordered it. It took about three weeks to arrive. I was very impressed. It's got wicked cover with a bare bum wearing a diamond g string.' She paused for a second to catch her breath, 'did you see the foie gras being force fed on the telly last night? Dreadful. No? We're going to Whitstable next week end, for the Oyster Festival if you want to come.'

'I'll put it in my diary,' said Tarquin, 'Hermione never says no to oysters, and discuss it with Garner on Wednesday.'

About an hour later some people were limbo dancing in the kitchen where Epiphany was taking a course in cocktail making.

'Could I have another chilled glass please?' requested Tarquin. Epiphany was becoming quite an expert at frosting the edges with sugar or salt if they were tequila slammers. Her tequila sunrise was perfect.

At 5pm they cycled back avoiding the bottlenecks and crowds who were dispersing down Ladbroke Grove and Portobello with the paper flowers. The floats had disappeared but music was still coming from about five different sources.

'Which way do we go to avoid the bass? Left.'

'No right. It's that way. Sound always comes from the opposite direction to where you expect. It bounces off things like clouds when it thunders.'

The rain held until they got back home. Hermione was reading.

Drapes.

Henry had two sisters Mercedes and Kaneda who were either working in Europe or busy with boyfriends and buried in business. Dubois found herself wanting to meet them when he talked about them in an affectionate way. It sounded like he missed them despite keeping in frequent touch by e-mail and having dinner when they were in London, single again. Christmas or the occasional celebration. Dubois reminded herself that you should start to worry when you meet the parents. She knew from experience how people's behaviour changed. Hermione and Sydney were a fine example of specimens for the behaviour psychologist whose name she could never remember and got muddled up with Morris or someone who could explain why your dog or cat was depressed. She just made a point of distracting herself.

Dubois was always amazed by the technical and physical accuracy of Greek sculpture. Greek boat head figures are less convincing and women were thought to be a bad luck superstition. The Greeks and Phoenicians replaced them with animals and the evil eye to ward off evil spirits. Asian Indians on the other hand preferred the eagle as a symbol.

Several examples of the figureheads can be seen at the Greenwich Maritime Museum although there are no statistics, which can prove the superstitions. Using statistics with conviction is a different body of satirical comment to the data collected by the Office of National Statistics, which uses it with courage of conviction – 40% of skivers' sick days are taken on Mondays and Fridays, the other 60% take the whole week off.

Henry's youngest sister Mercedes Michael lived by Vauxhall Bridge, the only bridge with figureheads greeting the boats from the river's source. From the apartment window you can see the pools of light made by the street lamps reflected along the Thames. The pools the lamps make look like the Star Trek transporter deck of the Enterprise. Depending on the position of the moon, the height of the tide and the size of the waves the pools vary in diameter. Mercedes sat at her laptop drinking tea from a Turkish tea glass, her left thumb absent mindedly in her palm of her right hand, half lotus state of contemplation. Her short platinum blond hair needed a wash and she had left her Calvin Klein glasses in the bedroom. She was wearing tracksuit trousers, a T-shirt and football socks.

'15 love.'

Venus Williams had just lost a point to Sharapova and walked back to the baseline concentrating on realigning the catgut on her tennis racket as if the ball had damaged it. Mercedes wandered if it was actually possible to do that or if it was just a deep psychological or nervous habit. Do the manufacturers test the rackets to see if 1mm displacement of threaded plastic off it's original highly-strung setting makes any difference to the line of shot.

'15 all.'

The umpire announced the next point.

Mercedes wrote for The Art of the State, an art newspaper she started to compete with the State of the Art, featuring new masters, features, interviews and an artist top ten supported by advertising and new technology sponsorship. She worked from her kitchen/office in SW9. Today, however, she was working on a concept to stage a season of Greek plays at the Proscenium in Embankment Gardens. Together with her connections at the RSA they had sought permission from the City of Westminster to run the season of tragedies and comedies for three to four weeks. Fairy lights would be hung in the trees and palms along the embankment and the WHSmith gardens from the Adelphi and Savoy to Hungerford Bridge with a stage lit by flaming torches. The actors would dress in traditional togas, satyr's goat legs and horns with serpent jewellery. Titian scenes of abundant fruit and wine – no leopards or live animals which were considered too dangerous for the Greeks, Americans and London tourist gods.

Sean Michael arrived back home and walked into the kitchen. He had just had his long Paulo Nutini style hair cut and was still getting used to his fringe. He had a fairisle tank top on over his T-shirt with his new Bulgari necklace ring showing and pin stripe trousers. This was quite coordinated for him.

'By walking twenty feet instead of thirty feet to boil a kettle to make fair trade tea at a typical sixty centimetre height kitchen unit [or lower for wheel chair users and dwarves, that's P.O.R.G's to quote Tom Sharp and be PC] the cloud will be .0000000001% the size of that made by the 3% emission of a 737 at twenty thousand feet using newly developed more efficient fuels to enable it to fly lower than the usual thirty thousand where it will harm the environment more. One thousand jobs are created for every one million air passengers. This helps to explain why the BAA subsidise cheap flights, which boost local industry. To quote the Guardian' the rail networks are on their knees.' Unless they take the BAA lead and use the global warming effects to their advantage, embracing the leaves on the line and snow delays to encourage passengers to boost local business, increasing sales of sandwiches and cups of teas and coffee during delays which could expand business ideas to British Rail mortgages and homes, exploiting the situation and increasing revenue enabling the reduction of prices. Do you want a cup?'

'Yes, please,' replied Mercedes.

'There were no buses at Piccadilly. They'd all been rerouted owing to a march of Indians protesting over something to do with freedom in 1984.

It wasn't far off a scene from Ghandi or how I imagine getting on a train in Delhi. I've only got guide books and travel programmes to allude to. 'India is only nine hours to go'. Madhukar Singh wrote that , top copywriter at CDP. I've never seen so many brightly coloured saris and turbans. Saffron, mauve, orange, yellow, pink and mauve. What was the name of that Bollywood film ....? Doesn't matter. Where was I?

They had a truck at the front of the march with a massive drum being hit with two boomerang sticks followed by four fierce looking men dressed in white and orange with massive swords. I don't know the technical difference between a sword and a knife but they looked very dangerous unsheathed. And less ceremonial than the British equivalent. Here's your tea.'

Earlier there had been another march in Hyde Park that was raising money for PHAB-Physiclly Handicapped and Able Bodies. The procession hit a bottleneck by the Lido path and any body walking in the opposite direction went slightly against the grain and flow resulting in near punch ups with tinsel clowns and sausage balloons in the afternoon heat. It was like back combing a B52 Rock Lobster without any choice. The march ended peacefully said a report on the radio, probably refering to the one with the ceremonial swords in Piccadilly .

The park was full of people enjoying the Saturday afternoon in the twenty five degree sunshine. Quite a few large picnics and children's parties were blanketed on the grass. One group by the lake sat in deckchairs, they looked quite organised with wine glasses, taking advantage of the supermarket packs of perspex flutes and goblets. He had passed a girl wearing a green and white stripped skirt which matched the deck chairs. She had probably worn it knowing but not bought it for that reason. A chorus of children singing 'Happy Birthday' broke out. In the shade of the trees by one of the less busy paths, a cellist was accompanying the birds. As it became louder,two women could be seen in the grass, one reading the other seated playing the instrument for the horse chestnut audience .

Mercedes' meeting was scheduled for 2pm on Monday. It was the first planning meeting for the Greek soap season. They had to discuss the Olympic torches, casting possibilities, agent contacts, a director, staging costs and publicity. Casting the approximate five actors and actresses was not Mercedes' problem. The alabaster skinned and Grecian aqualine nosed gods were Lucy's responsibilty. She would also have to organise their tonsored curls ,jewels and gems. Mercedes was general management and publicity. They still had to decide on exactly which plays would be most suitable. Odysseus and Euripedes. The little sunken portico amphitheatre could take three hundred people with enough additional seating for another two hundred.

Tickets priced between £7.50 and £15.00 were the going rate which would allow enough profit for the season's success. The Garden Restaurant could handle the wine and olive mezze refreshments and there were even garden toilets - no need to hire porter loos. It was small fry compared to Henry's city deals but it supported her and several actors quite favourably.

Mercedes opened her first planning meeting with a quote from a critic who argued that Greek theatre distorts from the original textural states. She had decided to wear her new Marc Jacobs top with her Gloria Vanderbilt indigo denim and Mui Mui shoes. She took her notes out of her Prada bag and tried to concentrate. She had spent hours researching and felt confident on her subject. And intelligent enough to ask the right question if somebody else at the meeting was an expert. Even experts could get it wrong, or lie she had learnt. Most Greeks were literate and their theatre was generally a reflection of their religeon and culture - whether questioning love or revenge, an eye for an eye, Thespis inventor of tragedy or Tragoida [goat song to be classically accurate - the cracking of male voices during puberty], Thespis was going to entertain Spiros. Mercedes short season wanted to revive those enertias for the five hundred ticket holders a night too, with her natural instinct for mercenary mimesis and imitation. She read Catallus' humorous Friend Furious to put them in the mood.

After about two hours of enthusiastic planning their instinct for mimesis and imitation of creation put them at the eighth day and nineteenth hole. They thought they had it all wrapped up; nothing would ever go that smoothly. They decided a few drinks were in order and went for champagne cocktails. Mercedes watched the bubbles rushing up from their central source. She had forgotten why some rushed up around the outside of the glass because that was at the beginning of the bottle when the iambic pentameters sounded more dadum dadum than dumdada.

She had a feature to finish for Wednesday and two interviews to make the next day, one telephone interview to a gallery in New York the other at a private view in the evening. The June artist's pop-top ten was nearly compiled based on no sales or votes, just the best second and third opinions she had depending on how subjective she felt.

She got home, took her shoes and jacket off and put the TV on. There was a documentary on the Trooping of the Colour. The soldiers had new synthetic fur buzzbees and sub machine guns instead of rifles. They're changing the guard at Buckingham Palace. Christopher Robin went home wearing his save the tiger T- shirt with the elephants that James I kept in St James' Park and had boiled egg with soldiers.

'Next morning on the coast of a tropical paradise, 'said Anthony Bates from behind his X ray specs.

It was one month later and the casting was complete. Valerie Trace and Pablo Bernice both had done TV dramas in addition to West End theatre work. Ray Burn was between two films and could fit the original opportunity in with pleasure. Fleur Young and Phillip Firman-Macintyre were both new actors.

'Exotic birds from interior and waves washing gently against the shore. Phillip, where's Odysseus?'

Fleur answered, ' His spirit is soaring, his gates of perception flung wide open .'

Odysseus arrived. 'These are the lotus flowers.'

'Those are the lotus flowers .'

'Those are the lotus flowers .'repeated Odysseus .

Mercedes sat and watched the reading. When it was over Anthony came and sat by her.

'Feasting on the potent ?'

'The lotus gets into your blood .'she said and added,' the masks are supposed to arrive tomorrow.'

'We're rehearsing the killing of the black ewe. The rules of Greek theatre say you have to take it to the back of the stage to kill it and bring it back to the front of the skene dead or the audience cry. A bit sensitive the Greeks but they knew a bit about acoustics. What time will they arrive?'

'About eleven or twelve. If your not here, where should I put them ?'

'Somewhere in front of the stage in our imaginary orchestra. Orchestra and opera are place names in different languages but we've decided to stick a bunch of musicians in chairs and name them after it. A bit like the hoover, which is a brand name.'

Mercedes' Burlesque masks arrived as promised. They were going to wear the leather sandals instead of the traditional actors 'buskin' boots .

The sandals won the vote and the management decided to compromise their pure art in favour of leather straps. The masks were also better for the actors than white lead make up, which they replaced after probably killing the first generation of actors. She had just completed an interview with an artist who was showing next month. He was famous for designing pop art album covers and T-shirts in the 1960's. His new material priced at between £5-10,000 was influenced by new technologies and TV commercials and included bank statement and cash machine print outs and deposits. His New York show last month was a complete sell out. He believed that it was important to consumer age kids to identify with art and it's value in a disposable age of instant graphics.To appreciate concepts and skills. Why suffer for your art? Was the title.

When will the stereotype world of notoriety, commission and investment, where fine art is an expression of passion and pain taken over by mercenary values, find an artist worth more alive than dead.

Mercedes' list of things to do included the difficult task of music and wine selection. They had bottles of Kourtaki, Karela, Bibla Chora and Boutari to try and then work out the budget for the crate prices. The music was even more difficult because research produced very little information on what it actually sounded like other than saying flute and lute were used and that the oriental quartertones were described as expressive. The comedy dancers were described as jumping and spinning to the music and the satyrs were described as doing lewd pantomime. Euripides, however, had to be tied to the mast of his boat to listen to the sirens whose sweet overtures and harmonies were pitched at the right note and stopped the sailors from leaving the island. Mercedes despite being sympathetic to sweet hypnotic harp music was somewhat in need of help, inspired to get a captive audience and without the need for MDNA, which she quite often got muddled up with her American Visa anyway. She had had some mock ups done for the proposed publicity. Greek patterning in gold and white with orange and black nude vase paintings, horns and satyrs in lewd phallus holding poses and goat skinned actors. The best performers were allegedly given a kid goat as a prize. Mercedes bought some chabechoue and vine leaf wrapped crottin to go with the wine for the meeting. She knew from experience the only curried goat shop in zones one and two was closed two years earlier. She was reminded of it reading the Nil By Mouth script during a period of estrangement from George. The curried goat shop was a front for drugs anyway.

Sean returned from work at about 8pm.

'Got the new sport brief today Israel v Arabia football for kids instead of politics and the footage of the kids playing. Don't know which player is going to endorse it yet. It's good sportswear sponsorship and good exposure.'

'You need some new trainers,' said Mercedes.

'Won't get any. We'll have to write some T-shirts into the promotions – football for ... how does Striking Football in the Middle East sound.

Goals –the new currency for kids instead of guns and oil. Evocative music and close up angles of prodigy footwork and expressive scoring.'

'How are the satyrs goat legs?'

'Like Sisyphus pushing his ball up the hill. Their pitches are flat are they? Or do they have to keep dodging the wells?'

'That's a problem for planning and traffic. Flat I think. A new account manager showing leadership abilities has just pitched for the Egg Marketing Inspectorate. We could be doing the new improved positive discrimination post Edwina Currie and 'go to work on an egg.'

'They had gull's eggs in Selfridges last week,' said Mercedes.

'Take an egg to work with you. We deliver the work. Come home to eggs. Stay home for eggs.'

'Quails eggs.' said Mercedes .

'Perchery, free range, organic, barn eggs, midwives for chickens, epidurals and then relaunch natural egg birth. What's for dinner? Have we got any beer? Or would you rather go out?' asked Sean.

'Yes and yes.' said Mercedes.

'Where are we going? Japanese, Mexican, French?' asked Sean .'Apparently in France 'you can't polish a pear'.'

'Is that a pear or a pair?'

'I don't know I didn't ask.Une pair d'aces ou pantalon - ne pas polir une poire. You can't beat two aces or perhaps it was two faced. Two little ducks, clickety click or is it quack quack?'

'You can't polish ducks unless they're on the wall and then there are three and then they need dusting and that's quack, quack, quack.'said Sean .

'You have to dust three ducks.'

'I need a triple barrel shotgun. Maybe we should go for sushi and noodles instead of French.'

'OK 'said Mercedes.' A stone mason could have chiseled a text message in less time than it took for Anthony's assistant to email Alfies for the spears and goblets today.'

'What's the time now?'

'8.30pm' replied Mercedes.

'Fine. I'll try on my new Pronuptia prosterneda Greek wooden wonderbra. Then we can go back to the lotus tree for the weekend, drugged with the honey sweet red fruit, white buds and pink blossoms.'

Sean smiled and kissed Mercedes, smiled again then went to the fridge to get a beer.

Sean and Mercedes spent most of the weekend in bed watching the Wimbledon Mellowdrama. Mercedes worked on her feature for July's Art of The State on her laptop.' Knowing your Opies from your Caulfields, from your Vauxs, from your Albers from your Rothkos' and investing in Bridget Riley. Plus the new unseen collection of Warhol's early work. Michael Craig was number one, the new Hockney was number two.

On Saturday night they met up with some friends on a wooden Horse of Troy NME guest list pass to see Werle and Stankowski a new German Indie band before going back to work on Monday.

15 out of 100 minimum age school leavers are convicted of a criminal offense. The other 85 get away with it .

Sean had to get his concepts visualised for a presentation 9 am Tuesday and was praying that the new Account Executive had confirmed the visualiser and understood what like yesterday meant.

Mercedes opening night was 15th July. She had sent some front row tickets to Henry and emailed him with threats of castration if he did not let half of the city know about the event, then she bought a Matthew Williamson dress and Vivienne Westwood shoes for the occasion. Olympic torches and fairy lights illuminated the gardens making the amphitheatre a very real experience. The atmosphere was fuelled by the wine and authentic mezze with olives and dolmades. An announcement interrupted the conversation, which sparkled over the flute and harp music and drifted across the Thames asking the audience to take their seats and switch off their mobile phones. The mobile phones bit had been Mercedes idea. She always found the 'turn off' request in theatres a bad stage direction just pre curtain up which destroyed the auditorium.

Penelope's suitor, Valerie Trace stood at the front of the apron in a white toga dress, which was just back from the theatrical dry cleaners in Mercer Street after an accident during the dress rehearsal. Her hair was piled up on her head in plaits and ringlets, which fell across her pale bosom.

'Then sing another. Not the song of Troy.'

Valerie played Penelope with a natural Mediterranean passion.

'It climbed my stairs, rising like smoke, seeping under the door and bringing me to tears, let me sleep I'm tired.'

Eurymachus [Phillip] – She's an icy one.

Antinous [Ray Burn] She'll melt.

The audience were enjoying the performance with laughter and other uninhibited reactions.

'My king you have landed us paradise.'

'I feel purple ecstasy.'

At the interval the audience made their way to the bar and enjoyed the wine and gardens again stretching their legs. Mercedes walked through the buoyant crowd. The event was sold out and a success. The press had taken some photos earlier and some during the performance. They would read about it tomorrow.

Mercedes had got Art of the State finished early to allow her concentrate on the play. Not as it had been occasionally to stop her stress levels going up and take her mind off it if something was going badly out of her control. She would be able to go to Henley now. Mercedes opened the critic's column.

The embankment gardens season opened last night with Odysseus directed by Anthony Bates. The play was literally a star-studded al fresco success staring Ray Burn, Valerie Trace and Pablo Bernice. Two newcomers Fleur Young and Phillip Firman-Macintyre added to a fantastic astrology. The use of open-air amphitheatre was well researched and true to the Greek original. The gods blessed the sometimes lewd performance with decent weather, it was superbly cast and the sirens had the audience held in rapture unwanting to be 'Homeward Bound' to their

Simon and Garfunkel living rooms but to remain 'Here where the fires glow.' Here where the stars turn, Here where the fruits burn, here where the heart grows....'

Sean and his art director had watched from the front row with about a dozen members from the account handling team and creative departments. He too could not live without kissing the mouths of sirens like Odysseus wailing and moaning to the harmonious chorus. They all toasted Mercedes with champagne and went out to dinner in Charlotte Street.

The next day Mercedes renewed her Oyster card and went to a meeting for next season's proposals following a large amount of financial investment and sponsorship interest. Sean emailed her from work.

Merc

'Stuffing O'Toole naturally stuffs with his tool, the stew – pot stews it's own mess.'

Catallus

Love Sean

Opening night was on Friday. Henry thought that he had the rest of the weekend to himself in front of the TV. If he was honest with himself he knew he would have preferred to have made plans but new that they would possibly get messed up if he was seeing Mercedes.

Steak.

Dubois had rung Henry about some tickets they had booked to confirm that they had arrived.

'I'm not used to the buttons on this yet. I have a new gold mobile phone. Am I driving? Yes, but it's OK I'll put the hands free on. That's better. I've just passed Camden's latest street furniture installation of CCTV cameras – a sixties - …….. fibre optic lamp, sputnik satellite confluence of design, which could be mistaken for last years Christmas decorations left up to save money for next year's budgets. The fact they have panoply on every lamp post on High Holborn and no others in the borough is an extravagance. Every other lamp post would suffice. They will probably end up Feng Shuing the red routes next and painting all the white lines black to be rebellious as a counter measure and at twice the expense. Vote for more trees, bushes, and topiaried tubs and bay trees outside civilised awning restaurant fronts. People who design their living rooms around the TV ignore the windows, views and have given up facing each other and any sociable society. The TV room is a more American concept, given the luxury of space saving the lounge for conversation and other sociable events like musing at the walls in my case. Which reminds me I've been given a print of a sixteenth century Dumonstier, 'The hand of Artemesia Gentileschi,' isn't that a wonderful name. You must come to dinner and give me some suggestions of where to put it and what to do with the place. What about lunch tomorrow? Are you busy, we can get the food in the morning? I'll invite Chris and Reese from next door.'

'Yes, I'd love to. What time?'

'About 11 OK?'

'Yes great.'

Dubois arrived at five to eleven.

'What do you reckon paella or rabbit with lentils?' asked Henry, ' I can't make my mind up. Maybe we'll find something else.'

After a glass of wine they walked to the shops through the park, stopping to pick blackberries, rosehips and apples. Then sat on a petite banquette with ornate ironwork to watch the cricket for ten minutes in the sun. A band with a big double base was playing jazz on the bandstand.

'The sound of willow and leather – English Summer – instant Karma,' said Dubois.

'Reassuring and relaxing despite the immense physical impact which would be potentially lethal,' She blushed almost as red as the cricket ball and was saved by a player shouting 'Run!' as his team player in bat hit a shot. This was then followed by a six then he was bowled out.

Plastic ketchup and mustard containers, bloomers, split tins, tins and cottage loaves in the bakery joined now by every European bread and brioche, put Dubois back in her Saturday job at school. Lunch time was always sausage rolls and filled ham and cheese rolls. This was before Marks and Spencer's food halls and Prêt a Manger coffee shops. Most of the bread was sold in the morning and the cakes, black forest gateaux, fresh cream éclairs and Florentines in the afternoon. And then occasionally someone would order a birthday or wedding cake from the selection of iced designs in the book.

One of the other girls who worked there asked her how old she was. She had to be fifteen. What was one year? 'You must have your o'levels coming up.' she said.

O'levels she remembered panicking having not yet had any detailed introduction on the subject. 'Yes.' She said. Later they sneaked through the bakery at the back and up to the empty flat upstairs. Dubois decided she was going to live there. It smelt fantastic.

As they unpacked the food, Dubois noticed a small insect on the coriander. 'Grasshopper! It's a baby grillo.'

'Jimmeny Cricket!'

It was very small, bright green with a red tail, very fine antennae, big black legs and black eyes. It did not chirrup like a cicarda and would not jump.

'Why won't he jump?'

Henry started singing 'have you ever seen an elephant fly.'

'I've flown first class in a jumbo,' said Dubois.

'Good. Keep it that way. I wouldn't expect anything less.'

'Why do they need to jump anyway? Would you pack his little trunk and put him on the window sill in the sun.' Dubois waved bye bye.

'Can I make the rose hip tea and then I'll make the apple gallette. I'll need a saucepan, a sieve, some sugar and two cups. You can make the ice cream.'

Henry put some Cocteau Twins on and broke two of the Road Island Reds, which Dubois had brought with her and mixed them with a pot of double cream, sugar and lime. He whisked it together then added the blackberries. They slowly orbited each other, maneuvering around the kitchen like planets with magnetic pull, preparing the food , as if they had done it a thousand times. They had found some rabbit and made a cassoulet which would cook itself in an hour while they left it in outer space . The others were arriving at 2pm. Henry put on his Hacket cricket sweater, poured some wine and introduced Dubois to the print of Artemesia Gentileschi's fine expressive hand with brush.

'A portrait within itself, ' he lectured, 'without a facial expression, it is not an anonymous body part, its lace sleeve and brush give it status and action. It's style and pose give it a character and expression. Where should I put it ?'

'Are you considering moving the big one over the fireplace'

'No.'

'I didn't expect you would. On the opposite wall near to the window? It's beautiful.'

They starred at it for about half a minute then he turned to her, close up. For a second she thought he was going to kiss her, then he walked off.

Their guests enjoyed the food . All the rabbit and lentils, ice cream and gallette were eaten with five more bottles of wine.

Chris and Reese, were a young couple. She owned a shop and he was a designer; mutual friends of Sydney who arrived with a lawyer friend.

'What do you think I should do with this room?' asked Henry.' It's bugging me, it needs some remodelling. I like the idea of a new shag pile rug and maybe new window dressing, curtains or blinds. I saw this. What do you reckon. There's more space now I have swopped these over.'

'Do you like Japanese. You could do takami mats and screens with bonsai. But you'd have to get rid of the brown leather.'

'Indian wooden furniture or low level credenza, low level everything.'

'Astroturf carpet and white sliding screen doors.'

'Submarine hatch doors would work well in the corridor.'

'I saw a nice bright yellow vase and maybe a matching melon yellow cushion which would go with the shag pile rug.'

Lunch was a success and they left by 7.30/8pm. Dubois multiple choiced herself.

a. taxi home with Sydney

b. taxi home in about half an hour

c. end up pissed and fall asleep

d. she did not want to consider the thought of any advances

e. she considered momentarily making an advance and played safe with plan a. knowing they were going out next week.

Henry was not sixteen any more but acted on the spur of the moment. He thought of the beautiful harmonies of the Italian Castrati and rang Dubois .

'Can you leave the chickens for the weekend? How long would it take you to pack and come with me to Paris this evening? I haven't had time to think if it's a good idea or not. What do you reckon?'

Seizure.

'Yes.' replied Dubois with a similar seizure.

'I have a meeting on Monday and the client wants to go to the Moulin Rouge. The rest of the weekend we can visit the Rodin and find some restaurants, the Buddha Bar sounds like it could be included as well.'

Dubois had to think for a minute.

'What should I be doing? Let me just check my filofax in case there is something. I'm probably supposed to be doing something. What do I have to do? Where should I meet you?'

'5pm Eurostar.'

'OK'

Dubois made a list. Feed chickens. Pack. Make calls for next week. It felt a bit secret, she had seven hours and needed to tell Hermione. Listening to other people's conversations was the most exciting thing she had done as a teenager. Telephone crosslines were possible before the fibre optic expansion of business and residential numbers. At first she hung up. Then the next time she hung on listening trying not to heavy breathe, only to realise it was the woman from up the road. Someone must have been making repairs at the junction box. After that she was aware of clicking and decided that she had seen too many spy films when she unscrewed the handset looking for a bug. British Telecom had never been so sexy. It's tower remained a great landmark wherever she was in London, despite the buzzing and potential radiation.

She emailed Hermione.

I'm accompanying Henry to Paris as a wife sub. I'll be back on Monday. You can keep your tracksuit on all weekend .
Love Dubois .

Paris.

Dubois paid the taxi driver and put her brown leather gloves, which went with her shoes back on. She put her purse in her Louis Vuitton handbag and walked up the steps of the main entrance to Waterloo Station. Her grey dress pulled where it was tight at her knees making her conscious of her legs and hips. Most commuters miss the grandeur of the main entrance as they arrive and depart by tube and platforms with numbered destination boards. She crossed the busy rush hour concourse, coffee shops and croissant bars, Boots, WH Smiths, passed the flower stalls, umbrella shops and the ticket offices and descended the escalator, putting her small wheeled case next to her. She arrived at the Euro star terminal where Henry was waiting in a navy pinstripe suit and similar luggage.

'Bonjour. Cava?'

'Cava bien merci. What's the time? It's not five yet is it? The station clock said about five to.'

'Vous devez parler a moi en francais. L'horloge dit cinq heures moins deux minutes et mon digital casio dit cinq heures exactement. J'ai les billets, allons y.'

They walked through the barrier to the train, which was pulling, into the platform.

'Alors!' said Dubois. 'Voyez la femme la bas qui porte un béret? Est ce que tu l'aime?'

'Oui, beaucoup!'

'Je doit acheter un beret pendant nous sommes en Paris.'

'Bien sur mon petit. Do I look like Roger Vadim?'

'Sydney would have a wig in her bag. Un perruque pour fair changer sa identite!'

As soon as they were in their seats and the hostess appeared Henry ordered two glasses of champagne and read out an article in the paper about recycling plastic and their biodegradable qualities.

'What's wrong with the environmentally friendly paper ones they had in Sainsburys, they take less time to recycle and cost twice as much probably.

Or expandable string bags? You don't see them anymore. They had some very clever wine bags with six divisions in Waitrose. Forget the shopping just eat there next time instead!'

The fields and trees rushed passed very quickly in the quiet train. From the newspapers, mobiles, books and laptops it appeared to be mainly business people in the compartment .

'J'ai mon ordinateur ici si j'ai besoin de travail. J'espère que tu n'as pas une probleme,' said Henry .

'Franchement! Non. Moi aussi. S'il est vraiment necessaire. Je peux aller trouver les oeufs français s'il y a du temps. Je veux essayer quelque chose differentes pour faire la jalouse de mes poulets. J'ai beaucoup des ordres à ce moment. Mais il y a toujours l'opportunitie nouvelle pour faire l'expansion. Aujour d'hui un poulet de Paris, demain le monde! D'accord! Contente?'

At Paris they alighted the train, took a taxi to the hotel and checked into twin rooms 254 and 255. Henry asked the concierge if there were any messages and he handed him a piece of paper.

'I have to make a call.'

A porter took the luggage.

Dubois made herself familiar with the room, the balcony and shutters, the bathroom and it's french soap, the TV and minibar. Then unpacked her trousers, T-shirt and shirt.

They met Henry's four market clients, and after the Moulin Rouge were taken to an elegant restaurant in the Champs Elysees and ate frogs legs and steak tartare. Dubois had the smallest steak she had ever seen and drank Brandy to Napoleon. Then they went back to the hotel piano bar.

Saturday was 86 degrees. The Indian Summer sun was streaming through the tall windows onto the gilt furniture and wooden floors and woke Dubois. She followed Henry's instructions and went for breakfast in the dining room at 8.30 am. Coffee with frothy French milk, brioche and eggs .

'Good morning.Did you sleep well?'

The proximity of Henry's head was paralysing next to her neck as he spoke to her softly. She forgot her headache for a moment and lost interest in her food.

He joined her and ordered his food. Dubois drank more coffee. From the hotel it was a short walk to the Louvre where they ran their hands over the entwined figures of Rodin's Kiss and contemplated The Thinker as he sat on the rough base block from which he was carved before going to the Eiffel Tower.

'I've seen and touched The Kiss.' said Dubois outloud. Henry smiled. The view from the two hundred and fifty metre observation deck was excellent. They located the Sacred Coeur and Monmatre beyond the grey roofs, balconies and shutters which curve around the Parisienne streets and watched the little boats on the Seine.

Before lunch they passed a milliners and Henry took Dubois' arm and lead her inside the chic boutique .

'Bonjour Madame. I'd like to try a beret.'

'Oui Madame .What colour?'

She pointed to a selection.

'I'm not sure. I like the camel one, but black is more traditional.'

'Would you like to try both?'

Dubois tried them on and stuck to her decision.

'Tres chic.'

'Let me see,' said Henry, then he turned to the assistant and said,

'Oui, je le prend.'

Dubois leaned foreward smiling and kissed him on the cheek comme une cocette. She kept the beret on and they continued along the road passed the perfumeries, couture shops and smart numbered gold panelled entrance buzzers with foreign residents names until they found a suitable restaurant.

 Dubois' friends in Paris had moved. She had emailed them yesterday to say that she was coming. Henry knew loads of people in Paris. For a moment she contemplated working there but did not think the chickens would agree. Lunch of oysters and champagne took about two hours sitting watching in the afternoon sun. Henry put a bet online for a race at Montpellier at 4.15pm. Then they walked back to the hotel with the shopping along the Seine where a group of men were playing chess.

'Echec et mat! A carreaux!' said one man.

Henry said something about the game which Henry did not understand. Another table were playing draughts.

'Qu'est ce que vous t'appellez en francais, cette joue?'

'Dammes Mademoiselle.Voudrez vous jouer? Essayez vous .'

'Oui merci.'

Dubois looked at the board. 'Blanc ou noir.?'

'Blanc.'

She moved the little piece and took one of the opponent's counters 'Merci mademoiselle. Nous gagnons.'

It was about 5.30pm.

'There's a sauna and Jacuzzi on the fifth floor,' said Dubois.

'I know,' said Henry. They put the shopping in the rooms and changed into the white robes and met by the gold caged lift with some towels to go up. In the lift Dubois tried to ignore Henry.

'It's a bit big,' she said looking a bit daft in the massive towelling robe. Henry couldn't resist and kissed her.

They sat in the bubbling water for about fifteen minutes trying not to giggle and had a sauna discussing what they would have for dinner.

She did not wake up in her room. She had just gone outside onto the balcony wearing Henry's suit jacket with her shoes as room service appeared with breakfast and champagne.

Sunday evening they went to the Buddha Bar. Large Buddha figures and black lacquer mixed with gold ornament, candles, rai music and masses of atmosphere.

Debrief.

Dubois spent Monday evening watching the cinemascope storm with Francis Ford Coppola clouds from her kitchen window. She counted the seconds between thunder and lightening, submissive to the powers of nature. It had obviously rained a lot, as the lettuce looked more like a paddy field. The chickens were dry and still had plenty of feed. She collected the eggs. The empty basket obsequiously waiting to be filled, it was nearly full, and needed a second trip. Dubois had only been away three days and her box supply was in need of organisation. Doodle, a Buff Orpington Cockerel was crowing impatiently to be let out, his long red tail feathers shaking at her as Dubois started talking to the muscovite ducks. Henry was going to the Lansdowne Club when he got back to swim off his Fois Gras and Calvados. He felt in need of a detox as his radioactive waste levels were exceeding those of the Selafield nuclear power plant and they were only five times the size of the Albert Hall which was the last statistic he was given up until 1980. He had spoken to Tarquin who said he would be in the bar after a meeting, which incidentally he added was where the Paris Treaty was drawn up and signed, which marked Franklin Roosevelt's American Independence. Dubois was happy debriefing the chickens. She also had an emailed invitation to a party sent with her Inland Revenue tax return. Amen personified something.

The comedy club on Wednesday started at 7.30pm. Dubois had sent her tax return on Monday. She met Sydney first at work. Amen was in a good mood as usual; he had arranged a table for about twenty five people and dinner afterwards in a restaurant nearby. The first stand up set was a sketch with two gallery curators.

'You may have heard of Dantes' Inferno and Rodin's Gates of Hell, but you don't hear much about his Walls of Hell because all the ice creams have melted.'

'These are the personifications of music and rhetoric with a book and an organ by Justus Ghent 1470. This organ had the first known notations of music written for it out of interest. The muse of music incidentally is called Enterpe.

The muse of song who holds a bird is called Polyhymnia. The muse of erotic poetry, Erato and Calliope, muse of music both hold books and the muse of astrology holds a telescope. The muse of comedy, called Thalia doesn't have much to hold on to. He wears a mask with a smile on it. And Melpo, muse of tragedy has one with a frown. What made the Greeks laugh? Obviously masks with smiley faces. They did not have much else to smile about with building roads, marching great armies into battle, playing sport naked, wearing togas and making peace with olives. Their toga party invites probably said dress 'formal'. There's always one gullible Greek who will turn up in a suit, when the rest are wearing casual dress.

Each table had a questionnaire on it. Amen read it out loud as he filled it in.

'What is your opinion of nucleur power? Who should make the decisions for it's uses - ME! We have to avoid having to make landfill safe and save recycling questionnaires. What's the next question? Would you like some more wine or a student grant?

When the club ended they walked to Andrea's and enjoyed spinach and ricotta filo spanacopita, swordfish, feta and olives dripping in golden oil, followed by honey and nut pastries with Debina, Greek rosé wine from the Klimata region, and Metaxa. Greek rosé is more caramel than French rosé, noted Sydney whilst not forgetting her Hard Day's Night hair. Her new shoulder length hair. She had had it cut in a modern interpretation of the sixties style with the ends dried in an upwards direction and was enjoying being a very dedicated follower of fashion. There was a plate smashing floor show which broke into dancing lead by a man with pom poms on his feet and odd Elizabethan style pants. Amen joined in the dancing first taking Dubois with him. She had bothered him and he betrayed his better judgement. He danced better than Anthony Quinn to Zorba the Greek and refused to let Dubois go. At first he denied himself an advance then smiling, kissed her anyway .

Sydney had experienced earthquakes in Greece and had enlightened them on the tectonic plates, faults and tremors, richter scale points and the pleasures of strolling around almond groves. And how she met the owner of a Club who owned the land she was trespassing on at the time. The bars in the village experienced bottles falling off tables and shelves, the villagers advised their usual practice of sleeping outside which gave the heroic tourist motivation to drink all night having little other choice. The British spirit at the airport in 90° heat the following day was slightly dehydrated as the DT's were scaled and overtaken by the tremors and vibrations, which shook your whole body. She read the personal messages out in the paper and said 'endaxi' as Amen ordered another bottle of metaxa. Then read out the astrology intrigued by the little white constellations.

'The moon is full on the twenty second, it is still in it's third quarter phase. The hazy area represents the Milky Way.'

Dressed crab.

Dubois, Epiphany and Hermione risked the showers and walked along Westbourne Grove. They passed a wedding with confetti cream rose petals. The bride who was wearing a cream silk dress got out of a big black Bentley and was being photographed on the steps of the church, probably for Tatler or Harpers and Queen. At the top of Portobello Road a sea of people with umbrellas laced themselves in a perpendicular direction down the hill and passed the stalls of silver toast racks, massive silver service plates and covers, etched and decorated with scallops, pairs of Pekinese, phrenology heads, pink patterned china, bird cages and canaries, a piano was playing from a room somewhere over the noise of the sales and interest that surrounded the pieces on sale. It took about ten minutes to walk to Holland Park. A children's party with pasta and strawberries had taken over the picnic benches in the café and a game of five a side football was being played on the pitches. The blackberry bushes had no fruit but an apple tree in the nature reserve still had some miniature apples on the very top boughs. They stopped to buy some food on the way back and lingered over the cinnamon chewing gum, interesting English goats cheese wrapped in leaves with funny names like Ticklemore, sheep's milk, hemp seed, harlequin pumpkins, squashes, gallettes, gingerbread people and chocolate motorcycles. Back at Hermione's they put the small blue swimmer crabs on ice to keep them fresh and made a big bowl of popcorn which they sat around with large glasses of wine trying to decide what they should do with the attractive crustations. Dubois made a note to bring a chillie plant for Hermione when she had separated the seedlings, which now had four leaves and dropped their little husks. She was surprised how quickly they had germinated and was intently observing their daily progress as the little leaves started to change shape.

It was about 5.30pm and Tarquin arrived back with Henry.

'Hi Epiphany!' Henry took some popcorn,' May I?'

Hermione got two more glasses.

'What do you get when you cross a mummy with a stereo?'

'I don't know, what do you get when you cross a mummy with a stereo?'

'Wrap music.'

Henry paused then started up again.

'Honda are creating 200,000 new jobs with pre-tax profits of 61% which shot to £39.5 million.'

'What did one flea say to the other flea? Shall we walk or take the dog?' Spat Dubios not expecting to see Henry so soon after their weekend away and realising she was on her fourth glass of wine.

'Have you any ideas for what to do with these crabs Tarquin?' asked Hermione. 'I'll leave them up to you.'

'Where are they?' he asked as he looked in the fridge and around the kitchen.

'Gone to the sea bed lost property.'

'The tickets for tomorrow are on the board next to the council tax bill,' replied Hermione.

'Where are we going, the Tropic of Cancer? I've found the tickets. What's this?'

'That's a flyer that someone left on my car.'

'Titanic Club Passenger Ferry night with uplifting music, DJs Winslet and Hovercraft playing iceberg hitting tunes. Train tickets for Cambridge, oh yes!'

'Just the place for a snark,' the Bellman cried as he landed his crew with care, quoted Tarquin from the book that Hermione had been reading which was opened and flat to keep the page.

'I'm going to wear my new shoes,' said Epiphany. 'Does anyone want to play scrabble while dad cooks?'

'Good idea,' said Dubois, ' a return match for yesterday.'

Henry and Dubois were staring at each other.

'I'll set it up,' said Henry, 'if you read some more Dubois.'

'OK the fourth is its fondness for bathing machines ' she continued for about two verses.

Dubois swapped the book for a glass of wine which Henry handed her and he carried on reading another verse. Then they started the game.

Tease – Epiphany got a triple word score.

Trains.

Gnat.

Procession.

Rose

After half an hour Tarquin shouted across the room.

'Food is in the complaints department.'

They put the scrabble on hold and ate linguine with small blue crab lemongrass and basil.

Bath.

Henry's other sister Kaneda was one year older than her sister Mercedes. She had been working in Paris and sent him her usual weekly email.

Hi Henry

'Engaged' his name is Francois. No date for wedding yet. When are you free for dinner this week?

Love Kaneda.

Henry read it again and looked at his diary. Once over the shock he replied. It was not out of character for Kaneda to give little notice for anything as she travelled at short notice for her work all the time. Neither was he worried because he knew that both of his sisters knew their own minds and would ask if they needed advice. He replied to her email then rang her to find out more, eager to speak to her and congratulate her in person. That's when he met Francois Curadell.

'Won't you meet me tonight?'

'Where you favourite past time's right round the corner at the O-de-on.'

Francois sang the matinee ditty song to himself as sung by the audiences at the first truly modern Oscar Deutsch Odeon's of the 1930's.

'Is everybody happy! Yes!

Do we ever worry? No!

To the Odeon we have come.

Now we're all together

We can have some fun!'

Francois Curadell had hazel eyes and light brown hair starting to go silver, which he quite liked. He wore either green Oliver Peoples or frameless silver Armani glasses, Mulberry shirts, rarely wore ties and either a black, grey or navy pinstriped suit. Or white shirt, Levis and a pinstriped jacket. He had heavy silver chain around one wrist and a blue face Tag Heuer on the other. He was enjoying the Bath Oliver biscuits he had brought back from his day in Bath placing slices of Somerset Goats cheese on the Roman soldiers heads, which are imprinted on their centres. The dry white biscuits are from the original recipe invented by Dr W Oliver, physician who left the recipe to his coachman Atkins along with a bag of flour when he died having established himself in Bath society from the profits of their success. Similarly Atkins left it to a man named Norris who sold it to a Mr Carter and he likewise to Mr James Fortt in the 1950's. It is now a brand owned by the Jacobs umbrella.

Francois had eaten nearly half a cohort with his wine, lining them up two abreast along the table.

'Now we're all together

We can have some fun.'

It sounded more like a rugby song.

Francois was forty two last birthday. He was still recovering from presenting his debtors petition order No.2809 0f 2007 which the Music Contract had caused to the Bankruptcy Court. He never wanted to see or fill in another form in his life. He delivered the insolvency made up of creditors and debtors lists to the Official Receiver in Room E01 in the Eastern Block of The Supreme Crown Court WC1 and then had the petition stamped in Room E04 and paid for it in Room EX60. He had a file full of Law Society advice, bank statements, Warrants of Execution and Garnishees for the Baliff which he had served on the Music Contract. The petition took half a day, the whole morning was a matinee feature to rank with a Kirk Douglas epic. The man behind the glass window looked at him coldly making him feel as guilty as an assassin with a concealed weapon not the innocent victim of circumstance. He felt like Edward Fox in The Day of The Jackal. Walking through customs with two hundred Marlborough and a packet of foreign tea is usually enough for most citizens to feel like a criminal. And worse than sitting outside the Headmaster's office waiting for the cane. He was with The Mercenary Bank, with Mercenary overdrafts, Mercenary loans, mortgages and cheque books not with WWF donations and cute tigers but 'Save The Source of Money' and 'Destroy The Threat'. No more Warmington-on-Sea and support a different arsenal.

He finished his goats cheese and opened another bottle of wine. He had drunk all the champagne he had bought returning from his duty to The Official Receiver Section 279 act. He now had one year minimum to get a sponsor and a new job then get a £60 certificate of release from the court, his mortgage was insured .

His day in Bath was the Ajax to remove the ring from around his bank account which the Music Contract had left.

Francois had read somewhere that French bakers put ice in their ovens to make the baguette crust crisp. There is an annual competition where the boulangeries battle to be the best. After kneading the bread dough the yeast in it makes it rise and then the air is knocked out of it and left to rise a second time. Francois' friend had used this analogy to try and encourage him in an optimistic way. It was his friend who had felt bad because there was nothing he could do, doing something positive was outside his means. French baking tends to be more attractive than the British loaf. They make light toasts and little brioche. The large thick sliced English white, split tin, bloomer and more individual cottage loaf appeal more to the 'cook until golden brown and firm to the touch' and the Italian Ciabbatta and Foccaccia tell tales of their own. Francois celebrated his renaissance of coach travel. He was unable to tax his car this month and planned his come back inspired by the Romans.

Rome was not built in a day, he kept reminding himself. He had a 10.30 am appointment every two weeks at the Jobcentre to sign on for his JSA until he found suitable employment. He Errol Browned himself and waited in the modern office with bright pictures of inspiring literature, courses and advice. Modern computer terminals with touch screens replaced the old job cards in windows. He put in his job requirements to see what was available then a woman called his name and told him to take a seat. He usually told people to take them home when they asked him if they were free. There were about half a dozen loud speaking stereotypes with beer cans a predictable percentage of youths and the occasional smart person who looked with justifiable reason for being in the mix.

Francois answered the questions and handed in the NS110 form, which he had filled in the day before. Then he signed his piece of paper and left in need of a drink.

He posted the competition form he had filled out earlier while waiting when he was early and went to the Audley.

He caught up on a few friends and then Francois tackled the bankruptcy.

'Don't you want to know about the bankruptcy?' asked Francois.

'No, not really,' said Rock.

'Good,' said Francois. 'Change the subject.'

'Mortgage?'

'OK.'

'My brother finished uni, started his first job last week and wants his own place – the wife thinks it's a good idea too,' said Rock.

'OK. A three month trial.'

'When will you have some designs?' asked Karl.

'One month,' said Francois.

'OK I'll look at them,' agreed Karl. Then they all took a long drink from their pints and changed the subject to the cricket. Grand Prix and whether they preferred Lily Adams, Kate Moss or Patsy Kensit.

He posted the competition form he had filled in while he was waiting. Having arrived early he had read a magazine and arranged to meet a friend for lunch to recover from his first signing. Two weeks later he received a reply. He had won the competition, a days clay pigeon shooting at Something House, with breakfast and lunch. He rang the number to confirm and was advised how to get the shotgun licence required. Francois collected the form from the Post Office. It needed a JP or bank manager's signature. His bank manager would enjoy signing it. He had discovered his sense of humour. There were customers alot worse than Francois.

'Why don't you have some business cards made up in Rymans.' suggested Mr Wilkinson.

'Something double barrelled like Francois Hamilton-Klein!'

'I could even buy a title online and change my name by Deed Pole!'

'Good idea.' agreed Mr Wilkinson.

He caught the 6.30am train from Victoria to Aylesbury and a taxi from the station to Aylesbury House. The sun was rising as the train travelled across the fields which were covered by morning mist. Francois had wrapped his Burberry scarf around his neck in a style that he had seen on the television, folding it in half to make it half the length and pulling the fringe ends through the loop that was formed. He was greeted on arrival by the Sports Car Magazine staff who would be covering the event, taking pictures and interviews for a future PR feature filling a double page spread with product placement and positioned advertising. Francois had understood the right hand facing, left hand reading, right side reading , wrong side down print terminology for about five seconds once, nodding alot to the person explaining it.

He noticed the other winners were all wearing similar jackets, polo necked sweaters and denim. He did not feel too unguerilla like. He had contemplated brand new Hunters, flat cap and tweed jacket but knew he would look like a dummy and he should not afford them either.

They were invited into breakfast which was toast and jam, kedgeree and bacon served on floral white Spode in a wooden walled room with a table which would probably seat about twenty four people.

'Good morning.' said Francois to the others, breaking the silence. And they all replied 'Good morning.'

'I'm Francois. Have you all shot before?'

One person had, the others had not.

'No never.'

'I tried it once before and missed most of them.' said one woman in a pink diamond Pringle twinset. He offered her the toast rack to go with her jam dish. She was looking a bit nervous. Then they sat and ate together. The magazine staff gave them a briefing of the day's events and introduced them to Lord and Lady Cosfoot.

'Would you like to finish your breakfast and meet outside the front hall door in five minutes.'

'After you,' said Francois to the pink Pringle who was called Anna.

As they were leaving the breakfast room Francois heard someone heckle an insult in French.

'Merci Madame ,' said Francois to the old woman who was now visible. Lady Sissy Cosfoot turned around and said, 'May I present Lady Tania Cosfoot.'

'Good morning.'

'Good morning.' Everyone in earshot replied. Then they formed a group outside by the higher taxed, higher fuel emmision, four wheel drive parked on the gravel. Getting two labradors and three children into a smart car would be much more environmentally friendly to society but not to the parties mentioned. It was slightly warmer in the sunshine where everyone was given earphones and talked about the guns. Francois missed the first one then hit a couple. He knew it was possible to and assumed he had been doing it for years to feel comfortable with the gun, making sure not to appear like an absolute novice or be over confident. The sagelous ape, he had heard, learnt what to avoid. He was enjoying himself immensely. It was a million miles away from the shelving in the Citizen's Advice Bureau he had stared at for an hour and a half when waiting for an appointment, which had information from everything from housing advice and homelesness, to employees rights and adoption agencies.

They stopped for lunch at 2pm and returned across the field to the house. They took off their muddy boots leaving them in the entrance in a style that was a cross between a ski chalet and a Japanese house or temple, and walked around in Wellington boot socks. Francois was of the opinion that slippers tend to be cliched as dogs toys or OAP territory, although the spa lifestyle was bringing them back and they are now being sold in shops like Muji. The inside outside shoe ethic seems to have bought a gym membership.

'What are you reading?' Francois asked Anna who he found looking at the bookshelves.

'Gunter Grass.'she replied.

'Every woman is a volume,' said Francois.' Confucious say man with slanted opinion - not on level. Do you think he was refering to graphology or standing on a mountain? Japan has plateaus as well I suppose. If you're in Amsterdam it's much flatter. It must be diffficult to have a slanted opinion if you're in Holland. You have to call a windmill a windmill!'

'There are men that talk like books and also books that talk like men,' interrupted Lady Cosfoot. She spun the globe around with her well manicured French ivory index finger and stopped it again.

'Addis Ababa! That's where the washing up brushes come from. Do you travel much?'

'Not as much as I used to,' replied Francois.

'My sister had one of her trips planned but she's broken her ankle and she's making everyone suffer. I was starting to wish someone would take her.'

Here you have a go.' She pointed to the globe.

Francois spun and stopped it again then read where his finger was.

'Helsinki!'

'Is her ankle very bad? How did she do it?'

'Fell over, now she's sulking. I might advertise for an escort to accompany her Grand Tour.'

'I have nothing planned for the next six months. It sounds great.'

'Do you have a card?' asked Lady.

'Yes,' Francois handed her his new business card.

'Thank you Mr Hamilton – Klein, I will ring you.'

'Is it true that Humpty Dumpty died off shell shock!' Francois rang his friend Ray from the train.

'I don't want to tempt bad luck but I might have just been offered a very good deal. Maybe I shouldn't tell you until it's sealed.'

'Never trouble trouble until it troubles you,' replied Ray. 'The best way to wipe out a friendship is to sponge it.'

Don't drink the water. A tourist's first purchase when arriving at his or her destination is a bottle of mineral water to carry around like an olympic torch. Bottled water, especially imported French brands like Evian, Volvic and Vichy are now a MISS rather than a HIT. It is considered unethical to drink bottled water as tap water is OK to drink and will probably become the new celebrity endorsed thing to do in light of the Thames being stressed and the leakage deficit. If you are going to buy mineral water in England it should be Buxton or Caledonian. Internationally the upstream areas are less populated and support less trade than the ports and flood plains which irrigate the arable areas downstream.

Francois put on his white cotton T- shirt. He did not know if it was organic or Fairtrade cotton made from thirsty crops or irrigated inefficiently in an age where water is the new oil well. He wandered if the microclimate possibilities for controlling the weather and making clouds would ever become a reality instead of relocating industries to new hydroelectric powerstations and reservoirs to get government Tax Credits points for protecting the environment. [Water metering]. He decided not to worry about his T-shirt or the water. Despite complaining he was hot, the 90 degree heat was very agreeable. He could still be positive about the new unifying business possibilities developing in Middle Eastern water supply and natural rather than political boundaries. There would be players to take the throw ins, corners and score goals in a more competitive and aspirational climate.

Francois changed five crisp £20 notes in the cool marble interior of the Banque de Maroc. There new design looked slightly like Bauhaus Gelders with the squarer borders and less spirogyra patterns and pictures. Then he asked the reception to organise a taxi.

The Corniche is a little known region of Marakesh, unchanged from the Belle Epoque when it was fashionable. The villas and houses may well have belonged to the cast of Casablanca with fishing trips to amuse the screen heros and seafood restaurants on the front. It has a Chinatownesque Studio City background, big deal and cigar feel to it's windswept front. Lady Cosfoot had visited some friends in the 1950's and knew some residents in the Expat and golf clubs.

They sat in the Expat Club gardens for lunch behind the big white wall and gate with it's little window. Women were parambulating babies in the afternoon sun. Francois was used to this having witnessed the afternoon parade of nannies in the London's park playgrounds, lakes and flower walks. A family was picnicking on the lawns their blanket was orbited by toys and a football. One boy in a little pale blue and brown stripey hat managed to walk, falling over and laughing one minute, crying the next. He handed a half eaten banana to his nanny.

There was a blanket of blossom and petals vignetting the edge of the neat square landscaped lawn and borders of bluebells and tulips with frayed edges. No one was paying attention to the 'keep off the grass' sign. The pigeons who were all listening to heavy metal on their headphones were suddenly chased across the lawn by an Airedale Labrador cross. What used to be a Heinz 57 now fashionably known as Airedor or Labradale.

This then bothered the Egyptian ducks. Their petrol blue heads and gold beaks moved back and forth as their webbed feet pulled alternate rapid strokes. If you can walk like an Egyptian then you can swim like one too thought Francois.

Lady Cosfoot was discussing the difference between the yellow dandelion flower and the dandelion clock.

'They're known as 'pusteblume' in Germany. 'Blow flower,' said Lady Cosfoot to the other people at the table, 'and the French call them 'pissenlit' their diuretic qualities are responsible for bedwetting. They don't say the same for celery sticks they're good diuretics but I usually find them in my Bloody Mary's. I haven't seen any in a salad for ages, so I can't really comment. Is that a rhetorical question? The old French 'lion's tooth' – 'dent de lion' is preferable. Don't be fooled though by the false dandelions known as 'catsears' they're much longer and don't taste the same with the burdock or have the modern ' antioxidant properties. Do people still try to tell the time by blowing the little parachutes?'

'I don't know. I seem to recall something like that. You know when they're ready to germinate if the wind has blown all the seeds off, so –one blow and it's the right time, two blows and it's give or take half an hour, three and four etc, etc?'

'Dandelions and daisies. They spoil a good lawn,' said a man in white shirt and Panama hat.

'Bunny dear!'

'Hello Cosfoot Dear!'

'They won't be as accurate as my Cartier watch. I haven't tried blowing that, it's kinetic, and my body movement keeps it going. Do you still like butter Cosfoot?'

'Yes Dear I still like butter,' said Lady Cosfoot, then her friend turned to the others and said, ' if you hold the buttercup under your chin your skin glows yellow if you like butter doesn't it.'

'They put jasmine behind their ears here for good luck. Odd bunch really.'

'Would you like some tea and Turkish delight?' said Francois, 'I'll order some more.'

'Yes please that sounds wonderful.'

'This is my companion Francois who's travelling with me,' said Lady Cosfoot. 'Francois this is Mr Tate. Stupid accident with the ankle. I have to suffer young men taking me out all the time.'

A waiter arrived with an engraved silver tray, a silver tea pot and tea glasses, and a plate of pink rose water Turkish delight covered in white icing sugar.

'I saw some being made on TV,' said Mr Eve,'the full of eastern promise enigma is slightly destroyed when you know it's cornflower, sugar and food colouring. It looked like blancmange or jelly liposuction before it set and was cut into little cubes and dusted with sugar. It always looks so pretty.'

They drank the tea with lemon which made a change to the thé du menthe and discussed the tickets to Carthage to visit the Phoenician Ports and mosaics.

'I ate grapes picked from a Phoenician vine once . Very warm and sour in the sunshine. I can't wait to get back to the Cap.' Lady Cosfoot took a sip of her tea and smiled .

It was about 1.30pm and the mosque started it's call to prayer. Francois was getting used to the loudspeakers having been there for nearly a week. When it finished they could hear the piano that was playing again from inside the club.

'That's agreed then.' said Mr Eve.

They would go to Casablanca for the weekend before going to Tunis.

'We can get the train tickets at the station. They're a lot more frequent than they used to be. So are the boats. You used to have to wait about a week sometimes.'

'What would the Barbary pirates have done if the Byzantians had had satellite navigation? Or the Titannic for that matter.'

'You may well ask. I always wander how the white piano from the Queen Mary ended up in the Lansdowne Club.'

'I read this morning that The Elgin Marbles are finding their way home and without the aid of a synthesised vox box.' said Francois adding, 'Go straight on at Dover, left at Spain, right at Italy and left again.'

'Don't forget France Francois.' interrupted Lady Cosfoot.' There's an election on there at the moment. The most important question is à gauche ou à droit .There's a photo of Monsieur Sarkosy on a horse on the front page of le Monde and something about his marriage having a problem. They're on the second round of voting. Je déteste les politiques,' added Lady Cosfoot. 'mais j'aime la parfum Rive Gauche et les vétements Yves Saint Laurent et Chanel. J'aime beaucoup le shopping au Champs Elysses, c'est le mieux diversion du temps en temps.'

Francois poured the tea carefully lifting the pot and positioning the cups and plates with the precision of a banquet place setting.

The party continued to discuss opinions and faults of anything from marriage to continental breakfast versus cereal. Francois particularly liked hotel breakfast as it required a unique social etiquette and behaviour. He liked the sound of teaspoons and china. It was completely opposed to luncheon or evening dining. People were generally hung over but at their most polite, they were not out to make, find or leave an impression. Good or bad. He also had a weakness for cereal packets and French pastries. Croissants and pain au chocolat. Lady Cosfoot was amused by her credit card room key and wandered why it was a preferable alternative to conventional keys. They were just as easy to lose and easier to damage. As they had left the hotel earlier they were entertained by a guest who was talking to his luggage as he wheeled it along. They got into a taxi and a scooter passed them driving with a two metre tall plant on his footplate that was half obscuring his view. Not so much déjà vue as jardin vue.

'He must be using greener unleaded fuel!' said Francois.

'It certainly looks environmentally friendly,' replied Lady Cosfoot.

'Remind me to call room service about the laundry and there was something about the minibar. Oh yes, it's out of gin.'

'I'm sure they will replace it.' reassured Francois.

'Mother's ruin dear!' said Lady Cosfoot.

'I'll get them to deliver another bottle.'

'You have to have the right balance in life. Can't go without gin.Somebody dies dear and someone is born. Don't ask me why. It just happens.'

El Efna was quiet in the morning when Francois and Lady Cosfoot had breakfast on the terrace overlooking tortoise sellers, snake charmers , sanskrit writers and henna. The medina was just setting up for the day, a row of horse drawn carriages were lined up along the road with freshly polished tack, ready for the tourists.

Lady Cosfoot's ankle was barable to walk on, using crutches, the short distance to the restaurant. They sat under the cream canvas canopy and ate pistacchio and honey pastries, sweets and saffron scented cakes with 'thé du menthe'.

Lady Cosfoot read her Financial Times as Francois smoked a Rothmans alibi cigarette called 'Business' brand. They were sold under a different name in the north African market on the stalls in the souk where beaded caps were juxtaposed with leather sandals and Nike ripoffs, hooded kaftans, beautiful jewellery, rugs with patterns woven in the maker's memory that took six months to make and six minutes to sell. Everyone finds a bargin between the hamam and the henna.

By 10 am the sun was getting warmer and they took a taxi to the cool palmed YSL garden with cactii and gravelled walkways. An oasis in the busy city where you can pick oranges from the trees which line the roads and the hum of the traffic reaches a crescendo of horns then gets quiet again when the call to prayer begins. They ate lamb tagine with coriander, cous cous, apricots and dates, chillies and yoghurt for lunch. Then smoked some charbon while playing chess in the shade. Lady Cosfoot was a mean opponent.

As the train pulled into Casablanca Station, it's large engine exposed by low platforms, Francois pictured the fez's, safari suits and the zebra tied gentleman and his wife sitting at a café from the film.

'What's black and white and red all over?' asked Francois.

'A newspaper dear. Here's looking at you kid. Could we get a table at the Hyatt for dinner?'

Dinner was at 9pm. They left the station and went by taxi to their rooms meeting up again at 8.15 pm for cocktails. Mr and Mrs Eve, Mr

Wilkinson, Lily, Lady Cosfoot and Francois. It had been a fairly anecdotal train journey south from Marrakech. Lady Cosfoot was readjusting her state of knowledge with new contacts and updated information. She saw in Francois untapped dynamic potential. His rusty French and relaxed adaption to the strange mix of people they gathered on their journey was probably what her sister had picked him for. Lady Cosfoot lit a Sobraine and sipped her Black Russian. She was wearing new leather sandals and had her toenails painted a dark spicy sumac red. Mr Wilkinson was entertaining the Eves about a half tonne meteorite rock, which he had touched when it landed in the Arizona desert.

'I've touched a piece of space junk, a piece of moon rock,' he said.

It had attracted the usual UFO press and religious extremists panicking that it was a sign for the end of the world. Nostradamus' predictions and the second coming of Jesus. Its surface was smooth with a very linear pattern inside the brown pumice exterior. The Eves were planning a trip further south to the Sahara souk trading post, now a ghost town at Ouazazate. It's riverbed is now dried up, its cracked surface now a garden of pink rose crystals and scorpions, four wheel drives, sand dunes, grasses and camel treks.

The German receptionist in the casino in Casablanca resembled a younger version of a school friend of Lady Cosfoot. An actuary with brylcreamed hair who had suffered a car accident. He was pulled from the vehicle by a group of youths. The engine had ruptured several valves spilling oil on the road.

Lady Cosfoot spent most mornings in an hour of diarist and epistomologic recluse. She joined Francois and the others in the casino for an hour playing roulette before they went for cocktails. Francois was an amateur on the tables, but he enjoyed himself, forgetting all the forms and finance. He gave himself a limit to antimacassar his bank account from potential spillage.

In Rome Francois put his suit jacket and trousers in the hotel laundry. He had made full use of the room services. He ticked all the boxes for socks, pants, shirts and the different levels of service on the list. His shirts looked like new with starched collars, folded with pins and tissue paper. He had dropped his hat in one of the fountains and it had not been the same since. He did not think that the hotel laundry would be able to help much. It would need a milliner's expertease as it looked like it had been steamed with the starch from a plate of mashed potato. The consierge, however, insisted that they help and returned it in perfect condition.

The fountain tour took in all the fountains in Rome. Fed by the river and mountain sources they were erected by the wealthy families as a display of their fortune and riches each one wih a different statue of fish, birds, cherubs and icons.

The fountain reminded him of the Sagefreda Church in Barcelona which had a tortoise at the base of it's pillars. They had eaten Don Quioxote's favourite Manchego cheese in a Moorish restaurant and drank Absinthe at the Quatre Gats whilst planning the next day's itinerary, where they would eat and who they would visit. Francois had also made a claim on his travel insurance for his camera. He dropped it when they toured the bullring and matador museum to look at the embroidered jackets, capes and weapons which had inspired Picasso and Debuffet. Francois had taken some really good shots of the bulls and stadium and lost the film when it jammed. Lady Cosfoot insisted on doing the Spanish lottery to try and save the day. They did not win. She had played Bingo once with the ladies from the village church and won a cookery book. They were raising money for the church stained glass. It needed a specialist from Camden who ran courses to stay and repair the damaged allegorical pictures. He said it made a change from the London pubs he worked on usually.

'Not many modern buildings use coloured glass these days.' he said. 'The Victorians liked sunrises, birds and flowered patterns. Stained glass has been around since the thirteenth century. It was popular in the 1540s when the reformation undermined the need for sacred art. Burne Jones did some nice pieces with the Arts and Crafts movement and the House of Tiffany are renowned for their lamps more than their windows. The

Italians were pretty productive too. How it ended up in pubs I don't know. One of my books says it creates atmoshere and retains privacy, somebody saw an obvious association with sociable communion and decided to put some in one day. Maybe to keep the glazier in business possibly. To pay his bar tab or the damage after a fight! Who knows?'

After about five days in Rome Lady Cosfoot wanted to be in the countryside again, with a particular desire to visit the lakes. Francois was filling in the car hire form and became stuck over the contradictory sounding 'collision waiver damage.' He had to get the representative to explain it a few times, then copied the licence number and gave him the keys and a map. They pulled away slowly, passing a school playground where the children were playing with a new toy that looked like the planet Saturn with an orbiting ring, pogoing on a footplate around a ball. Somebody had obviously had a problem with the literal translation of Spacehopper and the large orange 1960's horned bouncy thing now had an asteroid cousin. They drove through the centre of Rome, around the typewriter monument to the Unknown Soldier, passed the Spanish Steps and the famous piazzas. Sempre dritto, sinistra, destra. Francois was getting used to the Fiat.

'Can we have a Ferrari next time Lady Cosfoot?' asked Francois.

'Jarvis Maine took me to the opera in his Ferrari. We went to see Carmen. I wanted to see the version with the horse but he insisted on going to the Albert Hall. We sat in a red velvet curtained box with gilt chairs that had quilted cushions and buttoned backs. I can't go there without scanning the place for snipers. I think I've seen too many spy films. It was very good, they Bohemian Rapsodied the last scene. Do you go to the ballet or opera Francois?'

'Not really. I've been to the ballet once and my favourite theatre is the Criterion. I love the decor, it's a little bijoux treasure. A friend of mine designed a copper still installation in Whiskey Bar of The Edinburgh Festival Theatre. Christ Italian drivers are mad! Excuse me Lady Cosfoot. maybe we could visit the Lipozoan or Andalucian horses in Cadiz. We could discuss it over tapas.'

'Ooh! Paella with chorizo sausage and seafood, saffron, garlic and olive oil, potatoes, paprika, pulpi and sangria. Maybe we could find a square with some Spanish guitar music and a flamenco and some little birds singing in cages.'

'Beautiful.'

'Does your friend just design stills?'

'No sometimes he designs other things like willow tables.'

'To go with willow pattern plates?'

'Not in particular but they're very good.'

Francois changed into fifth gear. He was now driving on the main road out of Rome, leaving the suburbs where there were fewer buildings. Eventually the road opened into mountains and lakes, lined with poplars. After about an hour they stopped and enjoyed the scenery. The sky was very blue. In a small town they bought some local fragoli. They ate the fragrant strawberries with bread and coffee. The aroma of the espresso mixed with the flour and fruit in a instant hit of olfactory pleasure.

'I've just received an email from my niece. She can meet us for dinner tomorrow. Is your suit pressed? I feel like wearing something.'

Francois waited in reception. He had faxed his insurance claim and received a confirmation report. He would drink Vatican wine and say some hail Marys for getting the cause of the damage to his camera wrong when he told his insurance company.

Lady Cosfoot descended the large central staircase into the hotel reception hall. A red patterned carpet covered the stairs; the fanned steps becoming wider at the outside edge and narrow on the inside. Looking up, the floors above made ever decreasing circles with layers of metal rails and banisters, which appreciated numerous film scenes and dresses. Francois had discovered that staircases either made you grow up or down, walk badly or well and occasionally gave you the urge to slide down the polished banister which spiralled into a ball at their base.

'Good evening Lady Cosfoot. You look beautiful.'

'Thanks you Francois. I'm glad we're on the first floor.'

'I'll order the taxi. The restaurant is only ten minutes from here.'

'Caroline is going to be there at 9 o'clock. Does that give us enough time?'

'More than enough.'

It took the taxi about five minutes to arrive. They left the keys with the concierge who gave them a ticket in exchange. Lady Cosfoot put it in her small embroidered drawstring purse, which contained a lipstick, her Sobraine cocktail cigarettes and a lighter.

'Caroline, Darling!' Caroline was waiting at the restaurant bar.

'You look drop dead gorgeous as ever. This is my friend Francois. He's invaluable. They wouldn't let me go on my own with the accident, as you probably know. Sissy found him on one of the clay shoots. His French is lousy but he's good company.'

'Good evening Caroline and Kaneda,' said Francois. They organised some drinks then went to their extremely difficult to get table.

Caroline sat down with expert Lucy Clayton elegance having spent years in an institution for young ladies. It was second nature. She folded her arms in front of her on the table having absent mindedly put her dark chocolate hair behind one ear and moved her watch around off the fine bones on her wrist where it had slipped.

Her red dress had pleated shirt ruffles across the front and she blushed when she distracted herself by thinking of it. Haute couture snooker hall, premier red carpet, opera box boutique. Associations made for all dinner suit destinations, stand up, sit down and wedding dress code.

'How long have you been working in Rome, Caroline?'

'Nearly a year and two years in Paris before that. Tell me, is my aunt planning to spend the whole year visiting old friends and new places?'

'I couldn't say. Three to six months at the outside, depending on her ankle.' replied Francois.

'Which is much better thanks to Francois and the Tai Chi.' Lady Cosfoot interrupted.

'I haven't kept my Tai Chi up,' said Caroline, 'but I do a yoga class two times a week. I don't make the time as I should. It must be nice to travel at the drop of a hat. I've not really done that. Francois, my aunt is very secretive sometimes, I know nothing about you. Tell me about yourself.'

'I have a friend who is renting my apartment while I am away. I sold my business five years ago and my current import dealings have just been made bankrupt by a big US company supplying the French record shop I supply stock to in a buy out. I might be inspired to return to furniture design or something similar after the trip. I've been people watching and looking at a lot of bums! The Italians tend to go for high back seats, the chaise longue personifies the French, the Barcelona chair a Bohemian Bauhaus product of the sixties typifies most northern Europeans. There are a lot of gilt Queen Anne legged popular cover versions at the moment. The English Chesterfield, high or low backed button cushioning has retreated into the background along with the deep seated Indian ethnic seats.'

Francois checked himself.

'I've just started rambling. Hi I'm Francois. Taurus!' he said in his best Barry White. 'You must be........let me see, Aquarius or Libra.'

'Leo. Do you spend much timesitting on your butt?'

'No. And if I wanted a bad back I know how to get one. I don't need to stay sitting for long to understand a seat but I like to watch the natives they express them much better.'

'Do you have a favourite seat Francois?' asked Caroline.

' I have a ribbed Plunkett chair which is a hot favourite. How about you?'

'I like the Egg and Shell chairs, and the perspex bubble pendulum seats. They always look like the person sitting in them is in style heaven. What do you like Aunt Tania?'

'I like the clover shaped conversation chairs,'confidantes', 'love seats' or 'tête à têtes' whatever they're called. And deck chairs!'

The waiter bought the menus and they ordered the food. Centopelli and ribololita soup, artichoke and cheese rissotto, papadella with truffles, wild game, rabbit with pretty pink fagelot beans, la ciacci leavened bread, fried and powdered with sugar and castagnole cakes, coffee and rivigiolo cheese.

'Kaneda is an expert on Italian cheese.' said Caroline. 'Formaggi specialista!'

'How do you get to be an expert on Italian cheese?' asked Francois.

'I'm a travel writer. I was researching a truffle hunting holiday in Umbria and came across a slightly high shepherd, antiperspiranti e altitudi, who showed me his curd and whey separation. He introduced me to his very nice cows and goats and we made buffalo mozzerella. I sold a fantastic piece to Alitalia, Tesco magazine and the Observer Travel Section. Different angles of course. And keep finding more cheeses to add to my collection. I've not tried Ravigiolo.' she paused.

'I could tell you the history of the grains of rice in your orobia artichoke rissoto and seduce you with the irrigation of Italy's rice bowl, [seven gods in every grain if it's Japanese] the manufacturing is boring but the packaging is desirably authentic. I read somewhere this morning that Pierre Santo Stefano in Umbria is the Town of the Diary. It has a museum with four thousand autobiographical documents. One written on a bed sheet by a woman. I emailed a proposal to an editor I work for at lunchtime and he said yes. Now I'm going to Tuscany tomorrow to cover it and a car rally to go with the Grand Prix feature. Lots of Bugattis and Ferraris. They are also holding a mushroom exhibition.

'Will you send us a copy when it's done?' asked Lady Cosfoot.'Caroline has my email.'

'There are two Bugatti Brothers if I remember rightly. Ettore and Carlo. Carlo was the younger and designed some very African looking chairs with puff adder backs to them.'

'Any tables to go with them? Then you could eat with forked tongue too!'

The waiter arrived with the soup.

'Black cabbage . What a beautiful colour. Vince had a Halloween party last year with all black designer food. Black potato crisps with black pepper, black cabbage soup, fried black pudding, blackened cajun chicken, chicken and black bean sauce, squid ink tagliatelli with charred red peppers, sweet beetroot ice cream, black cherry and dark chocolate ice cream, with Guinness and blackcurrant and Black Russian cocktails. The pumpkins had black tea lights and everyone had black tongues by the end of the evening . There was a spontaneous tongue sticking out with hands up and thumbs in the ears Maori dance. Na na na na na! I promise to refrain from that tonight.'

'How's the centopeli?'

'Delicious dear.' said Kaneda.

'Per favori me passe il pane Kaneda.' asked Caroline.

'Grazi.'

'Prego.'

Lady Cosfoot was quietly amused by her niece and watched her across the table through the wine bottles, glasses and candles. The glass reflected the light in sharp highlights and the shadows and silver cutlery made strong contrast on the white linen in the dark setting. Lady Cosfoot was remembering Caroline's face. Her own was not bad for sixty years. She plucked her eyebrows a little and could not understand why other women insisted on removing them and then drawing them on. She limited her make up to a liner on the upper lid and a little mascara with red lipstick, occasionally adding a light powder. She had short silver hair and predictable pearl and gold earings. Lady Cosfoot's appearance typified the women Francois saw on the number 19 in Piccadilly, holding their Chanel handbags perched elegantly on their knees, twinsets and glasses on chains. Tonight she was in black silk and lace, with a cream paschmina, stockings and patent shoes. Francois was surrounded by beautiful women, wine and food. His silver Paul Smith cufflinks caught the light as he lifted his glass and smiled inwardly maintaining a calm internal asylum. Several months had passed since had felt quite so normal.

'Where should we go tomorrow? Does any one have any suggestions?' asked Lady Cosfoot. ' I've seen a wonderful cafe I wanted to try.' she added.

'I won't let myself near petit fours, I ate too many in Paris with grand tasses de café, brioche et chocolat petits déjeuners. Lazy packet food. Langues de chats, palmestiers, mielle feuilles, sweet cinnamon toast, viennese biscuits in attractive packaging with red, white and blue ribbons, gold crests and product shots. I got a bit carried away because they're different to Digestives, Rich Tea, Garibaldis and Ginger Snaps.' confessed Kaneda.

'Bourbons, chocolate chip cookies, Hobb Nobbs. Don't forget the Duchy Originals, shortbread, Wagon Wheels, Penguins, Club and Nice biscuits. Most French petits grow up with a piece of baguette and a slab of chocolat in their mouths, so Thè Riche and Digestifs are very English to them. The biscuit manufacturers aim more for mugs of tea than Tea at The Ritz which is also very English. It's ages since we've been for mini cup cakes and florentines with doilies, Dundee cake and Wedgewood.' Caroline reassured Kaneda with gusto.

'You don't hear much French music in England. Henry has a CD by Emilie Simon.' said Kaneda changing the subject.

'Unless you get a French chanteuse or Rapido style Plastique Bertrand playing in The Body Shop or a boutique where the girl serving doesn't know who the CD playing is by. The reason she doesn't know when you ask her is because she had tried to find the box when no one was in the shop.' said Caroline.

'There's alot of Italian minestrone in the clubs .' added Kaneda. 'But other than Air, some obscure ambient stuff, Serge Gainsborough and 'Je regret rien' Edith Piaf, we don't get much French music in England. Which is funny because our charts make it in other countries.'

'It's very unpredictable and subjective market and we don't have many commercial outlets for the stuff any way. A European radio channel would be nice in England.'

'That's how I practised my French. And watching TV. Textbooks don't help you get the jokes.'

'Neither do phone ins when you want to make a dedication. There is however a years prison sentence for DJ's and programme directors taking payola bribes.' Francois adopted a small print solicitor's voice.

'that's playing particular records with reasonable diligence. DJs give the public an illusion of spontaneous and genuine promotion. You'll have to bribe me to start a European Radio Station in England. I'd rather distance myself from the distribution people at Harry Fox and the NMPA, National Music Publication Association in New York. Since the buyout, I'm right off commissions and distributions. Although they have different people in supply for airplay from the exports department. Thank god.' he then added an aside and went into jingle voice over , 'No bootlegs, tributes or soundalikes. Call BritMusic Inc.Euro Music FM Salle de Jour - lounge musique et ambiente pour les femmes de Francois.'

The restaurant ordered two taxis. They said 'au revoir' to Caroline and Kaneda who disappeared into the night. They returned to their hotel passed the typewriter roundabout, the monument to the Unknown Soldier, The Spanish Steps and The Trevi Fountain. Francois was able to orientate his way around Rome now, he knew the landmark locations after a week without using a map and compass.

The airline seats had plenty of legroom. There were no sleeper seats on the 737 but Francois read about them in the inflight magazine when looking for the radio channel information. He also paid greater attention to the articles which supported the maps, duty free and destination information. He thought of Caroline, Kaneda and the shepherd. They climbed over the cloud base, up to 30,000 feet where the sky became a new blue on a separate storey. 'Up On The Roof'. Francois had a tune in his head. It looked like another world with it's own sky. He liked it best when the red eye flight was asleep and the sun was rising, a blood red sky in the distance. You can not see behind or ahead, just a great expanse of red. Francois in the sky with rubies.

The plane landed at Brindisi and they went to baggage reclaim. Anything to declare. Nothing to declare. Euro FM radio station was not a bad idea he thought and smuggled it through. It had not occured to him that he would want to see Caroline and Kaneda again at this point. It was not until he got back to England and heard that Caroline was in the country. Then he had to rationalise himself. It's up to fate, unless he could think of any real reason for him to reaquaint himself with her and find himself a new seating plan. He had enjoyed their company but he had not met them in the world outside the restaurant or for that matter received the email from Kaneda's Umbria trip.

They had seen the Calder in the Guggenheim in Bilbao and shopped in Milan where Lady Cosfoot bought matching handbag and shoes and a new hat. They visited all the sights in Venice and took one of the four hundred and thirty five gondolas on the Grand Canal.

Rome to Brindisi took about one hour. She had spent August with a family in their summer house in 1958 and stayed in touch, skiing with them in the winter or Easter months in the north near Turin. One year they went to Austria to a small friendly hotel with cuckoo clocks, wooden hearts and what Francois thought sounded like a Ludwig Von Rohe settee in it's reception.

François got a ten euro shoeshine at the airport. He was tempted by the thought of driving through the Black Forest, taking cable cars, drinking hot chocolate after sleigh rides in the snow and peach schnapps après ski. And he was tempted by the fruit of another. Kaneda emailed her feature, hot off the Umbrian electricity supply. No false starts and finish lines in Umbria.

Francois replied.

Dear Kaneda

Thank you for your feature.The south of Italy is very quiet compared to the Grand Époque, yacht clubs and smart hotels on the Riviera. The shiney brass and gold apartment buzzer plaques with smart names and well maintained window boxes are now usurped by mosquitoes and bugs, which are proving very insistent. I miss my Parker Knoll. I wrote this for you yesterday while drinking a Cataretto grape on a small boat anchored about half a kilometre off the rocky coast with some friends of Lady Cosfoot – an actress, a singer and her husband. It was a scene straight out of a Fellini film.

Knowing Your Onions by Francois Hamilton-Klein.

Onions tears? Just add sugar,
The caramelised onions make her smile.
Snow white Dr Zhivago shallots.
Gold leaf Taj Mahal.
Brighton Pavilion and St Petersburg Cathedral.
Both have onion towers,
Which made her cry for hours.

Silver skin, red skin, Indian rain dance,
White skin and green onions,
Fried onions on a hot chillie dog.
Mustard and cauliflower Piccalilli,
Branston pickle ploughman's.
Astro planet onion, another Dutch clog.

Born with a silver spoon in your mouth,
Your mother was peeling onions.
Water birth Nivana chopping them submerged.
With this onion ring I thee wed,
The bride's mother needs a Kleenex she said.
Walking up the aisle,
The caramelised onions make her smile.

Before leaving the town Francois bought a bottle of Limoncella from
of the large pink plaster fronted buildings in the square selling wines, it's
typical high windows had interior shutters and the floors were cool dark
marble. The heavily scented surrounding fields were full of the local
citrus and olive crops.

Francois talked as he drove.

'Bank holiday Mondays on English motorways, Camber Sands and copywriter's caravan names are permenantly engrained on the brains of seventies children. The piece de resistence of a copywriter's career then was the Bailey 400 - Airstream, the ultimate Luxuryline, Supersprite, Senator, Elite, Cruiser, Prestige, Crusade, Swift and Challenger. I must have been seriously affected by the overheating and traffic jams as a five year old. I started   drawing plans for Keisler utility living spaces with kitchenettes and pullout sleeping spaces aged serious five year old instead of the stripes of blue sky and green grass with pets and flowers.'

'Dali lobsters and sea urchins for lunch tomorrow. Did you ever build one of your dream caravans Francois?'

'No but I detoxed the fixation out of my system by staying in one in Ireland. They're very small, fun and functional. Extremely strange concepts but I'll stay in a country house hotel next time I go there!'

Every window at the hotel in Rome had window boxes with pansies, white with purple markings and purple with white markings and long stemmed lavendar with flowers that looked like bees. Looking out of the window the trees were blowing wildly in the fifty kilometer an hour wind.

The weather report had mentioned there maybe some gusts. It did not mention a New Orleans style hurricane . Francois had already Southern Comfort and Hemmingway Cubra Libras planned for the duration, playing on the pool table while Lady Cosfoot did her evening epistomology. A pianist played in the hotel lounge.

They had a flight booked for two days time.

From Brindisi they took the ferry to Greece. The port was industrial and large with anonymous looking buildings and containers lining the quayside. There was a stench of diesel and rotting fish. Large ferries, cars bikes, all jostled for position with the sound of loud chains, winches, fog horns and hooters .The taxi left the port . Within five minutes the taxi had driven them out of the town and was climbing the cypress and olive hill roads. In the next cove there was a pretty harbour, smaller boats, yachts, restaurants where everything moved at a smaller, slower pace. It was typical of most towns and villages they would pass through, about five in total and climb over as many winding hill roads to get to the villa where they would stay for the next week and which sat at the highest point. Lady Cosfoot had met the owner at a party thirty years before. The party had gone on for about two weeks and she stayed with them at least once every two years.

It was the usual eighty degrees. When they had unpacked they sat in the shade and drank wine for about an hour before starting to prepare dinner. This consisted of making fresh dolmades, wrapping the minced lamb, rice, oil, lemon juice and mint in the big vine leaves and lining them up on the platter. Then grinding the sesame seeds for the tahini and chick pea humous, the garlic was sweet and the olive oil golden and plentiful. Francois sliced some tomato and cucumber while Denis drove to the quay to get some freshly dynamited swordfish. They also made spanakopita with layered spinach and pastry, aubergine salad with garlic, lemon, salt and yoghurt with honey and nut sweets for dessert. They ate al fresco under the shade of the trees and then Lady Cosfoot organised a game of musical chairs for he children with the little bistro chairs. There were about ten children, five were family and the other five friends from the village. One of the elder children took charge of starting and stopping the music.

More honey sweets , pastries and unleavened pitta bread appeared for he children whose energy was exhausting. The pitta was fresh, like the packets in the supermarkets but made in a flat pan with flour, oil, salt and water. It puffed up with the heat making the little pocket perfect for the little kebabs or salad. When Francois emailed Kaneda, he told her, with great pride about how they had made feta with yoghurt and salt, leaving it suspended in muslin to drip and separate.

Kaneda replied,

Dear Francois,

I'm very happy to hear of your production of the feta. May I suggest some Indian paneer. This is made with milk and lemon juice in the same way. Delicious.

Caroline tells me there's a Greek band playing for a BBC recording at the Festival Hall this evening called Plastic Chairs.

Love Kaneda

Francois emailed Rock.

Hi Rock,

Have you heard of a band called Plastic Chairs? Please advise. Got an idea. Need your opinion. What to do you reckon? Euro FM. Magazine style format station with jazz, lounge, souk, sport – ideas welcome. Storm your brain. Ask some questions.

Francois

In the evening the company which had gathered at the villa made their way down to the square where a meeting was taking place about the olive farmers' dispute. A group of officials were sitting at the top table and did not realise that their microphones were switched on. They could be heard gossiping over the music and chatter coming from the people at the restaurants and bars. The local reporter was in heaven and the audience were in a very good mood. Francois noticed that the restaurant table was wobbling.

'Should we put something like folded paper under the leg?' Lady Cosfoot asked Francois.

'Most journalists are usually under the table,' interrupted the man on the next table, you might find one under there. You could use him or her instead. That's why they are attached to their desks.'

'Thanks,' said Francois, 'I'll consider it if I find one, but this is fine for now.'

'Do you need a hand?'

'No thank you, its ok now,' Francois levelled the table and straightened the red and white chequered tablecloth. He initially thought gingham but decided on chequered as it was more accurate and less Hailey Mills 'Parent Trap'.

'Men should always keep their hair trimmed short regularly if they are going to tan their necks. The white patch, which appears after a short back and sides, is hilarious. Or they should leave it until their tan fades to not offend anybody. Its awful some of the things that you have to put up with. Wasn't that Miller Temple the BBC newsreader?' asked Lady Cosfoot.

'What. I don't have my glasses on,' said Francois. He blushed a very bright red from the top of his forehead to his third button on his open neck shirt.

'I sat next to the drummer of the Heretics in a pub once without realising it and said that their music was rubbish. I hope I'm not starting another habit.'

He heard somewhere that people 'lived in their skin like a house'. He felt sunburnt, still blushing and wandered what suntan lotion they used. What protection factors and moisturisers, sunscreens and skin types – fair, dry, sensitive. He tanned fairly easily and sweated a lot on his top lip making a little pool of water, which refracted the UV rays and made it tan faster. He liked the idea of temporary patches to make two tone bikini mark tattoos. He had seen little hearts on apples in the supermarkets on Valentine's Day and a couple of girls on the beach had a flower and an anchor. When he told Lady Cosfoot she wanted to try one.

'Where am I going to put it?'

'Try somewhere boney like your shoulder or knee.'

She had now gone beyond the sexual revolution of wearing trousers but it was unlikely she would ever be found in the Church on the Earls Court Road or a tattoo parlour.

A mezze of cheese and lamb stuffed pastries, yoghurt and chillies,salads, tomatoes, onions and olives appeared on the table. The first speaker from the olive farmer's dispute, a fat man, stood up to speak, he was wearing a dark suit, holding his notes in one hand and adjusted the microphone with the other which had just finished a glass of metaxa. The band came to the end of a song and the music stopped. You could see the wind moving the silhouetted leaves on the trees around the square.

Occasionally a pippistrelle pippistrellus bat would fly out to feed. It's echo sounding screech making a flightpath as the soundwaves bounced back off it's prey. Flapping and swooping to catch mosquitos and maybugs, it almost disappeared sideways.

The fat man spoke for about ten minutes with the supporters in the square cheering.

'Endaxi! Endaxi!' he said over and over. Then the music started again and everyone got up and danced. They knew the steps and moved as lightly as the bats. Francois made a note to buy some insect repellent.

Two women walked passed the table wearing summer dresses which were a reinvention of the elastic cotton boob tube with smock skirts and no waist. Two other women had short skirts on with long legs, holiday legs for holiday dresses, bought for the week and put in the wardrobe until the sun comes out or worn with tights. Patterns were reappearing that Francois recognised. They had probably been in the wholesalers since the first time around. A backpacker walked passed with a goretex rucksack that resembled the one in his Highflyer magazine. Intelligent 'nano' compound materials developed for sports wear and the army, now available to the man on the street. Built in compasses, thermometers and altitude meters. There would be Sat Nav for pedestrians next. Lady Cosfoot lit a Sobranie. The top table were asking questions. The scene resembled a game show. A girl in a long dress handed a bunch of flowers to the fat man's wife.

'4 across - SUSDO YES - it's an anangram.' Francois passed Lady Cosfoot a serviette with a word written on it.

'Do you think they'd mind if I wrote on the cloth?' he questioned.

'ODYSSEUS.' answered Lady Cosfoot who wrote something down and handed it back to Francois.

'12 down - MORHE ?' he looked at it and guessed.

'HOMER!'

'We could always buy a Travel Scrabble.' he added.

'21 across- I SOUPED.'

'OEDIPUS.'

'9 down - APOLLONIUS.'

'NAIL POOL US.'

'1 across - SOPHOCLES.'

'COOL CHES.'

'3 down - EURIPIDES.'

'RIPE SUEDI.'

They played Greek God anagrams for about half an hour finishing the bottle of wine, then they all got taxis back to the villa and played cards until 2am. The scent of flowers and food were now replaced by pine trees, exhaust fumes and dusty road. Francois noticed his hair was looking lighter. As he climbed into the vehicle he caught his reflection in the rear view mirror where several crucifixes and chains hung with pictures of the driver's wife and family, typical of nearly every taxi. Francois' friend had a Feu Orange on his motorcycle fairing.

'The pine fresh alternatives were too strong,' he said.

Francois was handed an embarquation form to fill in on the aeroplane with questions about visas and country of origin. He was getting to know the different COO acronyms POB, place of birth, DOB, date of birth and EMG.

'Modern fabrics are made to withstand up to fifty washes. Would the new smart textiles eliminate washing? Eventually we will be wearing charcoal odour eater T shirts with fibres test driven by Olympic athletes.'

He finished reading the article on the plane.

Francois had spent hours choosing his washing machine. His priority had been the control buttons. He was a klunk klik button sort of person. It was one of his pet hates, expensive equipment let down by short lived, ineffective plastic buttons without a firm positive action and naf graphics. 1000 spin speed circuit board interior with curves and wavy handles was what most consumers wanted, but somebody decided to save money on the light weight plastic knob which you were not quite sure had depressed adequately. Vorsprung durch technik. Francois opted for a silver finish that fitted his silver catering style splashbacks and surfaces. It's only draw back was the small drum, but it fitted perfectly into the space he had, it gave him the best button reaction and least complex choice of options. He did not need a family washing machine designed for big loads of baby food, delicates and sportswear. It was a case of aesthetics not ascetics but it satisfactorally grounded the buttons. Purity of design versus spiritual purity achieved through the abstinence of worldly pleasures.

Francois met Karl and Rock at The Cow in Westbourne Grove for a Guinness and a pint of potted prawns.

'Great tan,' said Rock.

'Thanks. First stage designs.' he put the sketches on the table and went to order some drinks.

'Which ones do you like?' he asked when he returned.

'Give us a chance. Rock is just filling me in on a PR concert.'

'Great.'

'These. If you really need to know that fast.'

Francois smiled.

That day the waterfall in the water garden looked more like yeast waste from a brewery. Quite often it looked like someone had emptied their shampoo bottle into it. Francois had eaten a raw uncooked potato salad with sardines and olive oil, mint and sweet pea sprouts. Potato sushi, the latest new transference of styles. Quite an original angle he thought, and made a note to try some other potatoes raw. A potato degustation. They did not taste too bad. He prefered Pink Firs and Rattes.

Somebody said that poetry was the consolation of loneliness. Darwin , on the other hand was more in favour of 'instinctive thinking' of neuroaesthetics. Francois questioned if the poetry was an evolution, an expression of breathing without gills, coming out of the water and growing legs. And loneliness was the fear of non existence. Francois had tried writing some poems but was no Shakespeare. He decided to end his philosophy for the day.

He would not know what the loss of someone was until Lady Cosfoot died. Angry at not being able to fill the space that the person existed in. It was not there and he did not know where to put it. Taking a chair away at dinner and spacing everyone out instead of accomodating an extra guest at dinner, losing a little elbow room but invigorating the usual routine and stimulating the conversation. Lady Cosfoot died three months after they returned from their Grand Tour. Francois had settled into his job at the house as her PA while having meetings for the Eurostation. He had designed several pieces which he could get produced and place in the right showroom.

Caroline had called to say that she was in England and came to the house to stay for the weekend. Lunch was at 1.30pm and she arrived at 1pm. She was wearing a waxed cotton olive coat with a shirt back, a Fendi hat with gold and brown logos, a matching Fendi handbag and Sergio Rossi shoes. Under her coat she had a white shirt with a melon V necked sweater and black trousers. Her dark chocolate hair was tied back making a little triangular shaving brush, exactly the same length, precision and well cut. She drove up the long drive in a Peugeot 207. The ivy was overgrown on the gateposts and walls. To the left of the main entrance tall French windows were opened onto a small round balcony, part of a curved turreted feature of the building. It's castellations were silhouetted against the sunlit sky, making the little Chinamen in the spaces between the regular turned stone turned colomns. She knew this from smoking grass on the roof and playing amongst the chimney pots when she was younger. She always thought of it when she ate spaghetti a la vongoli and made little Chinamen's hats out of the clam shells. Lady Cosfoot did not hide how happy she was at seeing her and made a big fuss when she arrived . When it calmed down and the dogs stopped barking they went inside and had a drink.

Francois had found Kaneda's email. She had sent the piece on Santa Stefano and the Bugatti Rally in Umbria. He re- read it before she arrived. Caroline said that Kaneda had hated every minute of it. She had interviewed lots of people and was driven in a Type 42 to experience the Grand Days of Motoring. The Grand Prix feature and competition were a big success.

'She was bitten by Buggattis.' she said.

Lunch was purple asparagus soup, seabass with cress sauce and walnut ice cream. Caroline had bought some cheese in true Kaneda vein. A mozzerella and some Pecorino Romano. The mozzerella was young and not as firm as others. Your mouth tore the drier outer skin as you bit into the softer cream texture inside.

Francois put on his new CD. Lady Cosfoot liked him playing DJ. He had several meetings about the feasibilty of the radio station. It would be a mix of Eurotrash / Rapido music, sports and events.The silent partners liked the different French styles of Algerian Souk, Jazz and Lounge, Vocals and Ambiente. It was very different from the British music they were used to and felt there was enough P&O, Stella Artois, Danone, Muller Light and Sanex advertising invading our TV sets to make it work. The time was right to try the airwaves.

£49 to Paris on Eurostar deals made going to Paris for the evening clubbing feasible without the need for a hotel. They decided to test the water. Francois first tried a pirate station to try and get some demo tapes and feed back. Then they considered taking it further and making a commitment. Did the British want to know what was going on across the water culturally. Or would the typical British arrogant stereotype win. British complacent superiority versus French arrogance, which was quite different. They listened to our pop music.

Caroline sat at the head of the table with her unconcious 'Institute for Young Ladies' elegance.

'Will you play requests on Euro FM?' asked Caroline.

'Not many DJs do anymore. It's all mixed with ads alot of the time.'

'We will probably get people phoning in to dedicate a bench to their wife for their anniversary,' replied Francois.

'There will be a magazine format with topical stuff like film, Cannes Film Festival, environment, sport, celebrity gossip, food and drink, fashion,points of views and ideas, travel, places to go. Parallel opinions an stuff like the election that's just gone. With of course an oeuvre for the different styles of Euro music.' Francois scratched his head.

'I've not got the licence yet, not filled in or signed the form. We're with a silent partner who has one already, which helps. Let me know what you think.'

He didn't want to sound too pushy or salesman like. He was actually very confident but could not wait. We have a trial launch on the 15th. Francois handed over the flyer from his inside jacket pocket. It had a red, white and blue ribbon radio dial and Euro FM branding similar to something he had found on a packet of Langues de Chats.

After lunch Lady Cosfoot and her sisters were busy discussing something to do with the Japanese laquer. Everyone else decided to take the dogs for a walk then meet up again for tea in the Chippendale Suite. In the evening they went to the local village pub where they listened to some dreadful karaoke. It was a case of 'if you can't beat them join them.' And after about three drinks Francois and Caroline were singing 'Je t'aime' and 'Hey Jude.' They had hangovers the following day which Sissy tried to put right with a posset. On Sunday, Caroline took Francois and her 'Institute for Young Ladies' self to the village station where they took the little Pullman steam train a few stops over the viaduct, in an up train on the down track St Trinian style. Francois had watched the trains from the bridge sometimes but had never been on it. Caroline went back to London in the afternoon. Only to return six weeks later with Kaneda for Lady Cosfoot's funeral. Lady Cosfoot it turned out, had known that she was going to die and had amended her will to include Francois, having grown very fond of him, more than her bad tempered manner let on. She enjoyed the younger company, and his Jugenstil 'habitat' living and working world. He had Grand Duke Ernst Ludwig Von Hessed himself. Francois continued to run her affairs after her death.

Champagne, caviar, pearl oysters and white yachts with steamer seats. Lady Cosfoot bought out her white satin Indian parasol. It had an exaggerated teardrop curve, similar to the ones in the Raj. They sat in Monaco Harbour surrounded by elegant white hotels having lunch. Looking at the horizon her face was distant. She had a satisfied look of achievement, she had been somewhere and conquered something. She had seen things. She looked nothing like Ruteger Heuer but Francois understood and enjoyed his own internal asylum. Lady Cosfoot's enigma had a zen energy with 'Institute for Young Ladies' grooming.

Francois had no idea of Kaneda's past nor wanted to know. If there was one thing he hated it was hearing about relationships that started off in a consoling capacity for a failed previous one which did nothing for people's self respect. Why did they allow it to happen Why did it make them feel that they were special.

My ex boyfriend

a. had an affair

b. a bad temper

c. hit me

d. drank too much

e. argued over money

Francois would rather not know.

Kaneda had a successful life with no excuses, she had potential. Some women he had met were complete non starters or psychos with the desire to have someone bumped off. Kaneda had an 'I want to enjoy life' attitude' which was attractive with added, 'You're welcome to tag along or improve it.' Confidence in you is confidence in me. This is what Kaneda exuded from every pore. It did not make you question your adequacy, how good looking you were and you knew she was enjoying herself in your company.

Francois had done the I have to impress scenarios and did not always enjoy himself. They probably suited Rock better.

Francois' hangover needed a personal airbag. He woke up and ran a bath, sat in it with a cup of coffee, washed his hair and shaved. After wrapping a towel around his waist, he looked in the small cupboard for some cotton wool and found a tin of vaseline. Inspired by watching the boxing coaches stop bleeding between rounds he put some on his face where the razor had cut him. He left Nigel Benn in the bathroom and went to get dressed.

In the Telegraph there was an article about government and corporate investment in the future of driverless cars. He read it with his coffee and toast. The bleeding had stopped without the need for little pieces of quilted Bounty. 'Ultra' monorails, programmable destinations using Sat Nav, restricted speeds with accident sensors, he did not think people would trust it. There was also an article on Japanese investment with a skyline photo of the sweet potato shaped Phillip Stark Asahi Dry Hall building in Tokyo. Sweet potatoes, Kaneda had told him, contained traces of syanide.

He made a note to ring Mr Wilkinson, his bank manager, about investing what the executor had awarded him, trying not to get jam on the paper.

Aeroplane vapour contrails could be reduced by developing more economical fuels to enable jets to fly efficiently at 20 000 feet. Lower flight paths have higher pressure atmospheres which are less detrimental in forming the clouds and thereby reducing the damage done by global warming. Take off rescheduling to reduce bottle necks and taxiing time on the ground by grouping plane sizes is also being looked into to reduce turbulence and fuel emmissions at ground level.

England were 157 for 3.

Francois thought this sounded more reasonable than one Conservative policy proposal to ration people's flight allowances. If flight costs were being subsidised by BAA retail sales at airports to maintain business profitability, individual passenger polluters should pay an increased fuel or airport taxation instead of being told to take less holiday or domestic business flights. Francois thought about his date with Kaneda. The football match was on Saturday. They could go for a curry after at Ruby in The Dust or Chutney Marys. He made a note to ask Sissy's permission to plant an olive tree in the gardens. Lady Cosfoot had wanted her own grape vine too but that would need more consideration. He finished his breakfast, washed up the plates and cutlery. He noticed there were still some Bath Oliver biscuits in the cupboard.

'Only the minute and the future are interesting in fashion – it exists to be destroyed. If everybody did everything with respect, you'd go nowhere.' Karl Lagerfeld.

Snooker.

Hermione reluctantly followed Sydney into the Anne Summers Shop. She wanted to stock up on Ginsing Libido tablets. Hermione left with three sets of underwear and a vibrator. Dubois was going to the concert with Henry later. She had emailed her mission to the Hammersmith Apollo and eta for re-entry.

Sydney's office was still at lunch. A pair of the guys were playing snooker in the lounge area. Sydney and Hermione made some coffee. MTV was on in the office opposite as Sydney checked her messages. The pair of guys set the balls up, putting the reds in the trianglular frame and arranged the other pink, blue, yellow, brown, green, black and white in their appropriate places. One of them broke and potted a red, then went for he pink. He potted another red and potted the yellow. He took a sip of his beer from his highball.

Hermione started reading a market profile from a youth brand presentation that was on the desk. It was on the subject of confidence.

Red Lipstick

Shiney gloss or mat, bright red lipstick against pale skin, applied to a beautiful mouth is unavoidable. It says confidence. A colour statement. A statement of intention, attention, warning and love. A dramatic application of beautiful colour to exaggerate just one of a woman's features. You either want to kiss it, look at it's aesthetic qualities, watch it's phonetic sensual movements and listen to it's opinions, hanging on it's every sexy word. This photo was taken in Chinatown, you could consider the Geisha mask an art and skill and appreciate the traditional image of women's beauty, eastern eyes or a western mouth.

Shoes

A pair of retro 1970s platform shoes at least 15-20cm high or 7-8 inches to make today's youth nervous about conversion and putting their size nines in it. This is possibly a British style leader, remembering when Rock was young and Elton John's Rocket Man. They scream fashion and confidence, design, style and identity. With yellow heals and horizontal red stripes, sling backs and open sandal toes, lined with green leather they would need physical confidence to walk in them, carry them off as they carried you. Desirable today for their 'want it back' or second go clubbing as a confident thermometer of cool.

Barber's pole

The traditional red and white striped barber's pole is a helter skelter spiral, turning in infinity, an international identity, a known symbol for a short back and sides. The confidence of a smart haircut and something for the weekend. A traditional male bastion where gentlemen could be united and confide before unisex salons and TV condom ads. Possibly one of the first logos and recognised for something that has no complaints. Despite the rebellion of long hair and alternative hairstyles it still survives in today's fashion market becoming increasingly popular with the novelty of a cut throat razor and badger's brush shave, gentlemen's grooming and manicures.

Puccinella was hitting his wife on MTV as part of a pop promo, the band were getting involved with the sausages between the crocodile and the policeman's violent truncheon blows and hits.

'That looks painful,' said Sydney as player one potted the black. The game was over and the staff started to return from lunch.

'I wish I was going to the concert,' said Hermione putting on her lipstick. 'But I can't get out of my prior arrangement.'

'The Borgias used to kill their enemies with red cap or death cap mushrooms,' said Sydney. 'Now they sort it out with a game of snooker at lunchtime. It's easier concentrating on a belini and caviar or cocktail sticks and canapes. You have to develop a taste preference between sturgeon, ossetia, sevruga flying fish or Italian Botago salted mullet and tuna roe. Let them eat Avruga from Tescos and we'll have the full size table in the boardroom.'

'Do you want some more coffee Hermione?'

'No thanks. It's 2.30pm, I'll have to go. I'll ring you about Saturday. Rocketman looks a bit good at snooker. Have you got all your items?' Sydney called after Hermione as she left clutching her shopping.

'I have no idea if they're an item, let me know if I've forgotten anything.'

Cambridge took two hours on the train, the fog cleared and it became a brilliant autumn day with blue sky and sun. Hermione took the opportunity to take some photographs as Tarquin walked Epiphany around a familiar courtyard, this time without being caught for being there drunk. Hermione framed some punts then she turned through an arch and into an enclosed area where about nine or ten cats sat along the top of the wall. They looked at her as she entered and one on the ground wound itself around her ankles.

A few students who were by the river had been collecting chestnuts to roast.

'Can we get some?' asked Epiphany.

'The squirrels have got most of them,' said the boy. 'But if you shake the branches the bigger ones will fall down.'

Epiphany wrapped her scarf over her shoulders and smiled.

'Thanks. Where is the tree?'

'Over there. About three of them.'

'Marrons,' said Tarquin as Hermione joined them.

'Marrons.'

'We need a bag and apparently have to fight the squirrels for them.'

'They said the bigger ones fall when they shook the tree,' said Epiphany.

'Where are these squirrels? I could send the picture to the National Geographic.'

When the bag was full, they must have collected about one hundred chestnuts and went to eat before meeting Sydney and a friend at a clay pigeon shooting club.

Dubois checked her emails on Monday.

Dear Dubois

I can get tickets for the concert you mentioned and can you do me the honour of accompanying me to a wedding.

Iris and Dante Dimlot on the 20th at St Luke's.

I cannot forget the skilled way you play scrabble. I am left with the blank letter to add to these others MERACE.

I find myself drinking less beer and spending twice as much time in the gym. If you count the number of miles I have walked, run and cycled it would double those of Virginia McKenna. Please let me know when you are planning to go to Alice Springs.

Love Henry

Dear Henry

I accept. Excellent news about the concert. The chickens are thrilled.

Love Dubois.

Sugar coated almonds.

Dubois and Henry took a taxi to the wedding which was held at a church in Covent Garden Plaza hidden between the Opera House and market and surrounded by a garden. Dubois had bought an emerald green Phillip Tracey hat, emerald green Jimmy Choo shoes and matching handbag to go with a red wine suit. Dante, the groom, was one of Henry's oldest friends, they had started at the bank at about the same time. He threw rice with the other guests as the couple arrived. He would work out how he felt later, it was just a bit odd. Candles flickered in the church entrance. The service was longer than some weddings that Dubois had been to and the choir sang Italian songs. Waiting for the taxi to the reception they watched the children playing in the garden throwing leaves into the air like confetti copying the rice and walking up the aisle.

'You have to try not to let them get into your bones,' said a woman in a big fur coat. They shared the taxi to the hotel with someone called Antonio and his wife.

'Beautiful wedding,' said Dubois.

'Beautiful dress,'said Antonio.

'Women crying at weddings never ceases to amaze me,' said Henry. 'It's one of those involuntary reflexes. People get very emotional. It certainly looked like a typical group of displaced people you usually get at weddings.'

By the time they sat down to eat at the reception she was starving. The previous day Dubois had spent at an exhibition for small holdings and businesses at Olympia, looking at new chicken houses, the latest technology products feeds and breeds. She came away with a bag full of free pens, literature, badges, business cards, several Quality Street, a few Roses and some Polish fudge having entered a competition and shown a slight interest in a Japanese breed with amazing feathers.

At the beginning of the wedding reception there was the usual place name purgatory panic, reassured by a table plan and 'I vengo', I did reply to the RSVP and I can always blame my partner plus I have not gatecrashed a party since I was sixteen. There were alot of speeches and calls of 'baci! baci!'[kiss! kiss!]. Each place setting had a menu. Tuscany calves liver with lemon and rosemary, salted cod, papadella with hare sauce, broccoli and fontina cheese rissotto, lemon and banana ice creams with apricot pastry, coffee with cantuccini and confetti. In the centre of every table was a large pot of basil surrounded by green and white roses and crimson anenomes and peonies, the radiating stamen like mascared eyes watching from a Titian painting of Greek gods, food, foliage and flowers. The basil scented the air as the best man referred to the story of Vrinda and Alexander the Great where Liesabetti's lover's head was cut off and planted in a pot of basil, which she watered every day.

Most of the speeches were an Italian version of the Japanese craze for 'Pecha kucha', six or seven minute presentations with thanks and toasts. One of the speakers had met his wife in a café where she worked with an extra from one of the Fellini's films. He and the best man were very good at managing their task of looking after the brides maids as they shook their a) tail feathers, b) arses come over here, c) did the funky chicken.

'Di vostra condizion fatene saggi.' said the best man who Henry had met before as he stopped at our table. 'Let us know of your condition.' The afternoon passed in a heavenly feast of food, wine, champagne, dancing and conversation.

Braces.

India saw a man on the bus wearing the same navy Tie Rack braces as hers. She did not wear them that often and went off them rapidly for the duration of the journey. Then when she got home she liked them again. A woman sitting on the back seat was doing word search puzzle games, correcting them with tippex and a brush. India had always associated them with a friend's fear of flying to distract her from her nerves during take offs and landings. Sometimes her legs shook visibly.

India got off the bus and walked to the cinema passing a large white limousine. Two people stepped out, celebrities, prompting paparazzi and she reached for her telephone and photographed them though the back of the premiere style crowd in front of her as they entered a new French restaurant. India showed the little pixel people to Dubois as she told her about the courses of amazing food punctuated by different sorbets. Then they bought some popcorn and went to watch the movie.

Dear Santa Claus
This year I would like :
matching navy underwear
new hair straighteners
caviar
a duplex and money to spend ....

The lights on the Christmas tree in the gallery were bright red. It was decorated with red hot chillie peppers and roses. And the seasonal scent of cinnamon sticks was coming from somewhere.

'To quote Pablo Picasso,' said the buyer, 'the three most astonishing things in the past half century were the Blues, Cubism and Polish vodka. But that could come a close second. That and the existence of figgy pudding. They don't sell it in the supermarket. People only seem to sing about it and we all want it apparently.'

'Hermione has probably got a recipe somewhere.' replied Sydney, 'She's a genius in the kitchen. I'll make some for you. Where is she? Excuse my rhetoric. Invisible again. Do you have a card?'

Following a discussion with her dentist, Hermione had bought herself an electric toothbrush for when she was feeling lazy. She like massaging her gums with it to keep them healthy. They only bled when the scurvy got really bad or a mild vitamin deficiency. Then she knew the blood circulation to her teeth was still good. Being a dentist must be one of the worst jobs possible, she thought. Hermione only had to stare down the throats of pop stars on Top of the Pops when the cameramen did a close up.

Before she married Tarquin, a plumber had come to fix Hermione's dripping tap in her flat. She had shut her bedroom door and could still hear the radio.She made an extra cup of tea and took one in to an invisible man in the bedroom. There were two toothbrushes in the bathroom for the plumber to worry about as he tightened up the washers. It wasn't the first time Hermione had made up a husband and she even wore a wedding ring sometimes as defence against banal chat up lines in unpredictable situations. It started when she began noticing whether men on the tube were wearing wedding rings. All the attractive ones had rings. And a few unattractive ones too. It was something to do with her age. Just another phase. Tarquin had teased her about it and Sydney thought it was quite normal.

The tap dripped. Drip, drip, drip...............it had been like Chinese water torture all night, and she couldn't get The Cure's song out of her head. She was very pleased when it was fixed.

It was still raining. Earlier she had been caught in a shower without an umberella. She was resigned to the fact that her feet were getting wet in her shoes and her hair was wet. Gene Kellying herself was the only solution. Warm monsoon rain was preferable to cold London rain and puddles. You can swim with pelicans on the equator but the pelican crossing was only deep enough to paddle. A large Mercedes with a gold plated tissue box and crown on the back shelf did a three point turn in front of her.

Cyclone.

India emailed Hermione.

Hermione

Buttered yams with red onions and sumac.
1 yam
1 red onion
tbspn sumac
Butter

I have forwarded the statement from Prior Estates, the managing agents to you this morning.

Love India.

Hermione watched a report of the storm on the television news. Technically it was a cyclone. She had never been in a cyclone before. A cyclone, the weather girl said was a tropical hurricane, which is where the wind blows in an anticlockwise direction in the southern hemisphere. Not to be confused with a typhoon or twister. There was footage of damaged houses and people struggling against the high winds, almost blown away by the force. A man in a black rayon 1950's style mac was climbing the steps outside a building; the fabric was flapping against his body, as he had to fight to hold his footing, making little progress as the wind kept him in the same place. People gave up their umbrellas.

Sydney met the buyer for dinner in Shepherd's Market. He was interested in a new up and coming artist, a recovering alcoholic who had been made bankrupt and rehabilitated. The bank had requested his cards to be returned or cut up. Before they stopped his overdraft he found inspiration in his achillies heel and bought an undisclosed number of American Express Travellers Cheque on his credit cards. His latest show was sold out. 'A gibelotte of game' was the buyer's description of the hangings, a desirable brace of investable art.

It was just the broken 'mijotter', [that's the surface tension of the stew] and I'm keen to see what lies beneath!'

He looked at his glass as he swirled his laguna and watched the oily texture cling to the sides.

'This one has good legs.'

Sydney found him very entertaining.

'Did you know it was Burn's Night tonight. We should really be eating haggis. I nearly bought one earlier. It struck me that there's only one brand available - MacSweens - and they have put the price up higher than inflation, about 150%. Which got me thinking if they were to bring out their own competition at a higher or lower price bracket they would create a market, consumer choice, widening their shelf exposure, increasing demand and creating revenue for advertising and expansion. Then they could diversify their product range. People would be eating MacSweens everyday, all year round. What do you reckon?'

'It sounds great. What's in it?'

'What do you think of the show?' a man in a green Harris Tweed jacket, grey sweater and Gucci glasses asked Sydney as she studied a painting at the private view.

'The artist's muse appears to have toothache. She is holding her face in nearly every pose. I think the paintings as a whole obviously make a better picture of the artist than the one or two which I've seen before. I'm thrilled to have the chance to see them together. Are you an artist or a buyer?'

'Buyer.'

'Have you tried the mini bagels. They're heaven. A Lilliput taste of cream cheese paradise. They were first made by a baker in Vienna who gifted them to the King of Poland in the seventeenth century apparently.'

'Also a gift to a woman at childbirth,' interrupted Hermione.

'Please excuse my sister's ejaculations, she's reminiscing about the loss of Harry's Bar. Scrambled eggs and smoked salmon breakfasts, dinner jacket clad men and taffetta ladies after an evening on the ball circuit. A great loss to Kingly Street . It's a hip bar for the happening youth scene now who are more likely to get their bagels from Brick Lane after a good club and then grab a bargin bicycle from the market and a topiary heart from Columbia Road before stopping at Spittalfields Farm to stroke the goats and return home with their dance cards marked.'

'Show me the way to go home.' said the buyer.

'It's where the heart is .' said Sydney. ' Do you have a favourite picture. The spatial awareness and use of light really expresses his theatre work. I've not seen these before.'

'The dark red one is a favourite at the moment. It's easy to have an opinion but I can't make a balanced critique........I'm keeping an open mind. The artist was sleeping with a famous actress while he painted this one, that's why I'm interested in it.'

A tray of champagne walked passed them on it's tour of the room and they refreshed their glasses.

'Larger than average bubbles, not a delicate fizz, random and periferal not from a central source. I have no idea why or where they come from but I can watch them for hours. I was fascinated to learn about freezing the sediment to remove it during fermentation and topping the bottles up, tapping and turning them.' said Sydney, ' I exploded a bottle of Moet Chandon once by putting in the freezer in the absence of an ice bucket. Awful waste.'

Caviar, belinis, forcemeat and canapes were served with the champagne. The buyer put his caviar on his wrist, then licked it off. Sydney ate her artichoke and tomato belini.

'I love artichokes,' said Hermione.

'Italians call them Girasola - towards the sun,' said Sydney.Then she tried licking her caviar. The buyer had been asked a question by a gentleman in a red scarf and a beret.

'My most interesting find this week were some prints by Nelson Mandela, landscapes and statements from his infamous life. You should see them if you can.'

India usually only read books on holiday. A front cover promotion incentive, free with August Vogue bought at the airport. India enjoyed Hideous Kinky on the beach in Johanesburg. The author's baby, bestseller, publishing midwifary to go with the free bag and sunglasses incentives that came with June and July. She enroled at the library for her New Year's Resolution and read three books in one week. She also mourned the passing of the HMV chart. Technology downloads and sections had exploded into subsections of dance music, trance and techno. No longer was it simple rock, pop and indie with the 'Big Saturday Purchase Total', Top Ten and number one in 1980. Even unsigned internet bands were making the chart.

When Tracey Chevalier described her pleasure at letting go of the Pearl Earring to a director and film crew it reminded India of a woman she met on an aeroplane to Vietnam who was passionate about the freedom of her dependants. They were gone, she sounded in pain and in love, they were gone until they needed her again.

India had not had children but she had read somewhere that the body gives a rush of endomorphines following birth. She likened it to the pleasure dome of enjoying your Ikea kitchen and furniture having gone through the store and warehouse gestation period and delivery company. India was eating yams for the first time. Not a craving, just vegetable of the season in the supermarket. Soft and watery with creamy flesh. Hermione and Sydney found themselves drinking vodka toasts after the private view.

'V strtcha! [to the meeting!]'

'Za prekrasaik! [to beautiful women!]'

and anything topical followed by 'Davey vipiem! [let's drink to that!]'

Bump on the head.

India's head was full of party policy following an interview on the television in the casulty waiting room. Taxation proposals which encourage mobilisation of something along particular paths was a directive to reduce inequality. Efficient business centres with 'cats cradle' control contracts with local government. Telescopic communities where local government ran hospitals, schools and services with a view to taking a more strategic path of taxation along the lines of the congestion charge. Knowing the strategy, like the community charge, informs you of the value of the goods and bads from which you can chose to appreciate your improved quality of life. Alternatively you could complain about poor road maintenance and having to pay taxes.

Walking through the hospital, India passed an area of sensory experiences, mood environments of birdsong and slowly dimming bright lights . There was an area with someone playing the piano and enough room for a tea dance with a space age scanner next door. Her bump on the head was slowly becoming a Tom and Jerry cartoon with stars and tweeting birds flying around in Hanna Barbara circles. She was trying not to find her sense of humour after having spent two hours wound licking sitting next to a drunk blood transfusion who had been in a fight.

Hospital waiting lists for back operations could be reduced by putting health warnings on furniture she thought. India considered introducing bingo into casulty waiting rooms to make them less depressing and could not understand how smokers blamed the eighteen month hospital waiting lists and institutions for their 50% chance of survival. Their chances of survival would be better if they had been operated on six months earlier. Maybe they should not have smoked in the first place or used the health warnings as something not to care about. In America they take tabacco companies to court. India was not too sure what Lloyd George would do in his grave. She was reading about some glass sculpture by Max Jacquard and Angela Thwaites in her copy of Wallpaper. The couple next to her were discussing CDs they had swapped in the three for the price of one HMV sale by peeling off the reduction stickers and putting them on new releases. India wanted to know why the edges of coloured glass looked green. She guessed it had something to do with light refraction and particles but the article didn't say. She also knew that the yellow calcium dioxide glass was rarer and more expensive. After the confusion of the x ray, three in one ultrasound scan, reflex checking, blood presure and IV saline drip, India rang Dubois who collected her. They signed her release. She reassured them that she would be OK in case she developed concusssion. Dubois had a double vodka and tonic on top of her antibiotics to detox the emergency services.

This is quite normal for people whose immune systems are low from drinking and cannot not drink. The 'there there' antibiotics in fact probably do more harm than the alcohol anyway. India had never had a day off sick in her life and had to lie about getting the flu.

Epiphany uploaded a picture of a spider's web she had taken onto her MySpace. She had been reading about Machiavelli at school. She also had loads of spider blog.

'You never see pairs of spiders in a web do you,' said Epiphany to Hermione.

'No. The females eat the males sometimes and they build a new web everyday.'

Epiphany said she was reading some research from the US which used spider's web silk in bullet proof vests.

'These are good come and have a look.'

Epiphany had a page of webs made from spiders which had eaten injected flies.'

'This one was made on LSD, this one on hash and this one on caffeine.'

'It's a complete mess.'

They had gorgonzola and basil rissotto for lunch and watched a programme on the glass wing butterfly.'

India stayed with Dubois and the following day they went to visit Hermione for lunch. They took a bottle of Sake for Chinese New Year and made noodles with crab, mushrooms, pakchoy and steamed fish.

Hermione was working on a PR campaign for corporate responsibility and energy conservation. It questioned the possibilities for making personal lifestyle economies to help climate change.

Renewable biofuels and hybrid company car rewards, efficiency drives, equipment standby and light pollution in offices and supermarkets. Hermione was fluent in tide farms, turbines and hoover rig boats that would make 60% reduction in CO_2 emmissions by 2050 and the new discovery of gasification production of low carbon fuels by 2075. Hermione would be a hundred and ten with another twenty five to fifty good years left in her. She was writing up the Tesco sponsorship package research for the Pentaland Firth project which was to replace Dounraey. The peripheral Orkney and Shetland Isles Tide mills and turbine construction would mean a potential 25% increase in local contractors and new business to Scottish industry. She read a paragraph to Epiphany who had appeared with some green tea. She felt she was digressing slightly from her campaign message.

'We're working on tide farms and solar system orbital mechanics at school. We have a French model in La Ranch to learn about and I have to write about a divide and rule in Great Britain. If Ireland and the Isle of Mann self govern, why shouldn't Scotland?' she drank some tea and reached into her bag to get a book.

Kipling's Just So Stories. The Crab That Played With The Sea. She waved the book at Hermione, found the right page and read.

'Kun? said the fisherman of the moon..........

Sydney was holding her piping hot Starbucks, she adjusted the 'zarf' sleeve holder. She did not know where the word came from but it was another new 'stud muffin' piece of slang that would become part of daily life. It was her second of the day, an ordinal number, she usually had a cardinal three, an ordinal fifteenth of her weekly intake not a cardinal error. She made a note to ring the buyer, reminded by his penchant for caviar as she held the 'zarf' in her perlicue, between her thumb and forefinger. She placed the coffee on the mark it had left on her paper earlier making a Gilera logo. Another three and she would have an Olympic logo.

Sydney made arrangements to meet the buyer. She was going to Cheltenham Ladies Day for a PR event . Sally was taking orders for lunch. Sydney ordered Watercress Udon noodles and some dim sum before going to her meeting. It took an hour to go through the strategies and positioning for the Hertz Hire package competition and racing driver book launch. It was an 'I'm too pragmatic for my Prada' monday morning. She thought as she put her tampon behind her ear, trying to cope with the cubicle door. There was not enough space to get around the door as it opened without walking directly into the porcelain. Whoever planned the cubicle needed to think bigger.

The lights turned red and the taxi stopped. A Gone With The Wind wide angle passed in front of the windscreen at the zebra crossing, a girl on crutches, a five year old on a toy scooter being supported by it's mother, and not very good at using it, an OAP on an electric chair and a man with a limp. The lights changed and the cars moved away before the carts pulled by oxen and other pedestrians followed, fleeing from their homeland of domestic accidents. Maybe they should have taken heed of the saying 'Don't put all you eggs in one basket.' Either that or they were practising European Easter traditions where the oxen and white horses pull carts carrying chocolate eggs through the town piazzas. Sydney remembered the French Cloches de Pacques where you can hear the 'flying bells' from Rome in France and the children play a game rolling eggs down a gentle slope. The one that breaks loses and has to share his or her candy with his friends. Hermione liked the little poisson d'Avril chocolate fish they had. She had brought some back from Nice once and sang the B52's 'I'll give you fish, I'll give you candy.'

Sydney knew there was something she was keeping from her about that trip but she never pushed her on it.

Amen handed Dubois her set of completed accounts for the year end. A clean white document with title and dates in a smart plastic file.

'Thanks.'she said.

'Did you know that New Years Day used to be April 1st?' asked Amen.

'No.'

'It was changed by Charles IX of France.' he paused for a second and smiled to himself then added, 'What's the difference between Charles IX and Ronnie Barker........ One sends an April Fool to a fishmongers to buy fish out of season and the other sends people to ask for fork handles, a long weight and has lousey phonetic French. I await your next quarter. Where do you want to go to dinner?'

Dubois looked at him and smiled, 'Anywhere but Turnpike Lane. What do you fancy?'

'There's a new Moroccan in EC1 that we could try.'

'Which means you've been there and want to go back for more cous cous and shish.'

Dubois' skirt was slightly impractical for Amen's bike which meant taking a taxi instead. They arrived and sat at a side table. Amen ordered some charbon and raki. The diamond holes in the decorative ceramic lamps made glitter ball patterns of light on the walls and small candles flickered on the tables. A kaleidoscope mezze of capers, olives, chillies, vegetables and spices appeared from nowhere. Dubois was playing with a pale green chillie.

'Have you ever seen any green onions?' she asked.

'No I don't think I have. Or green ham.'

'I can't find any in the supermarkets. I even rang up Fortnums and Harrods, but they couldn't help and I can't remember how the song goes either, which is really annoying me.' she stopped for a second then added, 'Waitrose had green tomatoes, 'I've tried 'fried green tomatoes ' but prefer green tomato soup.'

She drank some raki and ate some chillie.

'Did you know the Lumiere brothers experimented with onion cellulose before making conventional celluloid film and treating it with chemicals. As a result film editors don't have to put a spoon upside down in their mouths or use a knife underwater to stop them from crying when they cut it. The cutting room floor ends up ressembling a hairdressers with a hippy after a short back and sides and out takes on the floor. It would be like crying at Easy Rider or Dead Men Don't Wear Plaid.'

She took a sip of her drink then added, 'People should stop and ask themselves why the world is like a great big onion. Maybe Kodak have the answer. I'll email them later.'

They ate lamb tagine with apricots, dates, raisins and oily flat bread. The bread separated into layers and rolled up into flower petals like a rose. A waiter brought some honey and tahini dessert which they had with tea and lots of sugar.

'Sydney was at Cheltenham today. We texted some bets and won £27 on an each way ticket and £5 on Pay Attention To Win.'

'Sydney is talking to you then?'

'Yes I think she's forgotten Henry exists. There's a mystery buyer she's mentioned alot.'

Amen took something out of his wallet. It was a diamond the size of a five pence piece. He held it up to let the light refract and dance on it's faces, then put it away.

'In case you change your mind.' he said.

Belt and Braces

Taylor, Laurie and Fred had a lettre de cache to the Linguine House siege, others needed a map to find a way out. There were tectonic faulted floors in the Greek doll's house where the unbreakable china was made of plastic. Paper was folded under the table leg to stop it wobbling or bring up old jokes about people with alzheimers and getting ketchup out of bottles. They discussed the didactic content of early religious and occidental art compared to the more recent typical landscapes and portraits of western art. The first impressions of the invited newcomers and their reaction to the Escheresque interior were noted with amusement. As malapropable as a plate of ganache truffles with syrah grenache wine under watchful eye of Ganeche.

Quietly confident waiting for the previous company to finish their briefing sitting in the government office reception, nine years of training and one full years practise, that's two more than a vet. Their approach to new town planning prioritised the inclusion of catflaps and dogwalking areas. Taylor read from an ad in the paper,

'Crusher Operator £25,000 a year. Temporary three months only required. The applicant requires a C.P.C.S. licence. No promotion prospects. The applicant will have trained as a crusher already or have experience.' and added,

'Business in this field is obviously greater than general public knowledge.'

'A bit contrary to the government's £2000 trade-in scheme against new cars to help shift the carpark stockpile of manufactured models .What sales incentive does the crusher operator have to work with ?' asked Fred.

'It doesn't say.' answered Taylor

'Do they take it off your hands and give you the price of metal weight or under it, pocket the difference, make a profit, or does the right off owner pay them to take it away?' Fred questioned persistently.

'It might be quite satisfying being destructive. Did it mention a pension? Is there a future in it with the advent of electric cars?'

'I don't think electric vehicles will necessarily have greater longevity than petrol engines.'

Some manufacturers might need to speed up their evolution in light of the recent Chrysler liquidation. Terminater Salvation , liquimoly man, life immitating fiction, an early warning of Cleveland City consolidation or prediction of a Detroit Spinners number one. '

' I'll dig out my silver nail varnish by Sinful .' sad Fred.

'Googled info says.....Forty five seconds per car, the Granutech Big Mac was invented in 1970 and can crush 450 cars an hour- it's saving environmental grace is it has an electric engine and scrap costs are up three times.

'Did you know that Andy Warhol was a hindu and is actually reincarnated and living in Caerphilly as a crusher operater.'

"Not alot of people know that ."

'Remind me of that next time I hire a Minimoke in the Greek Escheresque exterior. They obviously don't worry about their scrap metal salvage.'

'I'll shave my hair off to keep the hair in my eyes.Taylor put the presentation portfolio in the car, clutching the briefing notes. He drove back inspired and took the plans to bed .

'Ever had the urge to get out of your car and climb over the cars in the traffic jam in front of you like a pursuit or escape scene from an American movie Laurie?' asked Taylor.

'Is that like getting into moving vehicles and rolling under closing shutters with stolen paintings or laser beams?' replied Laurie.

'Yes. I suppose. The roof and bonnet panels usually only dent temporarily and pop back into their usual shape. Getting onto moving trains can involve landing in other passenger's laps. Try and avoid people with bunches of flowers, they aren't usually very accommodating.'

'On the subject of copying things, I put a plastic aircraft carrier missile up my nose when I was a kid mimicking an Indian princess with a jewelled nose piercing I'd seen.' said Fred.

'Luckily it didn't require any casualty attention.'

'Are we digressing from the requirements for hospitals and eco carbon neutrality or sparking and brainstorming from the underground heating of Roman remains in the area?' asked Taylor.

'I was interested to read about the Pygmalion effect – a biased observation versus expected enhancement of children.' said Taylor.

'Pygmalion was a Greek sculptur who fell in love with his statue. Not unlike a Robert Hughes documentary feature on aboriginal territories or French terroir cuisine. I came to the conclusion that men are probably like clouds, they form and stay with temperature and altitude and go with the wind, blowing over or precipitating, one or the other. This theory was inspired by Martin Amis' allusion to Margaret Atwood's Edible Woman and clouds and women obeying their natural functions.'

They looked a bit blank.

'It amused me anyway!'

The pitch briefing went well, apart from the parking ticket. Taylor, Fred and Laurie returned to the studio. Unlike most minimalist minded interior designers Laurie's desk was piled high with towerblocks and skyscrapers of paper that turned himself into a piece of archeology with each layer of 90gsm white conquerer. A nautical theme was building around submarine hatch and boat doors with step over thresholds, rounded corners and wing nut hinges, porthole windows between rooms, wood veneer and mapchart wallpaper. A spider had been busy building its web in a corner, taking the helm until it caught a navy uniform bluebottle or a housework cleaning storm blew the cobweb away with a feather duster at force nine.

Laurie played a plan and elevation game of Port and Starboard with his childish sense of design placing the required items on the left or right. Man overboard seating plans and ladder climbing storage. Three Men on an island trilogies of linear features, a plimsole line level of units and Captain's Coming piped doorbell .He thought twice about the novelty value of the last idea and stuck it with ringtones and lapping waves, cicadas and birdsong on his dictaphone tape before going to the local Friends of the Earth meeting. Food chain was on the agenda .

Taylor was busy working on some peanut shell double seating with half monkey nut hinges based on the original Eames egg chair .'See no !hear no! speak no! ' contra conversation chair floatation tank flight seat concepts with headphones and personal movie screens. He had eaten most of them and saved the shells to add to the organic compost fuel he was developing with Pat .Inspired by the self sufficient Good Life of Richard Briars laughed at by many for it's totally alternative ways they would combine the market serfdom longacres with worshipful citytraders marks and gates in the futuristic scientific ecoharmony intended.

The houses of the future would no longer be centered around the T.V. and video five plug socket adapter with fifteen cables to hide under the T.V. stand or Ikea low level coffee table with video compartment on wheels. How would laptop living affect the focal fengshuei of the furniture. What am I supposed to do stare out of the window, at a wall or have a special table for the computer. One each per household member, a joint office furniture system desk.Taylor had mentioned a fact he had heard about more museums being made in the 1970's to house the heretige and culture the T.V. was beaming at us. As ecoliving would be trying to reverse consumption and emission trends he had in mind to open a Community Culture Minimalist Nostalgia Museum with nothing in it for the Zen kleptomaniac nightmares he was dealing with.

Taylor also mentioned a comment about T.V. programming in the 1970's. Other than T.U.C. conferences, How, a lot of Apollo launches, pop music, pairs of comedians and news programmes he wandered what the programmes eliminnated consisted of. Was this the 15:1 concept origin and how could he get hold of them for a documentary. He doubted the file would be very large somehow as the programmes selected were that basic. Our visual identity was very underdeveloped and it was difficult to imagine, much as he tried, what variables there were beyond the things to do and make that were beamed into our living rooms .

Taylor had checked the Bloomberg figures to see what Japan had produced over night. As the plum wine bottles in his supermarket only have screw tops none existed in his collection of corks. A collection of gothic dates, names, numbers and coats of arms of wine houses and vineyards burnt and printed on the bark stoppers, herded together in a frame. A record of stories told, to be read by other happy magpies and Marvin Gayes. Taylor liked having something to show for the glasses until he discovered a webpage of like-minded blog collectors. He took his frame of corks down until he wanted it again.

Taylor placed a low risk share order having quickly analysed the lines of support, resistence and pressure with his new found experience, protecting his stoploss following an area of consolidation. It was sunny spells, light showers and isobars. He imagined Nick Leeson telling us to wrap up warm and wear a woolly hat while forecaster Michael Fish swopped his tweeds for a bright stripey jacket .Taylor finished drinking his Fairtrade coffee. A freetrial with 30p off his next purchase with the voucher promotion. He wanted some quince jam to go with cheese and spreadbetting but that came from the supermarket he went to on Thursdays and it was still Tuesday.

Tuesday evenings 5.30pm was the Kensington and Chelsea time for employed people in SW3 and 5. Anybody from SW1and W1 would need to go to Westminster. Wishing to get assistance from the Citizen's Advice Bureau requires a degree in patience, telephone menus, and sign reading. All other people would need to go on Wednesday or Saturday mornings at 10 am or ring the advise line that was never answered but gave a list of problems and general F.A.Q.s with common sense answers. Then it would still be necessary to get there an hour early to queue up and arrive within the first ten people to have half a chance of being seen within two hours. The service is potentially very good but lacks any of modern civilisation. It more accurately resembles queuing for a potato in the Russian Revolution.

Taylor was not going to pay the increased price on his parking ticket. Having been sent the reminder at twice the price. It doubled after fourteen days or did not double if paid within fourteen days. He had subsequently removed a ticket from someone else's car and stuck it on another car then sort advice. Unfortunately it appeared that no humans actually worked in the processing office in Camden. Further to this he progressed to learning about the sending of bailiff letters to people who owed him money on the property he rented. Having sat and read every leaflet about unions, housing and work rights, tribunals and benefits in the waiting room with a diverse mix of public, religions and ethnic backgrounds, ringtones, footapping radio taste and proximity preference for radiators, he progressed to learning the difference between a garnishee and coriander sprinkles on a korma.

Taylor also received a further ticket for parking with one wheel outside the box line, his ticket not displayed properly inside the car and the meter not registering the money put into it. He developed a persecution complex and hatred for all traffic wardens. Being told to ring the number on the meter to advise someone that you had just lost another £1 in it lacked any credibility. Why would it be reimbursed because it was put in writing? He had occasional lapses in self control that included stealing knights in white satin serviettes and cruet sets from restaurants and feeding items of food into parking meters to presumably stuff them and anybody else who wished to use them.

He laughed along at the funny sounding names like Melton Mowbray and Leighton Buzzard, famous for stilton, pork pies, cockfighting, gamboling, foxhunting and steeple chasing. In fact Melton Mowbray, the Leicester location of the cream cheese production and fermentation of stilton is different to the town of the same name that is a coaching stop on the way to London. A cream cheese diasporo. What Isreal is to the Jews, and Afghan rebels, a displacement of curdish masses finding it's way to the port and cranberries at the Feast of Stephen in exchelsis.

It is also interesting to note that while most celts know the chorus to most folk songs, the Brits know mainly regional songs sononomous with Wembley and Twickenham.

Taylor was following someone Canadian on Twitter bigmac@ and read an online travel guide on all things Canadian. Canada geese, it appeared, have migrated to London parks permenantly and only reside in the 2298 acre man made Wascana Centre Park in their native land. The Ground Hog Day beavers and tweeting Canada Goose took an information diversion. Bigmac@ was sitting in his Solomon Grundies. Outside the window some birds were feeding from his peanut butter fir cone and Kate Humble feeder made from an old water bottle with a hole cut in it and painted attractive colours. Taylor scrolled caribou moose, racoon and totem poles as the radiator rattled and hissed. A noise that would send wild cat and Indians running for their tomahawks. The first time the air bubbles had shaken the expanding metal pipes he jumped and looked around at the direction of the aural richochet that carried tales of frozen damage. On rational and logical reflection he became unperturbed by the noise. How this reassured babies in cots or why it was used to stop babies crying was beyond him. Rattlesnakes are deaf and babies do not come with instructions. Find something to shake, apply rattle and roll a joint. Freudien explanations to stop us from biting or boiling them. Crotalus is the scientific name for rattlesnake and Greek for castanet, the rattle ceases to function when it gets wet .

'look here ' said the photographer to get the papoosed toddler to appear more alert .

'look here' said the toddler I was quite happy being warm and inanimate. This makes a better picture apparently, Osh Kosh Begosh baby grow and stripey hat, more formal and less voyeuristic. Cinnamon cereal, molasses bread , potteries, enviable crafts, blanket stitched and handmade decorations scrolled up the screen .

Bigmac@ had grown up on Pete Murphy Bauhaus Hunger and Blaupunkt ads. Taylor got to Lake Eerie, 'cat people ' fishermen and imagined David Bowie on his hols, great eagles with huge golden eye trout in their talons and grizzley bears in the Pelee National Park home to the powder magazine officers quarters at Fort Eerie, site of the bloodiest battle seiges when America tried to invade Canada in 1812. He knew the overture canons from the limited collection of vinyl resource available to him when he was eight along with Bill Hailey's Twist , Great Balls of Fire,

Rock n' Roll Greatest hits and listening to Top 40 tapes of Seasons in the Sun in between watching the Wombles .

Taylor scrolled further. Nova Scotia cod tongue, seal flipper and Moose flea delicacies, poutine french fries dripping with cheese, chomeur or unemployed pudding, sugar pudding, Molson and Moose beers, maple syrup pancakes and tree tapping.

What are you doing now? Tweet.Bigmac@ was listening to Alanis Morriset and reading Margaret Atwood. Tweet .The radiator rattled and hissed. Taylor considered researching the finances involved in US surrogacy cases and making diplomatic proposals to abortion clinics in light of the arguments made against extending the twelve week limit. A highly emotive topic that involved mainly the opinions of people not responsible for taking decisions and giving opinions based on sensational statistics. By making more operations available immediately it would be possible to reduce the percentage of abortions made after eight weeks to 50%, the figure stated instead of arguing against a figure of more than twelve weeks. Ask the smiling woman with the six week old baby in the termination clinic waiting room her opinion.

Bigmac@ was fighting his Inuk indian spirit and opted for articles on cryognics a cinnamon latte and a mars bar .

The man who had doors for feet.

The man who had doors for feet had to carry his shoes in his bag. He couldn't find any shoes to fit the doors. Where other people had size nines he had number twenty fours. He had screws instead of toe nails and had to use a key to unlock them because they blew shut in the wind and opened and closed when he walked .When he stood still he used cheese wedges to hold them open and smell like normal feet .

When he put his feet or doors up on the table someone asked him if he did that in his own home? He replied that he had to because they wouldn't fit under the table. The person didn't seem very happy that his doors were on the table and said he wouldn't talk to him .

So the man who had doors for feet got very drunk and woke up with windows instead .

Taylor was setting up the game of Kerplunk [co2 emmissions saved versus watching T.V. 50] He was putting the multicoloured sticks through the holes at the top of the plastic helterskelter and he realised the balls should go on top not in first. He tried to work out how they dropped like a game of spoof when the sticks were removed. It reminded him of a crisis last week. Someone had put the filter coffee machine together wrong. They had put a full jug of water on the top to boil with half an existing jug of coffee on the hot plate resulting in too much coffee plip plip plipping and spilling on the work surface. Another time they had put the water on the hot plate and expected the coffee to steam itself and drip like sweat in a sauna . He took the Kerplunk apart again, scratched his head and looked at the instructions .

'Budgets for planting. What's this?'

He had probably sent the Kerplunk instructions to the Mayor's office instead of the letter lobbying for more fruit trees to fix the food chain. Taylor and his girlfriend had picked some miniature plums and made jam by boiling them with sugar and using a fork and sieve to remove the stones. Then ate it with some homemade bread while digesting some food facts.

'The average distance for your roast dinner to reach your plate is 49,000km and carrots take sixty times longer than fifty years ago.'

They had failed to find any hazelnut or elderflower trees for their green team ecomonth and realised like most things you never found them while you were looking for them, especially men and women. The additional jumpers were keeping the thermostat down and the rubbish and complacent water consumption was measured regularly before watching the TV having given up after two games of Kerplunk.

A startled untamed rogue shrew on The Discovery Channel was devastating the dried grass underfoot as it stampeded the termite and anthill communities resulting in the broadcast of helplines and set up of emergency funds to rebuild them.

'I'll write a shopping list of what I need to get then shall I?'

'New goggles and a pair of socks.'

'And some ski trousers.'

'We're going to the Ultravox cool empty silence city of Klimts and Viennese cuckoo clocks for Christmas, cake, coffee and schnapps.'

'And going to Kitzbul by train for a weekends skiing.'

'Can't you manage with your sunglasses and wear your bike waterproofs over your levis!'

'How many CO2 emissions will that save do you reckon considering we are getting the train and staying in a chalet hotel with a shared log fire and a lounge?' asked Taylor.

'Haven't you got a balaklava somewhere to go and gull someone with? The hippo is in the water cistern and my monitor is off. Drip, drip, drip.'

'You sound like a Russian spy. Don't forget to turn the tap off when you brush your teeth.'

Read meter and recycle. Recycling collected plastics, paper glass, metal and other waste. Paying for products and being criticised for bad consumerist spending. What does a misspent youth mean to this generation? Thought Taylor. It must be wasted on some people. Certainly not hanging out in snooker halls when they drink beer from carbon neutral breweries with natural water supplies and recycled heating in underground fully self sufficient solar panelled plants. The shiney ceramic tiles on the exterior of snooker halls and high ceilings to accommodate tasselled lights with score things and draughty windows are a cross between an Oscar Deutch Odeon style cinema and a Victorian fireplace. He separated the newspapers from the plastic bags and noticed a job for a Guillotine Operater in a print production finishers £15k shift work.................not just an hour ahead in France. It did not say how long the shifts were. He imagined a lot of French heads. Was the government bringing back capital punishment?.................He had knowledge of the Gutenburg printing press and gothic hot metal typesetting from college although it was more in the style of a Steve somebody or Neville Brody ransom note punk album cover experimenting with different fonts.The guillotine operater went in with the other newspapers and he watered the plants. He had grown them from seeds that he had dried himself having bulked at the price of the price of tomato plants and seeds last year. He wasted a punit of bright red tomatoes with shiney red highlights in a gratuitous and violent re-enactment of 'happy birthday to you, squashed tomatoes and stew.'

He had noticed the apples had started stacking themselves in the fridge in rows remenicent of a fairground gallery. He could not help acting on impulse, and in the absence of an AK47 he threw the tomatoes at the garden wall resulting in something that looked either like a passatta or misinterpreted Japanese 'NO' cover version of a failed teenage chat up. Any last requests for a cigarette or meal. Wait until you see the reds of his eyes then look for the small white pips after the light infantry wave. Painting the town red, he would have a forest of tomato plants next year and eat as many green ones as he could to keep the plant's productivity up at the Whistle Stop Cafe. [And because he liked green tomato soup.]

There were several rows of pumpkin, marrow, watermelon and cuttings he had taken then grown using rooting hormones and baby bio. Someone had tried to tell the heavy plant crossing joke yesterday in Italian by translating it literally – pesante piante 'camino e macchina con forchetta' per alzare i terre traversa i via - but it did not make much sense............He found his Rizla papers and sat down and tried to work out why glass Christmas tree decorations were the same shape as shallots and onions. Last Christmas they had decorated the tree with red chillies. Onions might be a bit too heavy he thought then decided to start drying the oranges and limes out that afternoon.

Dear Santa,

I want the Jenson Button biography

An elf or sheep sleepsuit from the Sainsbury's gift catalogue

A balaclava from the Heal's collection of wooden toys....................

'Have you ever been to Coventry?' asked Taylor's girlfriend Jo.

'No. Why do you ask?'

'I was wandering what people talk about there and where they send them if they're already there.' continued Jo.

'Probably pink football strips and what to do with all the socks that ran in the wash. Reasons for Everton to change their away strip to avoid being confused with Coventry's.' replied Taylor.

'There must be lots of work for plumbers at the moment with the floods in Cumbria. Jo's Tool and Pipe Works are making a fortune!'

Thursday night.

Taylor took a swig of beer from the bottle and put it down on the bar again. The lime wedge collected enough CO_2 bubbles fizzing at an increased rate, then rolled over from it's initial position and continued to break the surface. The liquid's viscosity continued to curve up the edge of the recycled light green carbon neutral glass bottle as he licked the salt on his hand and took a shot of tequilla to mix the sodium saline with the strong bitter spirit. Straight up. Some people prefered a tomato salsa chaser. He stuck to the beer .

No $300 saliva testkit, popular with the New York movers and shakers to check his stress levels, he could try his hand at some slam poetry to blow hole the pressure instead of the gaskit.

Overpriced beer. They were running up a tab with a card behind the bar .

'I could borrow, steal or beg ' or 'lend, give or plant. ' One of them was from Agatha Christie's Appointment With Death the other a horticulturalists guide to for Mother- in -laws tongue .

I saw you shopping in Europa .

He had shopped once with Cliff Richard in an overpriced minmalistmarket / convenience store in suburbia near a private park residence with lots of rhodedendron bushes and roads with humps, and played at the same tennis club but it wasn't going to live his life by the same sentiment. A different basket case altogether .

Sonny Boy Williamson, harmonica blues, played to an audience, the notes not confused. African masks and Osiodu seats. Chairpersons agendas, BUDGET, financial fiscal feats. Fleet Street, N.U.J.s, Harrier Jump jets - do a slammer and fudge it !

He opened the mail. It was always him that sorted it and put the junkmail of pizza deliveries in a pile, nobody else bothered. There was always a pile of unforewarded or redirected mail for the previous tenants and he had given up writing 'Return To Sender' with an Elvis tune in his head and did not have the balls to throw it away. So he decided to open it instead. It was total madness. Inside were as he had expected, a credit card, bills with an address and statements. A whole identity for an alien. Then he finished his bottle, smiled a slightly lunatic smile and ordered another beer .

Laurie had a hangover the size of the Empire. He had lost count of the number of beers he had drank. 9-4pm Civil Service red tape, in addition to the service in the Indian Raj where everything stops for tea and tiffin at 4pm. The Joseph Heller mission school of marketing – on hold waiting for council tax information. Making recognaissance calls that state ' this call is being recorded for training purposes' disclaimers means any advice given is not going to be accurate and cannot be used against us so don't bother making the call about the claim in the first place. Catch 22 or duck it. It's St Valentine's Day, chox away and do a scratch card instead, win a million and spend your disposable income on new products with must have sales advertising U.S.P.s like leg make up shimmer. Charbonelle and Walker Crème Parisienne with sympathy.

'Is that a freecall number. Did you get through?' asked Fred. 'They should offer a manicure while you wait, free makeover to make up for the wasted call. There are always a pair of girls on the makeup concessions in the big department store who don't mind taking full advantage of the testers, sharing the lipsticks and mascaras along with Jo Public while a different pair of girls look on and find the grossly unhygienic activity, potential eye infections, oral herpes and coldsores grossly horrendous. I wander what percentage of women put it on at home out of habit. Telephone makeup! It probably seems funny to some people if they're not going out.'

As the fog cleared across the Turnered Thames from zero visibility the sun struck a glass building turning it into a gold domino, a huge gold Braille 'stop.'

Hot metal bus buttons and a number one from the Ting Tings.

'When you do get to speak to someone on one of these highly manpower saving menus,' said Laurie, 'the differing advice sends you from department to department, protracts your problem longer than the employment of the average staff member that you have engaged in correspondence with and introduced to other new staff members.'

'The complimentary cotton buds on the cosmetic concessions reassures you that the Civil Service has extreme blood poisoning when they painfully hit your eardrum.' added Fred.

'The same effect can probably be obtained from drinking a capful of white spirit,' said Laurie, 'although nobody would do it. Whatever it is that you need the Civil Service will never adopt the pachinko slot machine hand over time etiquette to collect mobile phones and belongings, it will always be in the internal mail or will take ten days to process. The Civil Service will eventually die of a heart attack following the use of option one's betablockers, option two's bypass, or require the assistance of option three - Dr Madi Jacoob for a transplant.

'Does it want to be buried or cremated?'

'As it's already buried in paperwork with condolences, regrets and deepest sympathies, it would be better to opt for cremation than stick to an urn!' replied Laurie. Then continued,

' I never promised you a rose garden so why not set up a community kibbutz garden of remembrance or English vineyard, give everyone one share and enforce homebrew to compete with the breweries and make Lloyd George turn in his grave. Then send one of Boris Johnson's selection of e cards and T shirts or Boris Johnson Playtex Cross Your Heart line in bras and play the Bette Lynch Crumpet Voluntaire.'

Walking from the tube stop, black leaves fell from the silhouetted trees above her, touching her face and blown away in the wind. Snowflakes against a cliché sunset sky. The lake, normally round appeared as a silver blue line collaborating with the orange reflection of the sky as she neared it . When she arrived home Fred made beetroot and vodka soup and bulgar wheat with pomegranate, red onions and herbs .

Fred rang up a friend.

'I've just made a homemade bomb out of a six pack box, red and black liquorice shoe laces, digital egg timer and some tin foil. And some sausage dynamite with last years sparklers. It's more entertaining than the snooker on television set. New Mission – washing up.'

' Explosive device – which liquorice shoe lace did you cut?' asked Fred's friend.

'I don't remember, the red one I think, I ate them both. If it's fine next Saturday we're going to Epping Forest for a walk and maybe to Waltham Abbey, Enfield Lock or Walthamstow dog track. The haunted hollows of Henry VIII! Do you want to come ?'

'Yes. I'm starting a new job on Monday. I'll need to do something different at the weekend . Can you make Wednesday evening - bowling ? We're putting two teams together for the old green. I've never made a strike yet. I'm useless. I'm not the best example of the teams standard though .'

'Great ! Do we get to wear the funny shoes and drink beer ?'

'Of course! G&T's actually and sandwiches.'

Wednesday evening they met at a bar before the bowling and left the table covered in beer bottles waiting for a strike. Fred did not like the shoes , they were sweaty and old. Fred's friend fancied someone on the other team. She went to get the bowling ball feeling twice as self conscious. She rolled it aiming straight for the middle having no idea how to do curve balls or spins .

I'm going to do this really badly. I'll look stupid. I don't care, I care,I don't care. I hope it goes straight off the grass.

She hit one of the other balls . As she turned to walk back someone said ,

'What was wrong with that one?' remarking about the one she missed and he added, 'I hadn't noticed that one.'

Fred's carbon neutral eco centre corps plans were nearly all drawn and the scale model needed about another day. The centre was a living organism with biorhythmic flow, bone structure a regenerative reproductive system, facilities and features fed by the local waterways. The Augustian Abbey grounds were unusually active. Children dressed as Saxon knights were hiding behind trees firing little Saxon arrows as the serious archery took place in a safer walled area beyond the original 1060 cloisters. The church windows were gothic outlines from the exterior viewed from the graves of Banbury and King Harold where a man in a sweatshirt and a zoom lens was photographing the stonemason's work. Inside the church Abbey the bright colours, predominant areas of blue, pink, red, yellow and white told of the

surrounding histories between the round arches, which stacked in rows of reduced diameter up to the astrology ceiling. Fred's friend lit a candle by the harlequin pumpkin harvest display and read the engraved panels on the floor by his pale blue Kicker boots. Then he joined the others outside by the falconry display of hunting behaviour. There were five birds, an eagle with a bright yellow beak and feet, a falcon, an owl with huge orange eyes and a hawk. Fred's friend studied the line of the yellow mouth. At the sound of the whistle the eagle owl left it's stand and flew low to the ground for about fifty to a hundred metres before it's sharp flesh ripping claws landed on the trainer's thick leather gauntlet. Venison and wild boar filled the air with hunger for game as the mediaeval wounds effects department made up the tin helmeted knights in red crosses and red tunics. Inside the main tent a potter's wheel produced more victims as other kids made mediaeval snails. For some reason they were popular. This may have had something to do with the topical French menu of escargot and frogs legs as the England France rugby match was being played simultaneously to the re-enacted Saxon battle. Fred threw some clay at the wheel with some water and made a hole in the middle with her thumb. Then started pulling the clay up to make a vessel as see had seen on the T.V. intermission that filled the gaps between programmes before adverts and soap operas.

'That's good.' said Fred's friend.

'I hate you you're out of control!' she screamed at the turning pot trying to keep it on the wheel. Then said 'Don't ask me what it's supposed to be.'

'I spoke too soon.- They have asymmetrical espresso sets in the Conran Shop like that!'

Other stalls had make your own crown and homemade chutneys. They reformed in the ale tent to recover from the garden walk before heading to the birch , beech, pollarded hornbeam and oak of Epping Forest where the eleventh century horse trials of mediaeval knights were being usurped by mountain bikes. Watervoles darted for cover into the yellow gorse and holly as spiders and harvestmen made webs in the Banbury hobbyhorse sticks. She will have music wherever she goes. Rings on her fingers and bells on her toes. Then they set off to find the long horn cattle that graze in the forest. The swans and geese watched the dog walkers and joggers from the boating lake. William Morris and Ophelia were here.

She could think of better breeds to take for a run. A jogger wearing white sweatbands and a pulse gadget passed them followed by a Daschund running flatout.

'Should we hire some boats and invade the opposite shore. He wanted to land his boat with all the oars held vertically. Another woman was discussing her dogs. She had about eight to ten on leads.

'That's my bark is better than your bark!' she said, 'They also have playful, aggressive or attention seeking.'

They collected some chestnuts to roast later. Fred collected some foxgloves.

'Excuse me for being an otaku - Japanese anorak – I have an interest in pressing flowers.'

As it was National Cheese Week with the cheese truckle tossing championship, the man in the moon from the fairy tale not the pub, was a piece short. A quarter phase or a quarter pound of cheddar to go with his Jean Paul Sartre ploughmans.

'The stout old gentleman grunted. Mathieu was conscious of a thrill of joy it was all over. Tomorrow – Nancy, war, fear, death perhaps and freedom.'

Fred spotted a famous actress. Noting her pale blue suit she was surprised at seeing her. She was reminded of the occasion a year later when the actress' once screen husband was in a different drama wearing an identical pale blue sweater and shirt. They must either share the same agent or devotedly watch each others clothing careers she thought. They looked at a restaurant menu and decided to eat at home. When she got back she got out the recipe for choufleur au neige – cauliflower in snow.

Scald the milk with a piece of onion and butter rubbed in flour. Stir with a wooden spoon. Add the grated cheese and whisk in the egg whites. Pour over the cauliflower. Make four pockets and drop four egg yolks into them. Cook for twenty minutes.

Taylor told Fred about a trick they used to do as kids. They had placed two eggs, one in each pocket of his friend's jacket and then smashed them for a laugh.

Walking passed the restaurant, there was a cooled lavabed, a glacier of mail, overlapping junkmail, party political circulars, directmail, bankmail spreading across the floor towards the tables where the chairs were piled on top of the tables. Four to six months of scaled envelopes and once molten messages. Was there a dead body inside somewhere or had the owners returned home to Greece for a family event. They had stayed to take over the family business in her imagination following a death in the family or the business had turned bad and the lease was paid up, letting the staff go.

A full bodied man in a panama hat with county coloured ribbons and a matching blazer, pink shirt and off white trousers sat down legs astride a large brolly , throne and sceptred with both hands on top of the wooden handle opposite her. The bus stopped opposite the restaurant and she got off .

Fred got off the bus and walked the usual five minutes contemplating the recent Greek fires in Athens; the news showed helicopters dropping measured quantities of water and men digging 'Ha Ha ' trenches to stop the fires spreading further. She had invitations to pick almonds in shadey groves with gaggles of geese and ducks pecking at the seeds and fallen fruit in the dust at a Gerald Durrell reality show location. Historical Byzantium Greek earthquakes quickly cut to acupuncture appointments, Accies 0 - Aberdeen 3 and that afternoon.

Back inside the sculptor's studio a girl was using a jagged edged saw to cut a pomegrante in half .

"They look like genetically modified rose hips ."said Fred.

"Do you want some?" she offered one half and started eating the other raw .

" Have you ever tried them with duck or foul. One of the feasts from Like Water for Chocolate, I think or Persian soup ."

Eating it reminded her of a taped off C.S.I. Triad murder scene twenty years earlier causing the school smokers to find an alternative venue on Monday morning.

Her agent was making a deal on the telephone.

'He's not getting in or out of bed for anything less than fifteen .....one five .'

They chatted for about ten minutes then she dropped off the Wimbledon tickets to Robin for the next day .

The grass was already worn away after only three days and the queue of people waiting to board HMS Wimbledon and the sea of faces onboard the great liner was massive enough to make a pressgang shy. From the aerial shots, tennis whites fluttered like little sails on a green sea. A woman wearing an asymetric union jack jacket made a row of spectators stand as she walked to her seat. She made a perfect red admiral for the championship.

Most people had been queueing since 7.00am, some had camped overnight. PR giveaways kept them supplied with cold drinks and ear piece radios for the latest news and scores. Everyone was in good spirits singing and playing poker on the grass baise.

'Why do they pay £70 for a seat in the Centre Court?' said one girl in the queue who knew her favourite player was playing on Court 2 that afternoon.

Once inside they rushed passed the ivy clad building and shops selling merchandise, strawberries and champagne and went straight to the courts . They did not need the signposts to the museum and would probably have a picnic on the hill in the afternoon. They passed two players dressed in white tracksuits and sunglasses carrying bags and rackets .

'Thats Boris Leibnitz!' they giggled .

'Who's that dear?' asked the woman behind them .

'I didn't see dear.'

They located the right entrance and went and took their seats.

'Do they ever use the Centre Court as a concert venue like other sports arenas?' asked Taylor, 'Cliff Richard could do a concert - 'I'm not singing in the rain !' crazy not capitalising on potential revenue the rest of the year.'

'Spoil the exclusivity dear!' replied Fred.

'What Cliff Richard? '

The umpire called 'Quiet please !' and a pigeon flapped loudly disturbing the concentration .

They played the first set .The television cameras panned the painted faces and Mexican wave, a bit like a crowd of cock bating gamblers on 'e'.

'It must be awful being a linesperson .'

'Smart jackets.I like the white edging and striped shirts .'

'I understand they have to train at one of the major clubs for a season before they are selected and progress to being an umpire .'

'They've not been replaced   by computers yet. Like gold leaf leatherbound books and print on demand. Do you think they ever will ?' asked Fred.

'I doubt it .' replied Taylor.

'I used to play at lunchtimes at school. When the balls were white or yellow   and the courts were   grass or hard surface. You think you're playing quite well until you recede yourself when The Head Umpire's daughter starts playing on the court next to you.'

'Now the courts are either clay or blue and the balls are different pressures. What percentage of people do you think would   prefer it if the game was umpired solely by a hi-tech hawkeye?'

'67% apparently think that the linesmen should stay.'

An older couple arrived and sat in the seats next to them .

'Good afternoon. I hear Boris Leibnitz lost, is that right?'

'Yes we saw him leaving earlier surrounded by giggling girls .'

A ball boy raised his arm ready to throw a ball .

Another politician claimed expenses for another Wimbledon season ticket and the proportional representation of M.P.s got confused with the running of the 8.15am to Waterloo. Leaves on the line again. Signal failure at Clapham Junction.

Taylor took the chair for the new Milton Keynes project. He read out the points from the agenda as Fred took minutes.

'Proposals included for the new centre - sports facilities and traffic flow. We propose working with the local waterways to present a duel system with toll bridge to include both river crossings. Laurie is going to enlighten us with his research and knowledge of the Sandwich model in addition to discussing the new bus terminus. On the subject of buses, he has also managed to get a bus ticket fine to add to the existing parking tickets. Then we can hear about the G&T bowling green party and existing facilities before we level the old pavillion to make way for a larger football pitch.

Laurie had had a busy week compiling his research. At 10 o'clock the full moon was visible through an uncurtained window against a cloudless sky. Laurie was reminded of the bicycle thieves that half inched his Raleigh Apollo bicycle and applied some Tom Hanks re-entry tillemetry and calculated

how many degrees and the distance it had travelled around the Earth by the position it was in at 2am. In four hours out of twenty four it was a sixth of the way round. Sixty degrees or 4,150.02 miles /6,012.1km.The following night it was a higher orbital configuration in the window.

It didn't shed any light on the unanswered questions about corncircles or aliens but ....try walking in the middle of a vaste harvested stubbled wheatfield to see how big the round yellow bails are made by the combine harvesters and it's totally different from the view from a car experience. Golden Love among the Haystacks, tightly packed no chance of finding any needles and not a camel in sight. What any one would be doing trying to lose one in the first place was beyond him. They smelt dry and dull in need of sugar and water to make the wheat ears taste of anything recognisable .

The seaholly growing at the top of the tiered pebble beach at Sandwich had a few fishermen's cottages one way and hour glass industrial chimneys the other towards the cliffs. Blackberries lined the footpaths and hedgerows away from the tall bamboo like rushes that laid a backing track to the aural sound sculptured along the walk with wind, cicadas, cuckoos, reed warblers and sanddippers. Damsel flies and dragon flies made a distraction from the landscape and a disturbed partridge rapidly beat it's short wings to get airbourne. I've been watching too many Kate Humble nature programmes he

thought when he recognised an otter slide into one of the many Stour's tributaries. Coincidentally or not the same name as his great grandfather whose family possibly took it in Saxon times before the Dutch brought over silk,celery and other imports including elephants to wander around St James' park. And before the Earl of Sandwich put two pieces of bread around

a piece of meat. George Stowers of Tooting who told Laurie he took his bread and dripping on the bus to Queen Victoria's coronation and drank cold tea out of his saucer aged ninety eight going on eight ran with the soldiers had liverspots and massive ears that never stopped growing and he always wore a suit .

Distracted by red tape and parking tickets Taylor collected a fine for neglecting to touch his Oyster card on entering a bendy bus.

Passenger statement.

The passenger took a seat on the 436 at Marble Arch before swiping the Oyster on a bendy bus. I was asked to give my Oyster to the inspector immediately having swiped it. The Oyster card is valid. Inspector 3158 said that I technically was not paying for journey if I swiped it on exiting or getting it out of my pocket having sat down. She said that the Oyster was 'UNVALIDATED', that I paniced and got up to swipe it on seeing the inspector before the bus had started to move away from the busstop. If the technical 'UNVALIDATED' reason 04 for a fine exists, surely the passenger has to be leaving the bus, showing an intention not to use the Oyster or refuse to use it when asked to instead of a hasty accusation that I got up to swipe it when I saw the inspector and was accused and told that 'I was not going to.' The inspector said the only reason that I used it was because she got on the bus. Is there a rule that says passengers cannot sit down first?

I had already paid for my journey, had a valid ticket but was told the light had not turned green when I used the Oyster and the last journey on it was the 390 to Marble Arch. I would appreciate a withdrawal of the fine in writing as I cannot see any real fault, nothing has been done wrong to warrant it, the inspector might have pointed out it needed to be touch activated again to register the journey.

Fred tried to stop thinking about the project brief and meeting as she made her way home for the evening. The number 176 to Crystal Palace and Penge only moved fifty metres in half an hour in the afternoon traffic. A voice came over the bus radio advising the drivers to 'try and keep the yellow boxes clear to improve the flow.' Albanian flags with black eagles on red backgrounds were flown from nearly every car along Charing Cross Road, all of them using their horns in a constant, deafening, single note rhythm. The initial assumption was that the fans and supporters had won a football match.

Their celebrations added to the rush hour congestion.

'Hot dog! Jumping frog ! Alberqurky !'

Fred always enjoyed singing along to that.

Prefab Sprout knew what they were singing about. Thank you Mark Twain. On the 10 o'clock news it was announced that Kosovo was celebrating it's independence from Serbia. Maybe the traffic would move on with the nations post traumatic growth.

'I don't know said the great bell of Bow

You owe me three farthings said the bell of St Martin's '

National budgets and bus fares. Fred knew that you can abandon your Oyster journey for another day or take an alternative route. But Fred would never know what leaving the emerald green tie, crisp white collar, leaf green sweater and dark grey suit to continue on it's journey without carnal knowledge or to further enjoy his choice of colour scheme inline with the textile, texture of an abstract painting would produce.

Benefits of walking instead may include finding a geranium bush the size and age of India requiring Olympic Baby Bio testing and enjoying the biblical lighting hitting the houses in St James's, Hyde Park Gate and Fitzroy Square lived in by the likes of Pepys, Virginnia Woolf and other diarists who never had to complain about the noise. Two old chinese ladies were sitting on the back seat of the bus with SeeWoo carrier bags full of banana leaf, dried fish and noodles. They looked about sixty but were probably hundred and still lived in Kowloon despite going home to Folest Hirl and Clystal Parace. Tea and yum yum chinese donuts in the Kowloon café Gerard Street for the game theorists doing behaviour study dilemas. Were they on the wrong side of the road or going the wrong way up it, one is in breech of the Geneva Convention,

and neither were going anywhere. An earlier sitting included the local triads and a B.N.I. American Breakfast club.

Fred's new business had a start up loan secured, no snitching and pay offs. It was an evolving baby delivered with forceps and an epidural into the lifecycle of the different ages of man. Building customers from the existing market and adapting to stay ahead of the competition. It had focus tasks and deadlines, market research and cashflow. Charing Cross Road was waiting to be paid with 7% interest, the bus was being used as Copydex credit, other roads were getting paid by the congestion charge in the City Savings Bank. She got off the bus and took the tube and collected her business cards ready for the meeting she had with Laurie the following day.

Laurie was in early and checking his emails.

Dear Laurie

Jambo

Good wishes to you and god's blessings. Today the pineapples harvested are at the plantation. The machines cutting them in boxes and putting them at the cannery on the conveyor belts and in the trucks to going into the town airport. All our fields are now empty .

Michu sends his wishes. His wife has a new baby and the party lasts all weekend on the 16th. I send you a picture to see the joy in our houses for you and look foreward to your next visit .

all my blessings to you Moffat

Dear Moffat

Jambo.Habari?

Last weekend we walked into Brockenhurst. The walk to the village through the Manor fields, along the public footpath usually only takes about twenty minutes but the irrigation was particularly bad. Where the horses had rode earlier the path was a swamp between the clumps of grass and oak leaves. We named the field New Nairobi and longed for the summer again when we could play on the swing over the river, jumping off it into the cool water. The reeds are a pale gold at the moment not the lush green they were in July.

Have the pineapples been harvested yet ?

We were lucky to see a brown owl fly out from some trees near the nature reserve, more of a nightime hunter. Fred said it was a pigeon, but I'm sure it was a bird of prey. It's flight was silent , unlike the familiar beating wings of a pigeon taking off. It was something I had noticed at the demonstration in Walthamstow .

We cut through the windy stepped brickwall alley once trodden by sailors back from visiting Vasgo da Gama's ports and drinking quantities of Mateus and Portugese Vino Verde. My hair was windswept like a new forest pony grazing on the cold heather moors.

We bought some chips from the Fish and Chip shop and covered them in salt and vinegar, the smell is delicious enough on it's own but it makes you want some, even though you wouldn't eat the ingredients separately and one or two of the greasy deep fried potatoes are all you really want.The seagulls want them too. Any more than a couple and you're just eating them because you're agreeing with your weaker half. You've already decided they're nice and know that you like them. Taylor says I'm like the food taster in the Madness of King George. He is always hungry and can eat everything on his plate .

We rambled back up the cobbled street looking at the voodoo /charm bracelets and other jewellery in the windows, romantic Valentine presents waiting to get listed in practical contents insurance policies or thrown back at a lover in a jealous tantrum on a psychological guilt trip.

Kwaheri tulonana

Goodbye write soon

Laurie

'I was reading my favourite sports magazine last week ',said Laurie, 'and I noticed Mars has reverted to the old Stirling Moss ' Work Rest & Play strapline but now dropping the and and adding bullet points.The Mars ice creams are now however straplined as ' a little bit tasty'. The other thing I noticed is that Mars is now not a major sponsor of the

England team but official supplier to them, whatever that means.There must be a technical difference because it's not allowed on their clothes .'

'Maybe they should be given Minstrels instead.' said Fred .

'Other things I noticed. Andy Murray now has a brother who plays tennis, introduced to us by a Highland spring advertorial page. I fear that this might

reflect the average English armchair tennis fan [me included] who still believes that Wimbledon is the only championship and fed by the media foodchain '. Taylor knew the processes for organising a tournament by ceremonially pulling names of the seded players   out of a bag   and contemplated how we are now eating more cereal to fund the facilities to train them by collecting packet tops. A Man of the Match title is slightly more interesting and financially rewarding than sponsoring vegetable of the season he thought .

Jamie Murray we are reliably informed drinks lots of water .

Where do sportsmen and women fit up the foodchain ? he wandered. They have plenty of natural predaters but few of them would be seen playing in a wheatfield or harvesting a marrow .They are accompanied more often than not by beer and wine and sent off as dramatically as a grape harvest raised to the ground by bad weather. You won't hear it through the David Vine, you'll read it in the Grape Press.

Having left no stone unturned for the leisure centre and football grounds requirements Taylor presented their pitch sketches and said,

'This   brings   me to the conclusion   and the paragraph about sponsorship for the sports plans and facilities.'

Christmas shoppers were dressed for the weather, not for any particular event. Unco-ordinated hats, coats and boots shopped with a goal to accomplish. Alpaccha macchu picchu hat and silver fake fur overcoat, red leather boots, trousers and a red jacket, peroxide hair and a fur collar, a mass of brown, grey and blue, velvet hat with flower, camel coat, denim trousers, Agnes B bag, lots of Uggs and scarves, plastic bags from supermarkets and department store bags hanging from every handle and hook, shelf and pocket of Maclaren buggies. Indifferent bus stops, rushing on board suddenly, the tubes on time with the usual Christmas hats and phone photos of office parties.

The library opened at 9.30am. A computer class was booked on the A-E terminals. O.A.P.s learning Windows and one end of a mouse from the other, keen to be on Facebook and not let the grandchildren have all the fun. It was three hours until lunch. One hour teaching and two on the returns, the classics were in need of alphabetical order and philosophy and self help needed a tidy.

'Did you know you have cotton wool in your ears Fred ?!' asked Taylor.

'Did you say something? I can't hear you ! I have cotton wool in my ears.' answered Fred.

'What about – why did the dyslexic banker not get interest on his client's loan? Because he paid in arrears!'

They sat under the large antler shooting trophy on the wall in the pub at lunchtime and had a pint and a sandwich.

Fred's pint was nearly finished, it had been about fifteen minutes, then the cavalry arrived to fight another round. Frank appeared with his author friend who lived in the converted stables. His girlfriend had said how awful it must be with the smell and all that. He was going to get a ready meal T.V. dinner on the way home. It was the most expensive and dullest food to eat but the packaging said otherwise.

'My friend has some friends coming from Italy to study, to get out of their National Service.' said Frank, 'He said that they had no references, bank papers and bills and the rent down payments for a flat would be six months up front or there was a Russian guy who had an agency, charges £60 for a guaranteed flat search and introduction. He gave me a card. I thought it might help Gladis.'

Gladis had written at least a dozen letters to her local M.P. , Mrs Hetty Upton and made daily visits to fill in complaints forms to the D.W.P. Housing Office signing the documents and dealing with forms and red tape. Enough paperwork to compete with China's usual intake of recycled paper from the U.K., usually three million tonnes, although the figure has been reduced by 50% this year and many paper packaging plants are closing due to the climate change restrictions and views on over packaged goods. Gladis was finding it obvious that single women with dependency were the priority and everyone else was just a statistic.

Fred decided to invite Gladis to dinner with Frank and the Italian friends using the Russian card as an icebreaker. They went back via the supermarket to look for blackbread, vodka and pirowski. Feeling like freedom fighters they managed to drink a bottle of gin with a box of Gordon Ramsey's luxury chocolates whilst looking. It was decided that Gladis' idea for a P.O. Box was a good idea, she would stay with the fireman, airhostesses and agency nurse on a timetable of shifts, it beat the £35 per night in a hotel and avoided having to stop her benefit until she secured a new address and she could put her stuff in storage.

'It's a strange world, one jew dies but another jew, a counterfeit is saved.' Fred quoted from the Primo Levi he was putting back on the shelf in the library.

'That sounds more like a buddhist philosophy to me Frank. Someone dies and someone is born. How do you balance the population these days as people live longer. Sid's friend got knocked down in her twenties and got £50,000 in insurance for brain injuries. It gives you goose bumps and déjà vue just thinking about it .' said Laurie.

'It's one way of making your own path in life driving up the pavement. Last time you said you heard trombones coming from the garden next door. Are you sure you've not been smoking again?'

'Absolutely!'

'That's a relief.'

The next day they went to the Russian's agency in Brook Street opposite a flat once lived by Jimmy Hendrix from 1968-69. It resembled a naf cocktail bar with a silver art deco interior after the Palm Court of The Park Lane Hotel with faux Egyptian carpets. They took the deposit for six weeks and paid six weeks in advance, viewed the three flats and successfully secured an agreement. Gladis then had to complete a change of address form for the assessors. Still bitter at not receiving the £1000 back from her previous landlord who had disappeared out of the country, despite her own court order and Citizen's Advice Bureau lawyer's assistance in trying to retrieve the money. This was after having sat out the three months as listed in the Citizen's Advice Bureau form about Section 21s and Court Orders. Gladis was sick of forms, she had read the lot and redesigned a few as well.

'People always apologise for sending form letters. Which is funny, why do they bother. I have a file of rejection letters from publishers from writing my first book,' said the guy who lived in the converted stable. 'They're remarkably original with impersonal approaches. I think I might propose publishing them as a book on how many original and literary ways of saying the same thing.' The guy who lived in the stables smiled to himself.

'That's red tape for you or in the case of the publisher – read proposal! There's always the possibility they could publish talking books for the blind on any colour tape. My attempt at a joke. What next?' asked Taylor.

'Get another drink!'

The guy who lived in the converted stable went up to the bar.

'When do you get the keys Gladis?' asked Taylor.

'Tomorrow.'

'Airhostess doesn't mind, she's away for Christmas anyway.' said Gladis, then she said quietly, ' He's not called Joseph is he?'

'No, thank god!'

'All you need now is to have an accident and wake up in St. Marys!'

'Are you sure you want her as a girlfriend' asked Fred's friend at the bar.

'She sounds like bad luck to me. Hardly good luck unless you have a disability or dependency to make you a priority for the Red Cross, Sally Army or Community Housing.'

'Self help roulette! Are you coming round for Christmas lunch? I read a Jack Keraouac this week. Remind me to return it or it will be overdue.

There's that Oceans film on about the guys and the casino with what's that blokes name who had the bags of money with the three kings. He was in Dead Calm too.'

'Yes, sounds great what should I bring?'

'A packet of Rizla and a bottle of wine or beers.'

Fred put a reference book on the Hoover Building back in the architecture section.

'Those architects get everywhere these days. The garage I used to use was bought by one and he turned it into a designer flat. There's no where in central London where you can get a car M.O.T. or service. But at least your car doesn't end up on bricks when someone needs some tyres anymore.' said Taylor.

'No they're more likely to go for New York loft style exposed brick work and recycled tyre souled flip flops with headlight lighting.' said Fred.

'Here's something for Gladis, Fred. The English Tourist Board Heretige trail here has an interesting piece on John Wilkes and freedom of the press in the eighteenth century. And there's another on Maharajah Duleep Singh the last King of Punjab who was pensioned off to an estate in Norfolk when British rule took over. Shall I photocopy it for a present?'

'Sounds great she'll like that. Champions of libel or liberty. The Civil Service post colonial expansion – they only work from 9-4 pm these days. What once was a hangovered Hogarth cartoon –"nothing functions very well until after Tiffin and then everything stops for tea!" ' replied Fred.

Laurie's traffic system and toll bridge was well received. The toll bridge would pay for the upkeep of the old bridge and ease the major artery flow from the new river-crossing further north. They decided that revenue to build the new Milton Keynes had come from the parking ticket and fines departments that were totally unmanned, just red tape, recorded messages and system produced standard responses. Taylor got nowhere with his parking ticket. In fact it had doubled in price.

Fighting Weight

Jack sprat could eat no fat
and his wife could eat no lean
so between them both you see
they licked the plate clean

Jack Sprat came from a very large family. His temperate relatives, known for taking off their little silver jackets in the heat , liked to cure themselves in salt and called themselves anchovies.He had too many relatives to remember all their names but he always remembered what they told him. When the anchovies get out of the sea, it's salt cures amnaesic shellfish poisoning, potential smell and rot is removed by osmosis and they absorb the salt instead.

Jack Sprat decided to go round the world and visit his temperate relatives where some grew as big as herrings. Some were made into Patum's gentleman's relish and eaten on toast, others mixed with eggs, olive oil and garlic to make fresh Caesar salad dressing in Mexico and were eaten with fresh hearts of Romane. But they were best known for sitting on pizzas in Napoli. According to Jack Sprat, Patum's Peperium, The Gentlemen's Relish established 1828 42.5g is no longer unique. There is now a Poacher's Relish added to the individual product range in ceramic jars; although this does not detract from the anchovy's fame. Jack Sprat had believed for ages that the Caesar's Salad dressing was a signature dish from Caesar's Palace Casino in Mexico and not a story told to him by a pickled herring from Crystal Palace. He was put straight one day by a Roman Sprat who was more familiar with the fish knife back stabbing original and historical version of the story that refered to the famous Anthony, Cleopatra and Emperor Julius Caesar who was filleted by his own senate - typically more a kin to the angling school of jokes .

In India Jack Sprat's cousins thought he was definately underweight . His Hindu cousins said to cure his' kohlum' he should find and eat the healthy sesame seeds symbol of immortality. They described the green pods of the sesame plant and the white and purple flowers known in Urdu literature and proverbs for meaning place so crowded that there is no room for a single seed , 'til dharnay ki jagah na hona', and told him if he ate them then he would not have a problem with his fat but he might end up looking more like a sardine .

'Why should I believe you ?' Jack Sprat asked his Indian cousin.

'Because I'm telling you .'

'OK so why does your toque hat have the same name as a french chef's?'

'Probably because we are used to the English coming here and trying to boss us around ! Now go and look for the sesame seeds !'

Jack Sprat laughed and said he would find some straight away. He set off through the lush green countryside. Soft low cantations from the temples travelled through the streets and across the fields as the flowers dripped water from the early monsoon rains. He looked all day and watched the elephants drinking by the river hiding from the Keralan fishing boats with reed roofs that bobbed up and down on the water. At last he found a plant with a green pod. He picked one and walked back along the red earth road in the dry heat to his cousins .

Unfortunately the green pod he found had white seeds that fitted the description but when he ate them it was so hot he had to drink lots of water. His cousins said it must have been a green chillie. Before he left they made him a tomato and coconut curry and they listened to a concert played on a sitar and an instrument with eighty strings. He thanked them for their hospitality and carried on his travels to find the sesame seeds, symbol of immortality.

When he got to Italy, his Italian cousins in Napoli teased him about the chillie when he told them and gave him a caper instead to laugh about his silly mistake.They told him not to lose his cool, take off his jacket or lose his head if he wanted to keep going or he would end up in a big oven on a pizza lying around like a pair of Gucci loafers. Jack Sprat thanked them and told them that his Egyptian cousins also ate the latin black bread Picea seasoned with herbs originally made to celebrate the Pharoah's birthday. And when the anchovies kept their silver jackets on, the Napolitana was taken off the menu and more people ate

Margheritas. He said he would tell them how nice the capers were and that Italian pizza was the best in the world.

Not put off by his failure to find the sesame seed plant and symbol of immortality, Jack Sprat continued on his journey. In Spain he was told to look for the white' ajonjoli' sesame to boost his weight but the green vegetables he found were all cucumbers and olives. He told his Spanish cousins about his Italian cousins and they warned him if he teased the Spanish they would take him to the bullfight, make him fight the bull and then eat paella with lots of saffron and watch the hot blooded flamenco.

'It wasn't you that told the seis pescetas to return the six squid to the eight octopus then?'

His cousins were not too sure what he meant but did not want to look stupid .

'No .' they said, then told him that the olives were harvested by beating the trees and collecting the olives in nets underneath, then some were pressed to make oil and this was used to store the rest of the harvest. Sometimes anchovies were rolled around the olives, served as canapes and eaten with champagne. His cousins warned him to be careful of the farmers they might try to catch him and gut him like the fishermen as they went together really well. They decided to do something with the cucumbers he had found, as it would be a shame to waste them and they could keep cool in the sun. His cousins sliced them up and made a big salad then used some of the remaining slices to put on their puffy eyes to rehydrate and keep them shiney and bright. They also polished their fins with them like a manicure or 'finicure.'

Jack Sprat thanked his cousins for their wonderful hospitality and the sprat spa and set off refreshed and cleansed. He travelled to the port of Aligeceras where he disguised himself as a trader and enquired about the boats to Africa.

'There wouldn't be a boat for about three days because of an approaching storm ...' said some sailors, but they knew of an albatross that was flying to Tangiers, maybe he would take him. Jack had heard about Phoencian sailors who painted the evil eye on their boats to protect them from bad spirits and storms and he also knew he should avoid sea birds.

'It takes ten years for the crayfish to grow to full size, ten minutes to catch one and ten minutes for them to be eaten.' said one sailor before adding ,

'it also takes ten minutes to sink the fishing boat in a storm and he was not going to risk it .'

Jack knew he was in great danger, he felt his disguise had worked with the sailors and he was confident it would fool the albatross. The albatross flew Jack from Spain to Tangiers where he was going to see a friend before going to Venezuala where he had heard there was another albatross.

'Why are you going to Africa and Arabia ?' asked the albatross .

'To be as free as you and find the famous sesame plant.'

'Its more like a tin of sardines in the kasbahs, you'll get crushed!' replied the albatross who laughed to himself and flew away .

From Tangiers Jack Sprat travelled through Africa where his African cousins had also heard of the lightening seeds, symbol of immortality that popped when they were ripe, he found lots of gourds and beans but no sesame ' benne' pods as they were known. They drank some honey beer and worried about the rains instead. The farmers needed the Harmattan trade wind from the Gulf of Guinea in Ghana to bring the clouds and rain to grow a decent peanut yield and a good harvest of sesame to make the tahini paste, tatziki and sugary nut brittle that was very popular.

Jack Sprat got his honey beer hangover up early the next day and swam to the Spice Islands , but all he could find were green coconuts , vanilla pods , flowers and cardamom seeds . He climbed the coconut palms and followed the different scents on the breeze collecting the different spices to show his cousins but could not hear any pods popping dispite keeping his gills open. His cousins used the spices to make a big bowl of ice cream and several pina coladas made with sugar cane, spirit and cream from the village cow and he told them about the Africa rains needed for the savannah drought in the desert and plains of Africa.

'In the islands we have more clouds made from the sea in the equator, it evaporates and condenses over the mountains where it cools. That's why it's so lush here compared to Africa.' advised his cousins .

Jack Sprat did not want to leave the beautiful shells and beaches of the Spice Islands. He wanted to stay under the shade of the mango and palm trees all day forever and watch the pretty grass skirts walk past. But his wife who could eat no lean was expecting him back .Tainted love was for turbot and trout he thought, then he looked at his confetti covered wedding photo in his wallet and missed his home. He thanked the Spice Island cousins for their hospitality and waved goodbye and left the white beaches and cool scented breezes for the hot deserts of Arabia.

When he arrived at the dunes and deserts along the banks of the Nile he found his Arabic cousins and told them the story about looking for the sesame plant too. His Arabic cousins said the green pod sounded like a green chillie but he had to really listen hard for the 'jaljala' echo of the ripe pod going 'pop', then he would know it was definately a sesame seed pod, symbol of immortality, not a firey chillie in Cairo. They said if he found one they would get it gold plated for him to keep. Maybe there was too much jungle noise of water, birds, monkeys and crickets. The best time to listen was in the morning, and avoid eleven and four when they had the call to prayer, it was impossible to hear anything then. They also said it was why the actors opened the door to the treasure caves in the pantomimes by saying the ' open sesame ' speak and spells.

'I'll listen for the vibrations,' said Jack Sprat 'because didn't you know that fish don't have ears on the outside of their bodies, they have internal ears .'

He spent all day listening for the popping sound then returned to his cousins who reminded him of smoked mackerel. After a big dinner and lots of mint tea in a room with lots of woven carpets where they saw more than genies in the smoke coming from the from the oil lamps.

'Maybe there is a carpet with the location of the immortal sesame seed. My wife will make you a carpet about the story of your journey for when you return. We will make lots of carpets and sell many, telling of your adventures.'

'What would you wish for if you had three wishes?' asked his cousin.

'To.............. to find the sesame seed plant and get some ears! ' said Jack .

Determined to be a great adventurer remembered by his grandchildren rather than a diminished epigon, Jack continued to visit his anchovy cousins in Siberia and look for the Russian 'kunzhut' sesame seeds to cure his underweight 'kohlum'. He had brought some cabbages and onions with him from the souk to use as barter and bribes in his quest for the sesame. His experience told him this was a good idea as he had been to his cousin's wedding five years earlier. It was nice to be back in the USSR and see what had changed. They welcomed him with vodka, cheeses and pumpernickel. He told them about the Arabian prayer mats, mint tea and listening for the popping sound.

'We have Russian samavar if you prefer tea. Russian Sprats do not need ears to hear the sesame popping. We have listening devices from the cold war with the American Sprats at best black market prices. We can detect the sesame if it even whispers!'

Jack then told them about the albatross and the storm and the genies in the lamps and they replied that the Russian lamps used the fat from the fascist pigs and that if any genie appeared in his house he would have to drink vodka too.

'What would you wish for?' he asked his Russian cousins.

'Three Russian wishes - to drink best Russian vodka everyday, live in Winter Palace and own the best Russian football team .'

When he got to Japan in the spring he found the paddy fields beyond the cherry blossom and beyond that he found the endomame and green soya beans. One step beyond that he found his cousins . A step in Japan was like a zen kilometre in sprat terms. His cousins did not understand why he needed to be any fatter unless he wanted to be a sumo wrestler sprat, they looked at the soya beans and rice plants but could not see any sesame seed plants amongst them. They were impressed with his Russian listening device and said he should enjoy the nori seaweed while he was there and drink some sake and plum wine with his terriyaki and tell them more about his travels. Jack Sprat sang some karaoke and bowed good night. Turning Japanese was fun ! He was happy and decided to go back to Great Britain he would swim the Pacific then traverse America and swim the Atlantic.In fact he crossed the Pacific in the swimming pool of a cruise ship where they ate lots of green olives on plates and drank cocktails because they were scared of sharks. And his route sixty six he spent in the water tank of a Harley Davidson motorcycle looking out of a port hole wearing a jacket and helmet made from a wine bottle top and seal.

He swam up the Hudson River in New York to the Statue of Liberty where he met some cousins who had some cactus and tequilla. Jack's cousins thought maybe the cactus plant looked a bit like a sesame pod but they had eaten the mescalin worm that lived in it. This was meant to be a bit like taking LSD so Jack did not take their word for it.

'maybe it is and maybe it isn't a green sesame pod.' they said to Jack Sprat and smiled .

Eventually he returned home to his wife via visiting some distant Welsh relatives in Lake Llyn-y-Cau in Calder Idris, a high lake above sea level in the mountains near Snowdonia. Far from the manic streets of Marrakesh he could still feel the hot desert winds and hear the male voice choirs in the valleys. His cousins said the japanese seaweed sounded awful and nothing beat the camphor and seaweed on the welsh coast, they also said that sesame didn't grow in Wales but they had some in the local supermarket. Jack bought a packet for 20p and took them back to his wife who added them to their plankton and they listened to pop music instead and stayed away from the flock of seagulls.

The Case Of The Turn Up And Down

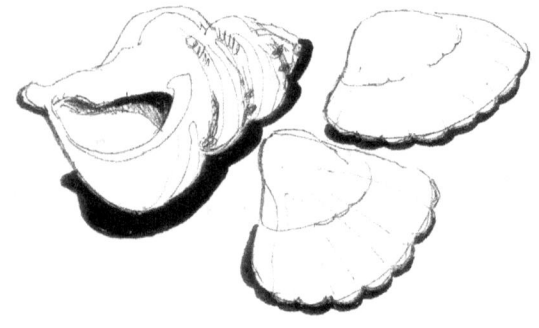

Poseidon was due to appear in the Whitstable parade the following day. A local school had made fish costumes and would be following the enormous papier mache headed sea god through the streets past the village shop and Post Office in the annual blessing of the catch. The parade usually stopped the buses for about three hours while the fishermen put on their traditional sweaters and bowler hats and sailed a smack ashore to be greeted by the Mayor and press waiting on the pebble beach. In the evening the pebbles were made into small piles resembling shrines with little candles as part of the villages fishing tradition. Pagan Morris dancing usually started at about 2pm with a white bleached horse's skull on a cloth covered pole. Mrs Partridge sat at the small desk in the village museum every day curating the displays and information on the boats and oysters.

It was Sunday morning at 11.45 am and Poseidon's neighbour, Alice had disappeared. She was due to be working on the chutney and jams stall starting at 12.30 am.

'She would have rung me if she was going away.' said Mrs MacKintire.

'I always feed the cat. And then there's the restaurant, who's going to open it. I'll call the waitress and ask if she knows anything.'

'Not appearing at the stall, Mrs West, is not enough reason for us to search her property or presume her missing, it has to be at least 48 hours before we do anything. But we can look through the windows and see if there is any disturbance.' said the police constable on duty at the parade who Mrs West had involved.

'There has to be a reasonable explanation.'

There was a small window open that the cats could get in and out of and a flower press and papers had been left on the table with some scissors and leaves. The room had a belle epoque air to it with grand tableau views of the countryside around the bridge and river. Birdsong twittered from the tree by the window and there was a strong scent of roses from the flower bed.

'That's a hobby of hers,' said Mrs West.

'Do you have any cat food ?' the constable asked. 'Maybe you could put some down for the cats. What are their names?'

'...Michelin....Pyrelli...and Dunlop.....'

Tourists and day visitors mixed with the village locals in the brewery owned pub and beach bars where huge quantities of oysters were consumed with tabasco and lemon.

'There's that man with the large sovereign ring again. Look .' said one of the locals.

'Reckon's himself he does !'

A week had passed.

'Is there anything on the body?' asked the detective inspector.

'Bag, purse and a mobile with several text messages.' replied PC Current.

'What do they say? Any leads?'

'This one says ....

SNAFU F2F something WOZ EZ SIT GG SUITM FR'

Situation normal all f**ked up, something was easy, see you in the morning got to go FR'

'Sounds like everything was OK and they were unaware of any problem.'

The detective inspector dialed the station and spoke to someone, gave instructions to the lab then put his phone away and straightened his cuffs. They sat in the car waiting for the Sargent Old to return. PC Current read the newspaper headline out loud.

'I thought you had lost your glasses.'

There was a picture of a woman in a French Couture naval style dress with anchors on the buttons.

'I can see through yours from this angle. That looks OK! '

'Oi! Get your own paper!'

'They are checking the numbers on the phone,' said the detective inspector as he got back into the car.

A week later there had been reported use of her credit card. They interviewed the shop and got a positive ID and description of a man with a sovereign ring. News spread rapidly; it soon became the regular topic in the barbers and tackle shop .

'It appeared she fell in love with a beautiful stranger like the Roxette song, ' the detective inspector explained, 'and took off without telling anyone. Nobody suspected she would ever do anything like that and she didn't want to spoil the excitement. They ended up in Ellen Vanin in the Isle of Mann. The car hire contract was only for mainland UK. The car hire company wasn't too happy it turned out. Seems they got a bit carried away. '

'When they checked the cottage to feed the cat, we found a Jazz album on the stereo, some salad and pigeon in the fridge, some baby doll pyjamas lying on the bed, not in the drawers, but not in a suspicious or evidently guilty way. There was also a copy of Thomas Hardy's Mayor of Casterbridge with notes in the margin and particular words and phrases underlined and an address book and notebook in her flower pressing equipment. It was written in French and we had to get a translator to sort out the chicken skittles and Coquilles St Jaques. It had us scratching our heads.

We've got the lab and Cambridge University analysing the Mayor of Casterbridge to see if it's anything more than o'level notes. It turns out Miss Alice Band, she's running a syndicate outside of Billingsgate with the fishermen and top London restaurants over the supply of oysters. Seems the syndicate has alot of control over them. She wasn't too happy about about her cottage being searched and despite the numbers matching those on the mobile we found there's nothing wrong .The syndicate are all like clams. Can't touch her or them. We have to be careful not to be accused of defamation says the Sarg.'

'What about the body on the beach ?' asked PC Current.

'Turns out she had followed him, Baroque the boyfriend here. He wanted her to see them together and she drowned herself. He's one of those golddiggers, he was stringing the girl along. He liked her being niave and dependant when he met her, then her dependency drove him mad. She didn't work, made him feel guilty all the time, the usual thing.

And he wanted Miss Oyster Syndicate to give up work so he could run her restaurant!' explained the detective inspector.

'What did she think of that ?' asked PC Current.

'Not a lot!'

The Case Of The Bolted Gate

There were already three people sitting in the bright waiting room, a small square room with one window, seating around the walls and a small modern pine table with magazines. Posters with Dos and Don'ts, A4 sheets of information about fire exits and what to do in case of a fire and a clock were positioned logically on the wall.

No petting, screaming, diving, running or ducking. The illustrated Dos and Don'ts rules from the swimming pool when you were eight, superceded by switch off your mobile phone, report to the assistant on duty, take a seat in the coral atoll waiting room on the modern pine chairs with padded upholstery, textiles and matching wallpaper pattern until called. A woman sat reading the newspaper wearing a small pad hat, it's tarletan covered crown had layers of short turkey and pheasant trimming with a foed single pheasant spine trim curled into a perfect arabesque. It demonstrated a modesty compared to the large ostrich feathers and long diamond tipped quills fluttering on the hats at Ascot. As she sat she studied the back of her hand and wandered why people said, 'I know you like the back of my hand.' How well do they know theirs? What could she really remark on. Less than the back of her knees and the French have a name for that, the jarret. It was smooth and fairly pale, the little knuckles were pink where the small sculptured bones articulated when she moved her fingers but she had not really thought much about it before!

An omnipotent official in charge of the jury escorted a fourth person into the silent room. Today's overheard telephone conversations that prompt a carphonewarehouse creche of broadcast dialing and texting, once an espionaged advantage, an infectious yawn, laugh or Lauren Bacall mirrored cigarette lighting.

'I spoke to Majorie Bramble. Yes the author. She was signing books in the bookshop. I don't believe I was talking to her. I've read all her books.'said the unashamed girl with the mobile phone without lowering her voice and blushing bright red.

A man in a brown herring bone suit took out his phone and pushed some buttons. The girl finished her call and said goodbye, the woman sitting next to her checked that hers was turned off as the official returned to show them to the preinstructed seats. It was not the woman with the hat's usual Film Society chair. She looked at the back of the coconut shy heads and prepared herself for the hoopla of questions to be thrown by the prosecution and defence. Exhibit 'A' was a sample of handwriting on a book of raffle tickets. It had been analysed by an expert graphologist as being aggressive and materialistic. He highlighted the lower third loop and tight middle third of the 'f', the missing dots on the letter 'i' and the mediterranean 'r' that appeared to be joined up like an English 's'. But moreover the line through the number seven was definately hegemonic of it's European hand.

The first defendant was sitting towards the front of the court with her solicitor. She looked about fifty five, had shoulder length styled hair complete with the oil and vinegar that went with the usual condiments that belied her years. I would not have been surprised if there was a bread roll in there as well. It was held in place at the back of her head with a lacquer grip and she was wearing an off white silk blouse and tweed skirt that fitted her position as secretary of the local Women's Institute and librarian.

Half the village had made the bus journey to the town court for the hearing, leaving the dry stone walls , footpaths, stiles, five bar gates with wool torn from sheep, now left as evidence in a CSI dna investigation instead of spun into balls to sit on the shelves of the local shop that had knitting patterns with pictures of fairisle sweaters, freckled faces and men with pipes. Monuments and water troughs punctuated the byways where the bakers, Post Office, butchers and dairy had heard more gossip in the last week than in the whole village history or at least since the church clock had stopped and Mrs Hobbs award winning roses had been sabotaged with greenfly, leading to an argument and punchup in The Farmer's Arms following several glasses of Montadillo Sherry.

The Verger's body had been found in his kitchen with the book of raffle tickets on it. The cause of death was determined as poison and the only food he had eaten was some buttered toast. Laboratory tests gave evidence that the bread had come from the village baker although it was not poisoned at source. This was known because nobody else had poisoned bread and the bread had all come from the same batch. In fact the dough was a continuous 'mother dough' added to in a daily and constant fermentation from the original one started in 1685, as old as the village shop. The investigating officer had found the source of poisoning to be the butter knife that also had traces of jam.

As one of the accused, the WI secretary sat listening to the prosecution. She knew the only crime she was guilty of was selling twice as many books of raffle tickets and declaring only half of them, pocketing the difference and burning the stubs. She knew there was no way they could prove this. It was no worse than the online click-on competitions, 20p a click, where there was no evidence that anybody won the signed Ronaldo football shirt. It was different in the days of 'finish the sentence in less than 12 words' tie breakers.

They had dismissed theft as a motive as none of the raffle prizes had been stolen. They had all played Little Red Corvette guitar by Prince on the Wii donated by the local Woolworths that had closed down and the church warden had made a joke about 'The Royal We' that made them all laugh.

In the village B&B, Mrs Jones was telling a young couple about the case while they enjoyed their kippers. They had Gretna Green written all over them, she thought, but in actual fact they were saving up for a flat deposit, and exploring the finer points of the English Tourist Board on a Housing Benefit misadventure. Mrs Jones' cat Montenegro sat watching the shadows made by a branch in the sun as the wind blew the lace net curtain and leaf patterns danced on the wall. She had taken Montenegro to the vets in the little caged basket last week for them to look at his paw. They clipped the claws and she bought a new collar. Mrs Jones scratched him behind the ears and grabbed the scruff of his neck, making him retract his claws and behave like a furry Jaguar gear box with the clutch in while she rubbed him under the chin. Then she let him go and he watched the beady orange eyed pigeons walk up and down the garden wall. She could hear the church clock strike across the square muffled by the wind.

'Would you like some more tea?' she asked the young couple holding the pink and white barley patterned tea pot with gold edging.

'Yes please.' said the girl as she reacted to the distinct aroma of Earl Grey while she took a spot glued sample of nude foundation to add to the perfume she already removed from the Vogue she was reading from the B&B lounge. They had also made full use of the trouser press and soap sachets available on their stay. Everything on the pale melon and emerald plates had been eaten and the pistacchio edge to the juice glasses had slight traces of kipper left from their need to slake their thirst.

She had said on the telephone that she could hear the clock strike three, which put her somewhere near the square and not the library. This was what made him suspect an affair.

Mrs Gate, the Verger's wife, was on the telephone to Mrs Pane arranging to deliver the raffle tickets. She had told her that her husband would be back at 5pm. This meant she was not any where near the library at the bottom of the hill.

'Can you prove it was 5pm not 3pm when you delivered the tickets? Are you sure you didn't leave the library and deliver them at 3pm calling Mrs Gate on your return trip?' asked the prosecution.

'Mrs Pane would have no reason to call to make arrangements if she had already delivered them, finding the Verger in.'

'But the Verger was not due back until 5pm.' said Mrs Pane.

The PC giving evidence read his report.

'The Verger's wife returned at 7pm and his body was discovered dead at 8am the next day. The neighbours said that they had heard an argument at some point in the evening about 9pm.'

There was a mysterious lacuna in the puzzle. It was suggested that Mrs Pane made two trips, the first to collect a book she had forgotten to return to the library and the second to deliver the raffle tickets.

The court asked the inspector what evidence he had found. He proceeded to give a factual narrative of the data the investigation had found.

'There appeared to be a trail of ants walking from the kitchen to the car which I followed to it's source at the radiator where a hole had been filled with jam and something else of a gelatine consistency. See Exhibit 'B'- laboratory report.' he paused as the paper was passed.

'It is an opinion that the radiator had blown and been temporarily repaired in the absence of a repair product like Radweld to drive it a short distance.'

The Verger's wife said in her statement that she had used a kitchen knife to put down some cyanide that evening to try and kill some ants that had appeared in the kitchen. She said the cyanide, sodium nitroprusside was for medical use in emergency situations prescribed for decreasing blood pressure.

[The jury retired and found motivation to do the washing up resulting in accidental death.]

The Pigeon Restaurant

The advertisement on the newspaper website said Restaurant Reception Manager / Front of House. It did not sound that sensational when she first read it , taking bookings and organising table sheets. Then on second reading the fresh spinach and haddock roulade tasted better as the thunder rolled outside, with a lightning reduction as the distant roll got closer and rain started dripping from the green roof tiles.

The coke machine in her office had started to sound like the techno electronic and ambient section in HMV with a note changing every thirty seconds instead of three. She worked out that she could afford to live on the £25,000 salary and invest in the £74,000 apartment in Dubai advertised on p.26 with £33,000 annual return from its company let , with a four week holiday home in the sun for her statutory twenty eight days off excluding sick leave. She would go to the Easter Egg Treasure Hunt at Blenheim Palace in the Capability Brown gardens and leave her chocolate egg packaging behind at the till in the supermarket in protest at the overpackaging of products to help with her green footprint. Many paper and board plants had already closed in and she would get in on the £390 m annual spend on media sponsorship increasing by 47.4% by 2012 . She was not sure how this would happen . A deal with Dubai airlines flight staff perhaps . Tidy ! She felt green global competiveness as she answered the ad and sent her submission in online. Vigilant of the Euro cratos she should have, she listed her languages that would benefit from use and her desire to repoliticise herself in the mix of Mediterranean food and wines while voicing her opinion that the UK as a whole should follow the slow food model being set for the Olympics in the sustainable London Loop and maybe cut cargo fuel emmissions rather than personal flights to help the nations conscience as a whole.

One week later she was asked to attend an interview. Was her suit good enough to pass the interview ? Maybe she would buy the emerald green silk blouse she had seen to go with the navy wool jacket with three quarter length sleeves and naval buttons . She had new shoes and a new Fiorella bag with a huge oversized silver purse clasp. Maybe a white shirt would be better.

She practised her joke as she was good at forgetting punchlines when she was nervous . How do you make a rabbit stew ? Leave it for three hours !or was it weeks. She was likely to walk in and tell them that the Eastern European country whose flags were being flown from every car in London had just won the Cup and then discover that they had just been given independence.

She arrived at the restaurant ten minutes early with maincourse Michelin star attention to her presentation, a caviar starter and spun sugar dessert. It was a W1 location with a roof garden and piano bar. She had to fill in a form before a woman in a Chanel suit with a pencil skirt and white edged jacket, cream silk shirt, fishnet tights and lots of gold chains and belts asked her questions   for about twenty minutes .

Why do you want to work for us ?

What experience can you bring to us ?

How would you deal with a suspect joke booking of 12 people that sounded like the preceeding person who booked one for 8 ?

How would you deal with a complaint by someone who refused to pay full price ?

Then she showed her a typical booking sheet with 3 tables of 6 , 2 tables of 8, 4 tables of 2 and an allowance for flexibility for another 10 at 9pm and asked her to plan 3 bookings for 2 hours ahead .

A week later she received an email to say that she had got the job. Would she be able to start straight away or next week. This amazed her as she had thought her table planning had caused chaos and wrecked the chefs budgets.

'Yes'. she said   straight away . Then she had a glass of wine, rang a friend and screamed quite loudly. She also rang the library to find out what they did if you had lost a book . As the price of replacing it new was less than the fine outstanding on it she decided to pay .Next question , would she seriously consider investing in the Dubai apartment, or was the sales pitch too good to be true .

The second night one of the rooms was booked for a debate event with a table for chair and speakers . There were photographers , guests coats, trays of wines and canapés.

I'd like to make a booking for 10pm on Monday 2nd .'

' Thank you Sir . How many people would that be for and in which name ?'

'Five people . Company Name .'

'Can I take the number please .'

One of the waitresses arrived with a payment and showed a table to their coats as she entered the booking .

'Could you inform table three that their mains are going to be another ten minutes. Somebody has put their foot in it about chef's something and he's gone off in a sulk. The new sous chef has also just wrecked a starter sauce. Don't tell them why but offer them wine if they are put off.'

A woman unzipped and opened her bag. The gold chain fell catching the light as it did and she took out a handkerchief, then blew her nose very loudly.

She replaced the folded cotton square and smoothed her fair hair. Her companion looked up,

'Do you have to stand there all evening ? I do hope you have something to drink !' and then she walked off to her table clutching her quilted Chanel bag .

'She's fairly normal dear !' said the waitress .

'How's the sous chef ?'

'I tink his Nike sneak is running comfortable now , miss manager !'

Table three was talking about the Olympic torch parade next week . A woman with red hair and a black dress had plans for their onion ring product relaunch in supermarkets across the country with a £15,000 sponsorship spend and branding on Linford Christie's T shirt .

'Excuse me for interrupting but your mains are now ready .'

Sea bass and pernod , lamb guard of honour with olive and parsley crust and Bresse Bleu risotto, toasted brioche and Woolsfery goats cheese with gooseberry and quince jam .'

The piano bar was very busy. A couple dressed in white stood out, looking like the Taj Palace Hotel in a sea of black.

'Is this your coat Sir ?' asked the waitress .

'It had better be only It might be more expensive than the others, 'said his girlfriend .

'Yes dear. But it's no good to someone else if it doesn't fit them, is it?'

'Don't worry Sir the restaurant is insured if there is a mix up .' she added smiling politely. The couple left as another order of sea bass in pernod went passed . The waiter balanced several plates perfectly on his arm. Less Statue of Liberty than a raised torch in TGI Fridays on rollorskates exercising calm control . He served the table and cleared another. The phone rang again with a celebrity booking .

One of the restaurants regular diners arrived, an A list celebrity who was pregnant and last in the papers for going into and leaving the Priory.

'What have you got for me today ?'

This was one of the things she had to do everyday , become familiar with the ever changing and seasonal menu .

' Pigeon Restaurant Toad in the Hole - Mini Yorkshire puddings with green sage sausages , saussison verts , 'Crapaud dans le trou' , that's like soufflé dans les saules , Wind in the Willows or ' my soufflé has collapsed ' and il y a le soufflé dans son saule , I have a double chin or something.'

'Oh good , delicieuses . I have to stick to one glass of wine.'

Her friend was saying something about needing an RAC tow truck to put her in the bath and its OK to still have sex at eight months pregnant as long as it's in the recovery position , presuming no drowning had occurred , but she was not sure what she wanted -' not a baby that's for sure !'

Her other friend added ' An Indian head massage, I had one earlier or a foot massage if they're swollen. '

'I actually have an urge to go and lie in a load of daffodils every time I pass Hyde Park but it was a bit damp yesterday and it's going to snow tomorrow. My lifestyle coach says that I should follow through with all my urges, however strange . '

'OK right Ski wear .'

They kept chatting at the bar as they were slightly early and their table would be five minutes .

'We never used to swallow our pills in the Priory – stuck them under my tongue and pretended to take them, then put them in a ciggy packet. I'm not taking anything they wouldn't take themselves and I'm sure they'd pass .'

The barristers on table eight were all wearing navy pinstripes , Pink shirts and short skirts , a Missoni dress with a diagonal pattern was a distraction from the mainly tailored camouflage. Her face glowed in the warm yellow light from the lamp at her desk as she watched them in the dark décor of the reception beyond which the tea lights flickered in the Piano Bar and the chandelier, chandeliered in the restaurant . It was the end of her first week and it felt as if she had been there a month . She was getting used to everything and there was always more to do. She had not found out anything more about the apartment in Dubai , but someone knew a conveyancing solicitor that she could speak to. She was wearing a large black and green pearl bracelet. She had seen one the day before with tiny seeds that would have looked more at home on a an individually hand sewn wedding dress or a Tudor Holbein dress worn by Anne Boleyn .The mirrored Chalmondly sisters with tightly wrapped babies had nothing on the uniform barristers.

One of them took a photo of himself and emailed it to someone . She heard a strong Ghanaian accent behind her and music from the Piano Bar. There was a slight draught from the corridor. At 11pm she took a break and had a plate of seared squid and coconut , green chillie and lime rice . With her first wage cheque she would invest in a new Hugo Boss suit and some Kurt Geiger shoes .

One weekend off in four in her contract which gave her two nights off a week . As it was Easter they decided to go away for the holiday and they booked into the Hotel de Paris in Cromer. From the train the fields looked waterlogged , there was still snow on the hedges and abandoned farm implements . Yellow primulas had been planted in the tubs on the station platforms along the line. The stations to Norwich were punctuated by farms and marine industries . Large freight rolling stock left in the shunting yard reminded her of the scene from the Omen where the man got killed and cut in half by two trains .

In Cromer the Tourist Information had literature for The Cat Pottery . She considered the results of a potter's wheel being operated by a tabby or persian pet then checked into the hotel before walking up the cliffs to the lighthouse . They needed to stretch their legs after the three hour train journey .

The one kilometre walk was not too much of a challenge and only took about twenty minutes . There was a steep short cut at the base of the hill where the lighthouse stood . People had worn away their own even path in the grass and gorse to invest in the view from the top of Cromer Bay - The Devil's Throat – hazardous to fishing and shipping . A light is visible in the tower of the white building that does not match the expectations of the traditional red and white stripey models in the souvenir shops where buckets and spades are sold along with the happy seagulls and soft toys . The eerie sound of the seagulls was audible over the noise of the wind and the crashing waves, spilling and dumping the tides and rip currents on the beach. Advice from the RNLI rescue station told people what to do in cases of emergency .

'Someone was killed by a train .' the news said as they returned into the lounge of the hotel . A resident guest had gone into hospital and the concierge was giving instructions on the telephone . They waited for the key while she finished her conversation .

It had started to rain and people persisted in their pursuit of crab fishing on the pier . They told each other jokes to stay sane beneath umberellas and pacamacs .

Why don't polar bears eat penguins ?

Because they can't get the wrappers off !

Why do crabs get caught by rowers ?

Something to do with their rollocks !

It looked easy winding the baited nets down into the water and leaving them just visible by an orange float. The fish shops were full of fresh Cromer crabs caught by the local fishermen who farmed them on shanks . She was looking forward to trying the samphire , crab, bloater, hare and black turkey. The concierge came off the telephone and gave them their key.

'Did you make it to the lighthouse ?'

'Yes and the museum .' she replied .

The rain beat against the window for most of the night and she thought of the restaurant . L'essuie de glace she thought – windscreen wiper ice cream . Then she thought about the apartment in Dubai and the guaranteed sunshine . The tinsel shrimp and lobster Christmas decorations and neon cinema signs on the front were a nice change from the front of house bookings and high energy calm and efficient organisation . She hoped it got messed up while she was away .They booked the light house guest house for Friday and took a huge white motor cruiser out on the Norfolk Broads for two days , navigating the fens and visiting pubs and hotel well kept lawns that sloped on the banks; not forgetting to put an online bet on the Oxford and Cambridge Boatrace .

After checking the hedgefunds and exploring the fens they bought a net and some bait from a tackle shop full of serious looking guns and fishing rods and had a go at crab fishing . The woman in the tackle shop said to tie the bait in the net and weight it with a large stone , then lower it into the water and wait . She had boiled small blue soft shelled crabs before and made lime, coriander and crab salad , crab and sweetcorn soup . She had also found their discarded shells washed up on the beach in SW9 where the tide had recycled the plastic and driftwood on the slipway . The only thing she was likely to catch in Cromer was a cold .

Back to work after a week off. The booking sheets were OK and after an hour she forgot that she had been away .

'Bookings were quiet in the afternoon and picked up later. She took a booking .

'Table for four on Friday at 9pm .' A couple arrived . The woman had blond ringlets .

'I want to sit somewhere away from any heat or steam . One or the other or they'll go limp. It's the humidity . '

'Yes of course, by the window should be OK'

'I musn't use too much Ellnet, it puts me off eating as well.'

I'll keep an eye on them. Let me know if there's a problem and I'll organise some temporary parmesan shavings until they spring back . OK.'

The next day she had a serious meeting with a conveyancer and the Dubai salesman . They signed the papers for £250.00 a month . It would pay for itself. 'Great ' She felt niave and young but went with her gut reaction, trusting something , probably money . They had a client ready to take the let in Dubai for a years renewable contract . She was both horrified and amused by her investment and could not wait to visit it in the summer . She started to make plans with swimwear and kaftans .

Table nine made a query about their bill. They had not received their starters they had ordered .Table five had to be told to keep the passionate kissing across the cheese course to a minimum .Would they like some passion fruit cocktails or bromide .

'Champagne please ! I've just got promoted .'

'Congratulations .'

She took a booking for Tuesday lunchtime as a group of eight Japanese arrived .

She noticed the different lengths and textiles of their clothes and the Asymmetric hair. Stuff not available in any of the shops in London that she had been to recently . Must be Yamamoto or something she thought as the pleats and wraps passed; the infuriating jet black asymetric hairstyles moved like the 1000 cc bikes at the Isle of Mann TT and returned to their original positions without the aid of any compressed air hairspray. They sat next to a table with a brat pack artist and model . Some of the few people still funding the tabacco industry , they had returned from a cigarette only five minutes earlier raising comments from the Olympic athlete dining with a well known musician. They had suffered lots of questions from the paparazzi about torches and doors lighting fires when they had arrived . She had seen some flame light bulbs in the Conran Shop and someone had asked if it was possible for it to play Light My Fire as it was switched on .

The musician's shirt looked like he had just dismounted the winner of the Grand National and judging by his spare tyre it looked like he had just eaten several winners .

'I could eat a horse .'said the athlete .

'You never hear anyone say 'I could eat a pig, sheep, fish, chicken or cow. So why a horse ?' said the musician .'If the person who said that first was that hungry why didn't he ride it to the supermarket and buy something .'

A restaurant critic from a newspaper mentioned a joke to someone about a chef tourant .

'Does he revolve or bend or what ?'

'I think he just does a few nights like a DJ . '

'Rotisserie chickens!' he said pronouncing it 'chicanes' as in racetrack circuit .

'Oh right !'

When she got home she washed her flip flop feet that were slightly less pink from their walk to the tube than they were in the morning. Chef threw a cucumber at the sous chef , quickly followed by bowling an overarm tomato . Drop the cucumber and catch the tomato or use it as a bat . No amount of management training could prepare anyone for a split second decision on concassing a tomato in midair and knowing which direction the exploding seeds would go . Alternative answers would probably be to use the larger moulhi or dudhi for novelty value .

'We took the DLR Docklands Light Railway from the Docklands Airport this time instead of a taxi .' said the man with an foreign accent on table six.

'It was great snaking threw the mirror and glass buildings and through the yacht basins from one satellite to the next .Then we had tea in Bird Street and went to look at an Art Collection .Is this a soup plate or a shallow bowl ? '

'They had wonderful hand painted Severnes cup and saucers and a lovely Giacomo de something pale blue, grey plate from Venice with a white lace picture on it .' said his partner .'The tube was full of runners who had finished the marathon . One girl was wrapped up in her foil Flora sponsored blanket and medal. Her grey sweatpants looked still wet from the rain . It must be difficult to know if new trainers are a good thing or not if you're running in a marathon . Brand new and they might rub, too comfortable and they might wear out half way through. You can probably tell I only run about 3k, I leave long distance running to the completely insane adrenalin junkies.

She was with her parents who had a bag packed with every possible item – blankets , Alpen bars and video camera .They must have met her at the finish somewhere and seemed very proud supporters . She was still miles away and about ten feet off the ground . She was rubbing her legs . They must get heavy when you stop . We could see the runners from the train by Mudchute below us . Their pace got faster as they passed the Radio Station playing music and they got into the rhythm running passed the allotments full of neat rows of green leaves and large cabbages and the strange triangular modern houses . For a moment I thought we were back in Holland as I saw the Dutch Bridge in East India Dock basin . Did you read the article about the Birdsong Radio Station ?'

'No '

'Remind me to get the frequency. Anyway , then there was an accident on the escalator with lots of screaming and a woman had to hit the emergency stop button .Two people seemed to take responsibility which was a relief I didn't fancy having to see if anyone needed resuscitating . I haven't ever had to apply mouth to mouth or do cardiac heart massage on anything live before – just the plastic things with out make up . The ones with make up usually need inflating more . I found a glass cupboard with a defibrillator in it, but there were no telephones down there or a number to ring with a mobile. Presumably their surveillance responds very quickly . We didn't hang around to see if anyone had redesigned their Wellington boots into open toed sandals . '

A bottle of vodka was ordered on table number one where a Russian author was entertaining people with Russsian fables . She had once heard one he told about a man and a woman who had first met in a restaurant . The woman was young , the man said he was very old . Then they began to meet everywhere . What does this symbolise ? The girl is as boring as the old man and they are going the same way in life 'How hopelessly ordinary , ' he said . ' You should understand this as a fable.'

A month before she had spoken to a man from one of the Government Ministries about the renewed growth in popularity of bowling greens in England and playing petang in the Mediteranean . She recognised him as he sat down opposite her in a tube carriage and smiled . It was obvious that the man was with someone as they were deep in blue stockinged conversation . She was unable to say hello to the man from the Ministry as they alighted at the next stop . She wandered what the probability of seeing someone again like this was and whether she would see him again as she alighted at Upminster. But she was not going to put money on it.

She took a table booking for a Children's Charity. Their budget expenses paid for by large companies with invested interests and tax losses in foreign countries to make sustainable and fair-trade products and to keep the footsie points appearing on her telephone and her foot print green .This was something she had learnt from Mr Hedgefund when they were on the Fens.

He had spent the afternoon racing wetbikes in the Docklands to raise money for a charity , like 'celebrity five a side,' he had said .'You keep a percentage from the Inland Revenue and spend it doing something you enjoy and it goes to your chosen destination instead of randomly to the economy's health and education .'

The ONS , Office of National Statistics listed a lot of percentages about detached retinas and cataracts caused by rugby scrums , boxing matches and diabetes . Both could be put right by the pioneering Russian laser liner cruise ships, the cataracts removed through a tiny hole and the retinas reattached with a bubble of gas, giving some one back the miracle of sight . The thought of being in the dark, seeing only the difference between light and dark left her cold and she drank a shot of iced Krepkaya in the piano bar on her break .

The Japanese table were busy talking figures and looking at something on a laptop. Their serious minimalism and zen meditation suggested a priceless Ming moment , broken only by the change in the raised glaze patterns of the linear cashflow projection and curves on the latest low profile Apple screen.

One of the Russians kept scratching the side of his nose , a gesture that could be mistaken for making a bid at an auction . He drank a shot of the vodka as their pomegranate and pheasant arrived and the conversation quailed .

She was on her way to meet a friend in the afternoon the next day and was caught without a bus ticket, her pass had expired. The ticket inspector needed a credit card to check her name. She gave the address of someone she could remember from school instead and said that all her ID was at home . In the panic being questioned in a bus full of strangers by a big scary woman in a uniform she drew on experience. She still went bright red .

When she returned the bar was suffering a minor disturbance as a music event by a duet called Great Wall was being set up. It included laptop accompaniment of computerised chinese percussian to a violin solo and took a while for them to set the sound levels and controls to the little pings and soft hollow wooden noises which were to form an alternative to the usual pianist.

She hung her wet jacket up to dry. The rain had been unexpected but she had an umberella luckily. Chef did not though .

Chef had made some little sushi starters and sake sorbet. The bar was full of the orchids and pink plum and cherry blossoms she had ordered from their usual florist who had delivered them in the afternoon .

'Where do you find the wicket on a boat ?' he asked the sous chef who had been celebrating a friend's birthday and had to towel his hair before he put his toc on to stop it dripping on the food .

'When the soggy matches dry out !Do you get it ? He's been playing truant from the English lessons again .'

One of the Russian women was taking sugar frosted fruit and chocolate from the large serious looking man opposite her and piling them onto her own plate in a game. Occasionally there was a cheer of 'Gorko ! Gorko ! ', apparently a football cheer and they toasted more vodka . She had noticed the woman's black and white shoes with disproportionate oversized floppy flowers on the toes and high square heels when they arrived . They reminded her of the grow your own mushroom kits she had seen in the slow food market between the honey comb candles and soaps, jars of blossom and clover, stilton cheese, and Guinness and wild boar terrine . There was a small crowd looking at the busy little worker bees crawling over the hexagonal comb . Some of them looked asleep or stuck as the others climbed over them covered in pollen chewing it to make their waxy secretions . She had tried to find the queen bee but she was probably back in the hive.

The next day she noticed all the blossom had fallen off the cherry tree where she lived. She picked a big stalk of purple flowers and studied the big flat helipads for the bumble bees to land on and the pollen and stamen protected by more wrap around petals .The small white 'peau noir masques blancs' daisies opened in the mornings and protested for equality in the grass putting on their little march across the lawn at the despair of it's owner who had pots of larger margerites on his patio .

As her Dubai finance had started to arrive regularly she decided to invest in a pale blue Givenchy handbag and some croc loafers from Franchetti Bond. The bag was pale blue leather with a chic little gold logo clasp. Staring at it was not dissimilar to bonding with a baby and she would not let it leave her side for about four weeks , it took priority over everything . At what age do baby blues change colour , six months ? She found it very difficult to deliberately leave the bag at home and take a different one instead.

Sunday afternoon, Mr Hedgefund had a birthday party at the City of London Bowling Club. Everybody wore a strictly white dress code and white gym shoes for the six rink event on beautiful manicured lawn. They drank gin and tonic in the Pavillion bar as the sprinklers watered the pansies and cucumber sandwiches preceeded platters of Indian delicacies to the vibe of a ninety two string santar and tabla drum. An umpire kept the scores . She watched as the balls rolled up to their targets and the figures were chalked on to the black board. Club fixtures and records were listed and displayed with the photographs of serious looking members and presidents dating back to the British Empire. An ice cream van drove past playing its typical composition of bells recorded for posterity by an unknown musician . Their information was only for the duration of the afternoon , unlike the team fixtures that usually played . She had heard cave paintings described as snapshots recording images as visual communication, destroying the need for traditional language . Certain profanities went ignored as the traditional language occasionally deteriorated into cave man grunts , defying perception and the eight layers of the cerebral cortex .

After the match they sat in the sun and watched the other games . Someone was building a house of cards on the next table carefully arranging the cards into leaning triangular walls with flat floors layered on top until they made a pyramid . His girlfriend wrapped her Nepalese Nettle pashmina round her shoulders as a light breeze risked the collapse of his carefully structured tower in the otherwise dry and windless heat . Her green woven shawl was from the now sustainable industry that spun, wove and dyed the green stinging plant, a remedy for many ailments and giver of health also dangerous to touch bringing instant pain and burning ; and as irritating as someone potentially jogging the table.

She thought of the Mappin and Webb case versus the designer copies on the stalls in Eastern markets as she sipped her Gordon's with lots of ice and lemon. An illegal street vendor was flogging stolen Mappin and Webb jewellery from a suitcase in the market square where she had lunch when she was a teenager at college. 'Not £5, not £4, not £3 but £2, only £2. Trying to get a quick sale and a quick getaway before a policeman arrived . Doing time after five minutes of opening his discount watch shop. A friend and her had brought matching necklace and bracelet sets each, 'hot' goods. Her innocent introduction to an exclusive Bond Street brand. The Tawainese copies of designer labels in tourist markets however, rust in the bath after five minutes and someone starts shouting ' not another £2' everytime he forgets to take one off. Not to mention the amount of damage to the real market or appreciation of owning a quality item .

As the tables were being set up with their usual royal banquet accuracy and measured precision , one of the serviettes caught chef's eye. He picked it up disapprovingly and started folding it into a wrap style more in line with an Angus Steak house wine glass that can stand up for themselves , then put it on his head and danced around the table clapping and singing the Baptist Gospel haleluliahs . He was following a woman going to church the previous Sunday and said, 'She didn't notice as I felt her headgear. I couldn't resist it, it was so stiff !

Stiffer than I thought it was going to be. Is she or isn't she ? What do they use traditional starch or hairspray ? It was like paper.'

'I haven't a clue, probably soaked in potato or pasta.'

'You've heard the one about the Italian rasta who went to the VDU clinic and told the Dr he had a round of applause then.'

'No . What did he give him the clap ?'

Chef confessed to having eaten a screwball ice cream earlier. He spotted one on the board of a Toni Bell with bubble gum in the base of the plastic conical tub.

'It used to be FAB's, 99's ,orange or strawberry, Mivi's , Rocky Roads with marshmallow or Tutti Futti with bubble gum bits but we never had the screwballs . We could make some if you like . '

'Ice cream or the gospel serviettes ?'

Mr Softwhip's hard balls and management soft skills – listening , problem solving , negotiating and team work . Lessons learnt from an accident insurance claim in a revolving door and enjoyed on a casino roulette wheel and Black Jack table . Chef returned to the kitchen through the opaque backlit glass door looking more like a shadow puppet from Jakarta holding his ladel handle to prepare the wood pigeon breast , baby carrots and pink fir potato plat de jour .

She had seen a wood pigeon yesterday with a large twig in its mouth on the way to work as she passed the fried egg tree that she passed everyday . Would making the pan fried dish make several speckled eggs into a single parent pigeon problem family ? There was also a moorhen on a thirty centimetre nest on the lake. She had seen at least one exposed white egg . She decided to keep an eye out for the ducklings .

The eggs hatched the next day and she took them chocolate ice cream and tuna fish sandwiches . Neptune's two prong fork for under the sea was also used for tuning and toasting . The three prong fork was used for his seafood and the four for his double vision . Any fork with a greater number of prongs was technically a comb .

Next payday she tried on some shoes called Kuckoo with metallic gold edging that looked like they came from a small side street shop in Milan or Barcelona that was patronised by middle aged women in aprons . The type of shop that had boxes that had sat on the shelves for ten years and collected dust , in an ornamentally protective way establishing The RSPS - The Royal Society of Protection of Shoes and a growing market for shoe trees.

What makes someone choose a career in philosophy ? Where do you train ? and what are the salaries like ?

Front End Of A Bus

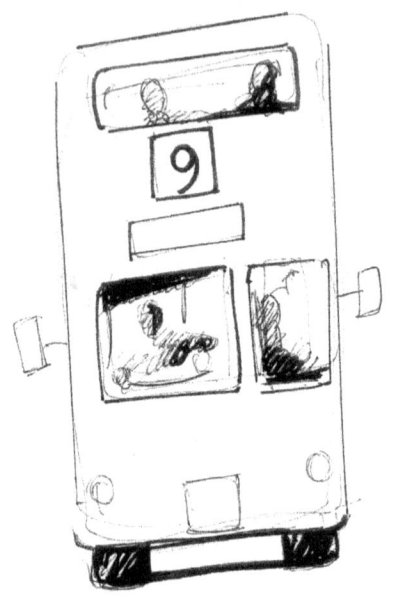

Every other person in Greece is named after St.Dennis, Dionysis, it's patron saint. Dionysis came from Zakynthos, green island of poetry, song and love. If you happen to visit there during August you can participate in the three day festival when his silver casket is paraded through the streets of the town centre of the same name followed by bands with the cathedral bells peeling from the tower which is a copy of St.Marcos in Venice. The island is also famed for it's contraband cigarette cargo shipwreck on an isolated beach only accessible by speedboat. Eric had met a few Dennis's during his stay on the island when it suffered from severe tremors hitting 5.5 on the Richter scale. Dennis owned the bar they drank the evening away in as bottles fell off shelves and he told how Dennis his father and all the other villagers had slept outside, safe from anything collapsing and burying them when the big quake had caused the whole island to be rebuilt. And Dennis drove the taxi which took Eric back to his apartment.

Dennis is also the name you find on the back end of a bus. They have other nicknames like Hoppa, Bendy and Double Deckers, not to be confused with American actors or chocolate bars.

It was a wet Monday on the usual number 94, different bus, same number. The hydraulic brakes of the bus were making a noise you would expect to be emmited by a plastic Christmas trumpet, one of the ones with streamers and a metal widget inside. Every time the traffic stopped the failed A.B.S - Anti Bazooka System gave an involuntary noise.Between five and seven o'clock the bus was always full. There were never enough seats, the crowding made it difficult to alight and sometimes people missed their stops. At the bus stops there were miserable queues too. Arrival times did not stick to the pressured timetables - 94 eta 15 minutes - fifty over eighty with stirrups to hang on to, D.R.T.V. to watch Evil Kenevil and bungy jumping and braille stop buttons. Buses cannot jump off buildings when they want to get off they concede to the ambulance response times to catch a ride to work and experience how they can pump your stomach if you OD on someone elses chips and walkman music. Fifteen percent more cotton buds are bought within tube zones and Eric had to complain about the uncomfortable back seats. London transport sent him an official complaint form. He was not happy that they had made the conductors redundant and retired the Routemasters which you could jump on and off. It is possible to buy a Summer Holiday Routemaster for £4K. If you find yourself staring at someone red with a number, destination, small window, a Dr Dolittle musical poster, insurance or underwear ad, a heating vent with Dennis, Bendy or Hoppa name badge then they probably look like someone's wife. The back end of a bus is an English idiom used for looking ugly. Actually the front end looks much the same these days. Eric found a website advertising the Routemasters and displaying photographs of 'unique back ends.' There are some fine shots of D1s, BN331s and native T272s. Carla's song is a good film to allude to if you need reference to their independant personal ownership image. It is also worth knowing that you should mind your American slang. You will find 'driving the bus' in the urban dictionary for selling drugs with the definition that there is little profit eg driving all the way to Egypt for $20.

Eric saw a man on the bus wearing the same navy Tie Rack braces as his. He did not wear them that often and went off them rapidly for the duration of the journey. Then when he got home he liked them again. A woman on the back seat was doing word search quizzes and puzzle games, correcting them with Tipex and a brush. Eric had always associated them with a friend's fear of flying to distract her from her nerves during take offs and landings when her legs shook visibly. Eric got to his destination and alighted. He waited for the bus to go. A school friend of his Justin, who had taught him to ride horses in a field near where he had lived, had actually got hit by a bus and died from a brain tumour. He walked to the cinema passing a large white limosine. Two people got out, celebrities, prompting paparazzi frenzy. He reached for his telephone camera and took a photograph through the back of the heads of the premier style crowd as they entered the new French restaurant. Eric showed the little pixel people to Melanie before they bought some popcorn and went to watch the movie.

At work the next day Eric decided to learn how to ride a motorcycle. He looked up a training centre, he had already passed his C.B.T. He fancied a Vespa or a Lambretta to practise on. Then he could park it for free before the G.L.C. found a way of charging for that too. At least the supermarket trolley gave him his £1 back when he drove that around Sainsburys. His girlfriend had put a pack of rump steak in someone elses trolley once when they were not looking to cheer them up. Eric bought his Vespa and helmet from a scooter shop, taxed and M.O.T.'d it. Two shiney dials and mirrors with a Piaggio logo in the middle. He was in control. He would have to put the reminder for his tax in his phone memory for next year. His friend's tax had run out and he was fined for not being road legal. The revenue from fines was obviously more profitable for the Government, depite the paperwork, than sending people annual reminders like a dentists check up. N.H.S. car servicing would probably be quite popular.

Eric joined a breakdown recovery. Then he was nearly driven to suicide at work by people complaining about the bus. His girlfriend became pregnant. They had decided to start trying for a baby when they had moved. She had had an abortion before because of the increased cost of the congestion charge and because their flat was too small. They wanted to give their child the best start in life. Eric decided to take up smoking as an occupation for his hands. He got nervous sometimes. His new pension plan had a mortgage attached to it which helped.

The urban dictionary also defines 'driving the bus' as throwing up, a more physical association than the previous one. Morning sickness is usually a request stop, three months of involuntary vomiting is not something you stick your hand up or out to unless a bulimic has an early breakfast. Eric drove his Vespa over Westminster Bridge back into the Bus Borough of Nivana, with his girlfriend on the back with the baby on her front. He wandered how long she would be able to fit on the back. They stopped behind a bus as the red lights came on. KEEP OUT OF BUS LANES £100 FINE said the sign on the back of the bus. Eric took extra caution between the red and black tarmac as he went round the corner, wishing he had S.I.P.S, where the apex is bisected by its perpendicular pivotal point longer vehicles take a different arc line needing a larger ratio bend to hug which he had discovered once when he became very close to an accident. It is a scientific physics problem that cars are less prone to.

He made a point of staying away from the raised white lines too. The paint was very thick to the receptive Vespa suspension. His girlfriend gripped tighter then let go. She trusted him. They had invited some friends for dinner and had had to buy some last minute things.

Eric made vodka martinis, making sure to chill the glass first. He had a cocktail shaker kit with a book from Debenhams and invested in everything he needed - Angustura Bitters and Grendine included. They ate rissotto and had a cocktail making competition, the Tequilla Sunrise won. He put All Of This And Nothing on the CD player and the girls danced in the kitchen.

Eric had parked his Vespa badly on a partial yellow line and got a ticket as a result. He knew he should have bothered to find another space and had fourteen days to pay or the price doubled. He saw another ticket on someone's Porsche and quickly peeled it off and stuck it on the Peugeot next to it. He would have hung around once to wait for the owner to return just to enjoy his or her reaction but he had to be somewhere. Somebody was going to receive a ticket for twice the original ticket when they sent a reminder or bayliff request on receipt of non payment. Camden's red tape is renowned for being deaf to any reasoning. Then someone else could get upset for no reason when they got a ticket on their car and a] send off £40 to pay for the offenders P.C.N. without checking the number plate written on it, b] realise it was not for their car when they calmed down, c] question why they had received it because they knew they were parked illegally. Eric was glad he did not have to get angry at the London Transport bus ticket machines anymore which frequently failed to dispense any tickets.

He put £7 of petrol in his Vespa tank, enough for the week and went to pay in the modern petrol station shop. He stared at the apple scented windscreen wash and read the headlines as he was waiting to pay. No use of mobile telephones allowed for safety reasons associated with the pump electrics. They had manual counters instead of L.C.D. to avoid any sparks which could ignite any fuel.' Oh I do like to be beside the seaside' was the tune in his head as he noticed the C.C.T.V. by the till.

'Good movie?' he asked the man behind the glass. It was a Shell station in the Bayswater Road but noone expected Ursula Andress to walk in wearing a bikini. Eric put his helmet on then realised he had a problem eating his Bounty choc ice. He also thought about the way the Indian had held his hand out waiting for him to pay the total of his petrol. He was offended by him asking physically and wanted to ask him if he was trying to catch a bus. Eric knew some people reacted against cultural differences like that making them condemingly racist. Eric found 90% of white people equally offensive, especially Brazillians. He was not happy when they won the World Cup and took over Trafalgar Square. Firstly because he kept his goldfish there, he let it go in the fountain and the noise might upset it. And secondly because England should have won. He had arranged to meet a school friend there on new year's day 2001 12pm, but Eric never turned up. When he had made the arrangement he worked out that he would be thirty four which seemed ancient. He always wandered if his friend had turned up but did not want to stand there and wait looking like an idiot. He was in no state to go anyway.

Eric spent the weekend pulling woodchip wallpaper off the walls in the small bedroom only to be told by a friend that it was coming back in. It had been featured in the property section of The Telegraph and Elle Decoration. He painted the nursery walls marble white with a baby blue fire place and blind. Melanie spent ages in Baby Gap looking at the cute towels with hoods and butterfly mobiles. They had bought a toy box, a globe light and some luminous stars, an alphabet, a toy boat and a grass green shag pile rug for the natural wood floor. The soft toy sheep, cows and pigs sat on the shelf above the cot. Eric also made a spaceman lamp from an old white crash helmet. He filled it full of Christmas lights and put a N.A.S.A. logo on it. It looked like the universe was in the bit behind the visor. Then he did a Fosbury Flop backwards onto the settee, the style of jump started by the U.S. athlete trying to avoid breaking his neck. Eric liked presents. When he was five he had taken a piece of his brother's Lego and wrapped it up for him for Christmas as it seemed the thing to do. He did not get out very much to the shops. He must have felt guilty that everyone else was experiencing the act of giving and experienced the wrong Dr Spock's guide to dyslexic warping paper. Melanie was very big. It looked like the baby could be twins, the omnibus edition, or would three come along at once? She eventually went into labour pains two and a half weeks later with contractions every ten minutes, doing her yoga to stay calm. The exercise classes at the pool had been worth it and she looked foreward to the mother and baby classes with the first introductary class free. Eric watched as the doctor smacked his baby's butt and heard him cry. Eric and Melanie called their baby Dennis.

'It's not catastrophies, murders, deaths, diseases that age and kill us, it's the way people look and laugh, and run up the steps of omnibuses.'
Virginia Woolf.

Eric worked at Unlimited Ltd, his secretary Polly Bored had an alias for days when she was not being interesting. He had worked there for five years and his social audience mapping was gaining altitude. He was not on the board yet but he would be in another five years. He had started as a junior executive, one of the company cosmopolitans, who kept the information inertia spreading it's halo effect. He was a hungry executive with baby blogg, podscroll information on the environment, motorbikes, sport and travel filling his thirty gigabite deadtime and Christmas bonus.

Eric and his brother visited a Russian exhibition of rockets, satelites and other orbital orthodox icons at the Science Museum. They viewed the lunar hardware and Soyez cosmonauts missions from a future space tourist's perspective. During the Cold War the long range ballistic missiles destructive power and vulnerability provided a so called Mutually Assured

Destruction -M.A.D. - the cornerstone of Soviet/American relations, now they were more interested in the shuttles and deep space. Then they went and had a pot of tea in the Gambol Rooms of The V&A, where the ceilings and walls compete with those of the Sistene Chapel but are a little known treasure. Eric did not predict that the buses would be on strike.They took a taxi and enjoyed a taste of taxi T.V. with breaking news and adverts for hotels and underwear. Polonium 210 radioactivity level scares were topical news all week. Eric's geiger counter detected a new level of interest in Melanie. He could count on her to keep him sane. She made roast partridge and pear tree desert for their first Christmas in the new flat. Their bouteilles de Hermitage rouge would have the 'length' [a new wine tasting term he had learnt] to linger longer than a Phill Collins drum solo. Dennis liked his presents and had milk. Next year he would probably manage pureed cranberries, Christmas pudding and brandy butter sauce. They watched the countdown to new year on the T.V., sang Auldlangsyne and drank red label Piper Heidseck with some friends.

The White Elephant Stall

The sign said the Post Office closes at 2pm. It was 3pm and thirty two degrees in the suffocating humidity. Monkeys were foraging in residential gardens then returning back across the road into the bamboo and palms. Tiny babies clinging securely to their mothers' undersides despite their dangerous missions. A few cows wandered about looking a bit lost. Jones had walked one kilometre to find the red roofed Post Office building, one of about five places of importance marked on the town map. Having failed to find the Post Office in the last town he was in he followed the instructions given to him very carefully. He had spent about an hour dodging bicycles, buses and rickshaws whilst eliminating the numerous sari and jewellery shops from the Indian highstreet until he was incensed. The monsoons were about two weeks off. They were probably going to be early due to a cyclone on the east coast. The India Express slid under the hotel room door at 6.30am had said a weather station could predict them within five days .

Jones was thirty five, average height and had brown hair in a style that looked grown out and in need of a cut. He was wearing a straw stetson, a lightweight charcoal pinstripe suit jacket, that was too small for him over a sports T shirt with the number twelve on it and indigo Levis. He had slipped his Birkenstocks off as he sat looking at the uninviting green water in the swimming pool at breakfast.

'Is it OK to swim in?' he asked the waiter as he put his satchel diagonally over his shoulder.

'We have a filter,' replied the waiter. Obviously they needed someone to ask them to use it and it would take slightly longer than his proposed stay to clear the suspension of algae. He wandered how long it had been since it had been used and decided he would swim at the beach early tomorrow morning with the men who swam in their white dhotis then dried in the sun, tying them up and untying them as they talked. Before 7am several small fishing boats and the strong undertow threw the clams underfoot up into the waves. If you caught one they opened and snapped shut contracting quickly and nipping your fingers like angry castanets. He had spoken to a local man who had told him the clam fishermen's lively hood was being threatened by tourism. The delicate ecosystem was endangered affecting the lime shell mining. The shells are used for grinding into a fine calcium powder for cosmetics which was vital to their income. They had sat on the rocks, listening to the crashing waves and chatted while the beach sellers set up their fried banana stands and tried selling camel bone jewellery and shells to the green tourists. One seller was demonstrating how to blow into the large elephant ear conch.

The sea continued to eat away at the beach, slowly eroding it and leaving a high step in the sand .

Jones and his local companion digressed from shellfish to insects, cochineal beetles inparticular and whether vegetarians were aware of the cochineal blood in food colouring that was used in most sweets, lipsticks and clothing dyes. Although it is now virtually impossible to get the genuine article and everything contains the replacement E129 .

'Does this affect the Tandoori ?'he asked. 'Is the Cochineal beetle being protected or threatened with extinction? The little cactus parasite cochineal beetle has been emmigrating from South America for many years - its one way of getting through the Mexican customs, most of us are trying to get in.'

'Did you know that the Ladybird, coccinela septempunctata is also known as the Virgin Mary or Our Lady's Bird?' asked Jones. 'In Irish it's 'boin De' which is 'God's Little Cow', in Croatian its 'God's Sheep' and French 'God's Little Animal', in Yiddish 'God's Little Horse' and Russian The Little Messiah.' He stopped to think for a second then added, 'Do you think it would be jumping to conclusions to assume that drinking plenty of Bloody Marys would assist in the preservation of the Cocchineal or just result in a lot of pissed entomologists ?'

The shell stand with the elephant ear was very simple compared to the air conditioned gold shops that insisted you were seated to make your purchase and the insane sari shops, at first sight a crowded confusion of colour. It took a while to work out the system of ordering, packing and paying at three different counters where the items bill was officially written, stamped and processed. Each piece of folded silk was individually embroidered, no two pieces appeared to be the same pattern or colour. Two toned, shot, paisley, flowers and abundant use of gold.

A lace wing butterfly landed on the palm tree beside him and he was reminded of the desintergrating displays in the museum that looked untouched since the collection was installed, probably in the early nineteenth century. There was no electric lighting and a thick layer of dust on the doolies, artifacts and fine examples of taxidermy. Jones had needed to sit on the curator's chair to catch his breathe and drink some water having climbed the spiral staircase.He put some water on his neck and wrist pulse to try and cool down and stop sweating. Everything was slowing down in time with the early morning bicycles and yellow butterflies that all moved laterally, occasionally interrupted by a man in a white dhoti carrying a bag of rice home on his head from the local delivery.

Returning from the beach there was no glass in the windows of the bumpy bus, allowing a constant breeze to blow through it and the babies and small children to sleep on their squashed mothers. A group of school girls wearing the same coloured ribbons in their hair stood in a row holding the overhead handrail in the packed interior. The bus driver hit his hooter to add to the non stop caberet of horns from rickshaws and scooters beep beeping, in the inescapable and familiar racket. The bus passed a stand selling bamboo juice. It had a mangle type wheel that crushed the vertical branches several times and squeezed a whole lime to extract a glass of juice. Rubber trees lined the road and valleys as far as the eye could see or eight kilometres with the strongest pair of binoculars for hire from the kid with an incredibly well practised sales technique. He started by offering a pair for fifty Rupees with a two hundred Rupee deposit, then hit you with the eight kilometre range pair for two hundred Rupees and a two thousand Rupee deposit. Problem. This meant a half hour walk to the ATM. Where's my PA when I need her? Jones was not in the habit of carrying much cash around and should have learnt his lesson. He was used to Emma, his Production Assistant, organising his daily finances and had come on the short trip to find locations for the tea brand commercial on his own.

Every rubber tree had a uniform spiral cut made with a special knife allowing the fresh latex to helter skelter drip into a small plastic cup attached to the tree and collected by agile rubber tappers. Wild elephants roamed the Cardamon Hills and working elephants with mahoots commuted between the sawmills and logging areas in the forest grazing on roadside leaves from the cannonball and red barked cinnamon trees covered with parasitic cheese plants. A horticulturalist rickshaw driver had pointed out the fragrant lemongrass and pale green touch me not mimosa whose comb shaped leaves close up if you prod them and told him about the flower that only bloomed every twelve years covering the Cardamon Hills in violet flowers. Jones thought he was either moonlighting from a nursery or had probably won the Indian version of mastermind. Further up the hill there was a small group of tea pickers at a weighing point with a tall tripod construction used as a scale. Different coloured headscarves and blue aprons were tied around and knotted on the heads of the pickers, normally only visible from the waist up between the bushes skillfully removing the top leaves. They still had another half day to work before emptying their bags for the second weighing. Come the red Keralan monsoon rain, the eight thousand employed pickers would need additional migrant worker help to cope with the rapid growth rate.

The hill roads had reasonable tarmac but the rural roads were bare red earth, a clearing made in the forest with no distinct border and usually just a lone figure or cyclist in the distance. Jones noticed the overhead pylon cables that were the only clue to modern existence. The bus ride was only about fifteen minutes and they went every ten. Back in the town every other stall near the station where the disturbing amputees and beggars sat on the pavement, were either selling lottery tickets or jasmine. When he first arrived he had been shocked by them and amazed by the length of the trains. It took about ten minutes to walk from one end to the other and felt like they were a kilometre long, stretching from the banana market at the large junction with carts and trucks piled about two or three metres high with unripe, green bunches of produce to the chai sellers by the park with silver pots on bicycles that weaved their way in and out of the traffic. Jones would have some cardamom tea and burfi when he got back to his hotel. The small coconut, cashew nut and ghee sweets had fine decorative silver leaf that made them look too good to eat. The bus passed another shrine with plastic and gold flowers and a pink lightbulb outside a temple that had a red conical roof and gold spires sticking up between the other buildings.

Jones arrived at the Post Office at 10.30am. The main gate was open and he walked up the twenty or so steps to the door of the small bungalow. It was shut. He walked back to the gate and asked in a spice shop opposite if they knew when it would be open or where the postman was.

'Try again in ten minutes to half an hour.' the assistant told him.

This seemed fairly normal. The Indians appeared to spend all day waiting for some things. Everything was in the hands of God, including the near head on collisions and low bridges on the backwater canals. Jones looked around the local shops for half an hour then returned.

Eventually the Post Office was opened. A white haired postmaster sat behind a counter at a desk wearing a checked shirt. It was a bare room with red paintwork, a set of scales, a cash tray, book of stamps and some Camel brand glue in a blue bottle. Jones took a letter out of his brown leather satchel and handed it to the postmaster. It took about half an hour to weigh the letter and individually separate the perforated stamps of Ghandi and stick them on with glue and then rubber stamp them. The man kindly glued the envelope flap that had been opened once and lost its adhesive.

'How long does the mail take to reach England ?'asked Jones.

'About a week,' replied the man shaking his head.

Jones wanted to say something as he waited and watched.

What did the hindu say when he trod on a beetle and broke his leg ?

'Don't worry we'll put him in a cast.' sprung to mind .

Later in the afternoon he took a packed, twenty five pence ferry along the backwaters from the main harbour overlooked by modern hotels to do some work. White ocean going cruisers and old Keralan fishing boats with woven roofs navigated and positioned themselves in the sea lanes and calm waters. He photographed a woman sitting on the jetty in a violet sari selling green and purple chard and a man dressed in white carrying a black umberella. The noise of laughing children and music coming from behind the coconut palms added to the rhythmic beating of washing against rocks and the boats engine. Colourful saris hung drying in the sun. Vivid reds, pinks, greens and orange. He took some pictures of a woman with a silver pot standing up to her waist in the water wearing an aubergine sari that spread out and floated, turning a deeper colour in the swirling current while she washed and beat some cream fabric. A few small fishing boats were spearing bubblefish that hid under the mud in the air pockets they made and cormorants were diving for pearlspots and mussels. A few water gypsy children paddled passed in their round woven coracle boats that they could carry on their backs. The only other movement was the occasional kingfisher or white snakebird flying left to right across the water or a dragonfly dancing about the pink lillies and water hyacinth. Jones took some recce shots of locations and made some notes, then he downloaded the photos onto his laptop and emailed them back to the production office in London.

A small bug took about five minutes to crawl across the marble floor of the hotel lounge. He was tempted to stamp on it but couldn't be bothered to move. It was Jones' excuse for karma. It might have a little family somewhere he thought.

What's the difference between United v Liverpool and a broken home?

One's a home fixture and the other one's not !

Jones was on foreign territory and held his tongue, he had once said that being without transport when his car was in a garage was comparable to losing an arm or leg! Many a true word said in jest is not a saying to be taken lightly. He decided to buy a VW Beetle to fullfill his   Herbie

Lovebug experience as it would cost less money than hiring something for the week. Unfortunately the Beetle was possibly one of the Mexican models on the US Department of Transport's Grey list of imports that used floorpans from earlier models and did not meet safety regulations. The car nearly killed him. He was driving at about 50 mph and one of the wheels fell off. This fullfilled a slogan on a mug his girlfriend had that said 'MEN! I had one once but the wheels fell off!' He had to sit and wait for the RAC in the dark for 45 minutes having narrowly avoided a nasty accident in the underpowered little box.

'Take me away and lose me forever.' He thought. The last Beetle that rolled off the Mexican production line was serenaded by a Mariachi Band. It had probably been crushed and come back as something else like a pink Vespa, plastic hairdryer, prosethetic limb or pair of Chanel sunglasses. It is incredible that 'a car so small can leave such a large void,' to quote the Mexican ad campaign .

Jones ordered some food and a beer. A vegetable kofta arrived on a little silver dish. The bright yellow turmeric coconut curry had small black mustard seeds and fresh, mild, green curry leaves. The honey and chillie paneer and red chillie fish were quite spicey.

Useless facts from his chat on the beach earlier came back to him. The cochineal beetle can bury itself in the sand to avoid dehydrating like an Egyptian mummy. He needed a welcome drink and some moisturiser.

Jones read an email from his girlfriend Alice. She was used to him working and travelling odd hours. They rested and played just as hard.

Hi Jones
saw this and thought of you.
Crematorium Manager
salary £29,500 - £30000 permenant
days [not graveyard shift]

An interesting and varied vacancy with the opportunity to work with funeral directors, meet the bereaved and stressed, run services and the cremator process with two technicians. No pension details.

Q. How would you describe the difference between stone angels on graves and normal sculpture?

Where do you draw the line between a first century Greek Aphrodite and a contemporary marble model with a hymn book. Why not have a nice reclining Epstein, Giacometti, Frink, Henry Moore or Barbara Hepworth on your grave. Or a Calder mobile. Where do you stop!?

How's the weather?

love Alice

Start with a mescalin trip and take the cochineal on a cobwebbed ghost train with skeletal fingers stroking your face, then go and laugh at the vampires! He thought.

She was obviously in a good mood.

Dear Alice

Miss you too!

love Jones

It was Jones second day of shooting locations for the tea brand commercial. The client was extremely difficult. She had verbally put the previous director and agency down; her vituprous tongue synonymous with a wife perpetually condemming previous bad relationships with a vitriolic attitude and vociferous foment. His production manager had been very understanding and diplomatic. The schedule allowed for three days of location photographs. Everything was tight to allow for the beginning of the monsoon rains. A production meeting was scheduled for thursday with a stylist, casting assistant and storyboard artist. Filming would start in two weeks .

Back the hotel Jones sat and imagined a long, karmic meditation bowl note in his air conditioned freezer before getting some food .

He had finished his Kingfisher beer in ten minutes and ordered another.

An indian family on the next table were talking to a Canadian about their picnic and pleasure boating on the PXXX Dam reservoir. Jones had seen the massive 48 m by 450m curved Dam wall and immense pipes to the generator of the hydroelectric powerstation yesterday. Dense rain forest had camouflaged the huge pipes in the patchwork, panoramic tea plantation scenery which spread as far as the eye could see to infinity and beyond. The energy to the turbines must be incredible he thought. The still water was a tideless, concentrated mass of energy and big calm.

In Marrakesh he had wanted to sit next to his hotel swimming pool with a drink but it had been emptied for maintenance. Imagining the 1000 cubic centilitres of chlorinated water was quite surreal. He felt quite philosophical about the disfunction of the white tiled hole that seemed more like a building site without the attraction of the floating water.

The dam had taken fifty years from conception to completion and supply of power from the generator. Everything in India appeared to be in the hands of the gods.

Civil engineers must be very responsible people, thought Jones. His friend's father was one, he distinctly remembered his firm handshake and talking to him about football for an hour at his son's wedding.

After his fifth Kingfisher the night before Jones had done some internet research on the dam and discovered that in 1922 the head of Araya had guided the tea estate manager and his friend on a hunt in the mountains at the existing location of the dam. The guide had told them legends that kept the hills alive with the sound of wild animals and spirits. The tea estate manager had been impressed with the supply and flow of water in the forest and conceived the idea for a dam. There were already several dams, some built by the British Army Engineering Corps but not to today's quality standards of design and construction, monitoring and maintenance, seismic resistance, spillway capacity ,and strength of foundation.

In a country renowned for landslips, evacuation had to be taken seriously. It took ten years for a construction and power supply report to be put in front of the Government in 1932. Then another ten years for a preliminary investigation   on the Government's request in 1945. Eventually in 1955 a detailed investigation was made by the Commission for Water and Power.

A coconut can survive up to a month at sea before it is washed up on a another beach and grows into a palm. After six to seven years they are mature enough to make the coconuts, producing up to sixty a year. It takes another thirty years for the tree of life whose flowers have to be present at Keralan wedding ceremonies, to fully grow. The difficult to crack nut is also known as 'millionaire's cabbage'. In addition to the sweet water and milk, the toddy made from the sap is distilled into a strong spirit.

The PXXX Dam project report was finally prepared in 1960 and it wasn't until 1968, eight years later, that the water stored was actually converted into power. The hydroelectric distillery process of pulped and shredded paperwork had taken three generations to ferment .

Jones finished his dinner with a cup of tea then went to the bar. He ordered a fresh coconut with a straw like the welcome drink the hotel had given him one when he arrived. He was booked on the 10am train to the airport the next morning. The production meeting was on Thursday. As he held the coconut in the palm of his hand with the nine planets of vedic numerology, he consulted the mounds of venus, luna, mercury and saturn about his reconnoitre mission and his future fulfillment. His heart, head and life lines were as precise as his production manager's budgets and planning.

www.ingramcontent.com/pod-product-compliance
Lightning Source LLC
Chambersburg PA
CBHW071134260626
47162CB00003B/784